An Oath

Also by Diana Cosby

An Oath Broken
An Oath Taken

MacGruder Brothers Series:
His Enchantment
His Seduction
His Destiny
His Conquest
His Woman
His Captive

An Oath Sworn

Diana Cosby

LYRICAL PRESS
Kensington Publishing Corp.
www.kensingtonbooks.com

LYRICAL PRESS BOOKS are published by

Kensington Publishing Corp.
119 West 40th Street
New York, NY 10018

All Kensington titles, imprints, and distributed lines are available at special quantity discounts for bulk purchases for sales promotion, premiums, fundraising, educational, or institutional use.

Special book excerpts or customized printings can also be created to fit specific needs. For details, write or phone the office of the Kensington Sales Manager: Kensington Publishing Corp., 119 West 40th Street, New York, NY 10018. Attn. Sales Department. Phone: 1-800-221-2647.

Lyrical and the L logo are trademarks of Kensington Publishing Corp.

First Electronic Edition: December 2015
eISBN-13: 978-1-60183-311-2
eISBN-10: 1-60183-311-3

First Print Edition: December 2015
ISBN-13: 978-1-60183-312-9
ISBN-10: 1-60183-312-1

Printed in the United States of America

At times in life I meet the most amazing people. This book is dedicated to Frances McElwee, a gracious, incredible, and inspiring woman. I appreciate the gift of your friendship and I will always cherish the special moments shared with you. God bless you. *Hugs*

ACKNOWLEDGMENTS

I would like to thank Jody Allen and Cameron John Morrison for answering numerous questions, as well as their insight into medieval Scotland. I would also like to thank The National Trust for Scotland, which acts as guardian of Scotland's magnificent heritage of architectural, scenic, and historic treasures. In addition, I am thankful for the immense support from my husband, parents, family, and friends. My deepest wish is that everyone is as blessed when they pursue their dreams.

My sincere thanks to my editor, Esi Sogah; my agent, Holly Root; and my critique partners, Cindy Nord, Shirley Rogerson, Michelle Hancock, and Mary Forbes. Your hard work has helped make the magic of Colyne and Marie's story come true. A special thanks to Sulay Hernandez for believing in me from the start.

And, thanks to the Roving Lunatics (Mary Beth Shortt and Sandra Hughes), Nancy Bessler, and The Wild Writers for your friendship and continued amazing support!

Chapter 1

The rumble of hooves filled the air as the contingent of knights closed.

Lady Marie Alesia Serouge ran faster. Dropping to her knees, she shoved aside the tangle of brush and started to scramble beneath. Stilled.

Fragments of moonlight exposed the outline of a large, muscular male form.

The man turned. His face, savaged by shadows, focused on her. Even in the feeble light, his gaze burned into hers with ferocious intent.

Twigs caught in her hair as she jerked back. Her breath coming fast, she dared a glance toward the advancing riders before facing the lone warrior. She couldn't leave cover, nor could she place herself in new danger.

The thrum of hoofbeats grew.

With a prayer, and careful to keep her distance, she pushed her way beneath the brush.

The knights thundered past, their mounts' hooves casting dust, leaves, and sticks in their wake.

Through the branches, the stranger's gaze remained riveted upon her.

Pulse racing, she edged back.

The stranger lunged toward her. With a groan, he crumpled to the ground.

Marie hesitated.

Another soft moan echoed into the night.

He was hurt! On edge, she scanned the darkened woods where the riders had disappeared over the horizon. Mayhap she'd erred and the knights were hunting this man? However much she wanted to believe that, she couldn't take the risk. Furious that King Philip's bastard daughter had escaped from his imprisonment, naught would deter the English Duke of Renard in his quest to recapture her.

On a groan, the wounded man rolled to his back.

She should leave. Flee while she could.

Marie grimaced. As if she could walk away from the wounded man without a care. The scent of earth melded with that of leaves and the warmth of the late spring night as she edged closer. A hand's width away she halted.

An arrow extended from his left shoulder!

By his unsteady breaths and soft groans, she could tell he was in pain. The shaft must come out.

She must go! Even were she afforded the luxury of time, he was a stranger, nor did she know what had led him to this desperate end.

But what if he was innocent of a crime?

Blast it! She pressed her fingers against the well-corded muscles of his neck. His strong pulse beat against her skin.

A wolf howled in the distance, another replying nearby.

In the silken moonlight, she withdrew the dagger secured within the folds of her dress as she scoured her surroundings. A wolf could detect the scent of blood from a great distance. If attacked, this man would stand no chance of survival.

Unable to discern any immediate danger, she sheathed her weapon and refocused on the stranger. Her whole life had been devoted to helping those in need; how could she leave him here to die? Nor could she linger. She'd help him until his recovery was certain, then she'd depart.

Now, to find a place for them to hide. Marie scanned the grass and tree-shrouded landscape.

A dense blackness loomed through the tangle of limbs ahead.

A cave!

Twigs snapped as she crawled behind the warrior. Careful to keep his left shoulder immobile, she slid her hands beneath his shoulders.

He groaned.

"I must move you, monsieur," she whispered. Sweat beaded her brow and every muscle rebelled as she dragged him through the brush.

He was a goliath of a man, taller and more muscular than she'd first believed.

After several brief stops to rest between tugs, she reached the entrance of the cave. Muscles aching, she collapsed against the rocky ledge and glanced skyward.

The moon had set and the first rays of sunlight streamed across the heavens in a prism of blues and purples. Marie frowned. Moving him had taken longer than she'd expected. Ignoring her body's protests, she dragged him inside and then shifted him onto his uninjured side. Opening her water pouch, she pressed it against his lips. "Drink."

With a grimace, his mouth worked as he swallowed, then he shoved the water away.

Rubbing the fatigue from her eyes, Marie secured her pouch and set it aside. 'Twould hold him for now. "Rest. I will return shortly."

A quick sweep of their path with a pine bough erased any sign of their presence. After, she picked several herbs that she'd need to treat the man's wounds and then gathered pieces of ash, wood that would burn without a trail of smoke.

Sunlight trickled through the forest by the time Marie coaxed the first embers within the pile of dried moss and twigs into a flame. After feeding several larger branches into the fire, she turned.

Her breath caught.

Until this moment, she'd caught glimpses of the warrior through flickers of moonlight. Now, embraced by daylight, she took in the fierce warrior. Long, whisky-colored hair rested upon broad shoulders honed by muscle. Hard, unforgiving planes sculpted his face. Unease trickled through her. Until she reached her father and informed him of the Duke of Renard's treachery, she could trust no one.

Turning to her task, Marie knelt beside the warrior. She clasped the arrow firmly in both hands.

His mouth tightened as he glared at her through half-raised lids. His gaze, even sheltered beneath dark lashes, burrowed deep into her consciousness with a potent reminder of the risk of helping this stranger.

Nonetheless, if he were to have any chance of survival on his own, the arrow must come out. With a jerk, she snapped the shaft as close to the skin as possible.

He gasped and then slumped back.

Thankful when he remained unconscious, she divested him of his mail and gambeson, careful to avoid brushing the embedded arrow.

As she began to remove his undershirt, she paused.

Whorls of dark hair swirled around aged scars, unknown stories chiseled across a battlefield of sinewy muscle.

As a healer, she'd aided many a man injured in combat, but this war-ravaged fighter exuded a dangerous edge. She eased farther back. Only a fool would allow herself to offer this seasoned warrior her trust.

Trust.

Her heart tightened as she recalled the price of allowing herself to have faith in any man.

A mistake she'd never make again.

Marie shoved her thoughts away. She must finish removing the arrow, not wallow in painful memories.

After taking the arrow from his shoulder, she cauterized the torn flesh. Once she'd applied yarrow and toadflax over the wound, she secured the poultice with strips she'd torn from her undergown and prayed he wouldn't grow feverish.

With her body screaming its weariness, Marie lay down and closed her eyes. A warm haze fogged her mind. Images of her escape from Renard's knights, of the terror guiding her every step as she'd fled, flickered through her mind. Exhausted, she pushed her fears aside and fell into sleep's welcome embrace.

Chapter 2

Colyne MacKerran, the Earl of Strathcliff, shifted to his left side. Pain tore through his shoulder. On a curse, he rolled onto his back, and his body nudged against a soft, pliable form.

What in blazes?

Groggy, he opened his eyes and sat up. Sunlight streamed into a cave he had nay memory of entering. Ashes of a recently used fire smoldered a short distance away. And at his side slept an incredibly beautiful woman.

A woman he'd never seen in his life.

Hair the color of honey tumbled in a silken mass around her, and her full mouth was curved into a smile as her lithe, shapely body pressed against his. A sword's wrath, who was she? He would have remembered bedding such an enchantress.

More importantly, how had either of them ended up here?

He fought past the pain in his shoulder as he searched his blurred thoughts to remember. Like a merciless assault, images knifed through his mind. An oath sworn to Douglas, as his friend lay dying, that he'd deliver the writ to King Philip. Being pursued by the Duke of Renard's men. An arrow shot into his shoulder and his narrow escape.

Then blackness.

The writ!

Like a madman, Colyne grabbed his undershirt, thankful when his fingers bumped the concealed document. Careful to keep quiet, he withdrew the bound leather and removed the rolled parchment.

Robert Bruce, Earl of Carrick, Guardian of the Realm of Scotland's seal remained intact.

Grief burned his throat at thoughts of Douglas. He hadna even had time to bury his friend. *A sword's wrath, his life wouldna be given in vain.* The writ to King Philip of France would be delivered! The woman at his side released a long sigh.

He shot her a hard look. Had she seen the writ? If so, she'd left it untouched. Where had the lass come from?

Her simple garb attested to her life as a beggar. Or mayhap a servant. From her healthy glow, he'd choose the latter. Had she stumbled across him while out gathering herbs for her lord and saved his life? If so, he would thank her. But before he allowed her to leave, he would discover whether she had seen the Guardian of Scotland's document.

After concealing the writ, Colyne nudged the lass.

Her nose twitched in a delicate flare and she continued to sleep.

"Lass," he muttered, mistrust roughening his words.

"*Qu'est-ce que tu fais?*" she murmured.

Stunned, he narrowed his gaze. What was a Frenchwoman doing in the dense forests of the Highlands? Disquiet edged through him. The French king's bastard daughter had been abducted by the English duke's knights and hidden in the Highlands. This was the very reason he carried the writ to King Philip, to explain the Scots were nae behind this treachery.

Could this be Lady Marie Serouge?

Again, he assessed the dozing lass in her mundane garb. He scoffed. Aye, as if the English duke would allow his captive, dressed in little better than rags, to be roaming the hills without an escort. A wash of dizziness swept him, and Colyne struggled to clear his mind. Wherever the Duke of Renard held the king's bastard daughter, she was well guarded.

As if a fairy summoned, the woman's brow wrinkled in a delicate arch as she lifted her lids. Eyes the color of moss leveled on him and cleared. Surprise, then fear widened them.

The lass shoved to her knees and started to scramble back, but Colyne caught her wrist. "I am nae going to harm you."

"Release me," she gasped.

"You tended me?" he asked, his voice rough with impatience.

Shrewd eyes studied him as if deliberating the wisdom of a reply.

"Fine, then. First, promise nae to run." His shoulder ached from his meager exertion, and he inhaled a deep breath to remain alert as her image began to blur. Slowly, his vision cleared. Bedamned, with legs as long as a king's prized filly if she fled, Colyne doubted he'd be able to pursue her, much less remain conscious. Before he passed out, he needed to discover whether she posed any kind of threat to his mission.

She angled her jaw. "I could have left you alone and injured."

Which spoke well for her character. Or indicated her presence here was planned. "But you did nae."

"*Non.*" Her gaze flicked to his fingers curled around her wrist. "Now release me."

"I will have your word that you will nae run."

After a long moment, she nodded. "You have my word."

Colyne let her go and braced his hand on the ground. "Why did you care for me?"

"You were hurt."

The sincerity of her words surprised him. "Most would have left a wounded man to die. Especially a stranger."

Her eyes narrowed. "I explained my reason."

A reason that invited more questions.

"You need to rest, monsieur. If you move about, you will reopen your wound. Please. The arrow went deep. Your shoulder will take time to heal."

He stiffened. *Time he didna have.*

An angry mark across her cheek caught his attention. Colyne skimmed his finger atop the darkening skin, curious as she jerked back. "You have a bruise."

Her lashes lowered to shield her eyes, but nae before he saw the fear. "'Tis naught."

"You have been hit," he stated, incensed that any would dare touch this gentle woman who had offered aid to a stranger?

"I . . . fell."

Fell his arse. By her evasiveness, neither would she admit the truth. Colyne studied her, and his gut assured him that something was amiss. Long ago he'd learned to heed his instincts. Until they parted, he would keep her under close watch.

The woman started to rise.

He caught her arm. "Your name?"

"Unhand me!"

At the dictatorial slap of her words, he obeyed and she stood. What the devil? He shoved to his feet, wove, and steadied himself.

She'd spoken to him as a woman used to giving orders and having them followed.

Was she in league with Renard? Colyne's suspicions grew tenfold. Had she turned against her king and joined England's fight to claim Scotland as its own? If so, why hadna she broken the writ's seal, read the contents, and then carried it to the English duke while Colyne lay unconscious?

He shoved to his feet and stepped closer, dwarfing her in his shadow. "Who are you?" At her hesitation, he shot her a fierce scowl. "You will answer me!"

"I—I am a missionary," Marie blurted out. *Mon Dieu.* Though the knight's frown declared his confusion, judging from the intelligence in his eyes, he wasn't a fool. But a servant of God was the first logical explanation that had come to mind.

"A missionary?" the Scot repeated, his brogue rich with doubt.

"*Oui.*" *Please believe me!*

"A French missionary in the Scottish Highlands?" He shot a skeptical glance toward the cave's opening, then back to her. "Alone?"

She fought for calm. What more could she say to convince him? Though he looked like a god, with his eyes the deep blue of the ocean and his cheeks hinting of dimples, the warrior's sharp gaze assured her that he was not a man to trifle with.

"I am waiting," he stated, his tone dry.

"It is difficult for me." *An understatement.*

His expression darkened. "I am nae going anywhere."

Neither, it appeared, was she. At least not until he'd received an explanation that left him satisfied. Once she'd appeased him, she would allow him another day to recover. Then, that night while he slept, she'd slip away. Though with the men scouring the area to find her, travel would be difficult.

Through lowered lashes, she regarded the fierce knight, a man with the power to intimidate and the strength to back his claims. His finely crafted mail, which she'd set against the rocky wall of the cave, bespoke wealth. Surely he carried the funds necessary to arrange for her passage to France.

Marie hesitated.

Was this man too dangerous to risk not only her life with but the safety of Scotland as well? Perhaps 'twould be better if she traveled alone.

But as a Scot, he would know the terrain and, if necessary, places to hide. In addition, his presence would add another layer of safety. The knights searching for her sought a woman alone. Regardless, she must keep the truth of her royal lineage hidden. Though a Scot, he could still be an enemy of her country.

"While returning from Beauly Priory, our party was attacked and our people were slaughtered." Marie closed her eyes against his stare, her pain real in that if she failed to reach her father and tell him who'd abducted her, more Scots would die.

Silence.

Marie lifted her lashes and found his gaze skeptical, though not totally dismissive. "During the attack, I escaped," she continued. "I was terrified."

He nodded. "Aye, you would be."

"I—I went back to . . ."

At her shudder, he lifted her chin, his eyes dark with regret. "Oh, God, lass. 'Tis nae the likes of what a woman should witness."

Caught off guard by his sympathy, for a moment she leaned closer. Shaken to be offered trust when she'd earned none, she stumbled back. "I am sorry," she said, fiercely regretting her lie. She despised untruths, but life had shown her the lengths to which people would go, lying, cheating, and murdering to achieve their goals.

"Do nae be."

The sincere concern on his face tempted her to admit the truth, but she remained silent. She knew nothing about this warrior, except that his actions deemed him a man of compassion. Did his conduct extend to honor as well? "I must return home to my family." Her quiet words echoed between them, and his gaze softened.

"I understand."

Hope ignited. "Then you will help me?"

The warmth in his expression faded to caution. "Help you?"

"*Oui.* As you are aware, travel for a woman alone is dangerous." Refusal crept into his eyes, and she spoke faster. "I only need your escort to the closest port. From there I—"

"Nay."

She touched his arm. "But you must."

Dry amusement quirked his lips. "I must?" Blue eyes studied her with unapologetic interest. "Lass, you have a penchant for ordering people about."

"I do not . . ." She withdrew her hand. Heat swept her cheeks. He was right. The woman he believed her to be would focus on serving those in need. She glanced toward the opening of the cave. Renard's men, along with miles of wilderness, stood between her and a port city. "The last few days have been terrifying."

The truth. Her abduction, imprisonment, and learning of the English duke's plot to use her as a pawn in hopes her father would cease support to Scotland, had torn her life apart.

"I am distraught and am being impossibly rude." She paused. "Forgive me."

Pain flickered through the tiredness in his eyes. "That is the second time you have apologized to me, and with nay reason. I am the one who is sorry that you have been subjected to such carnage."

"I . . . Thank you." Moved by his genuine concern, she struggled as to what decision to make. However much she didn't wish to involve him, fate offered no other choice. Somehow she must convince him to escort her to the coast.

His brows furrowed in pain as he started to turn.

"What are you doing?" she asked.

Honed muscles rippled as he leaned over to pick up his gambeson. "As much as I wish to rest, I canna."

Embarrassed to find herself staring at the powerful display of strength, she turned away, but not before he caught her perusal. By the grace of Mary, she was acting as if she were a dim-witted maiden! Frustrated the man muddled her mind, Marie tugged the quilted garment from his hand and tossed it atop his mail. "You need to rest. You are pushing yourself far too fast."

Mischief warmed his gaze, as if he were amused by her show of will. "I always take care with what I do, regardless the task."

Awareness rippled across her skin at his claim. Of that she had no doubt. "I am going to pick some herbs that will help relieve your pain." She walked toward the cave's entrance.

"I have yet to thank you for caring for me." The softness in his voice had her halting at the timeworn entry. She didn't turn; though a stranger, something about him invited friendship, akin to trust. Neither of which she was in a position to give. "You are welcome."

"You have nae told me your name."

Her entire body tensed. Her name? Drawn by a force she couldn't name, she turned and faced him. A mistake.

As their eyes met, the warrior's gaze narrowed.

"My name is Alesia," she blurted out. Panic swept her as she waited for the flicker of recognition.

After a long moment, he nodded.

She exhaled. Why had she worried? Few would know her second name, especially those in the Scottish Highlands, even more so a man who lived by the blade.

"Alesia. The name suits you."

Her body shivered at how his deep burr cradled her name. As quickly, she dismissed the foolish notion. It was exhaustion, naught more. Curious, she arched a brow. "Suits me?"

He inclined his head, appreciation simmering in his gaze. " 'Tis strong and beautiful."

Unsure how to respond, she remained silent.

"Have you nay wish to know my name?"

The splash of humor in his eyes assured her that he was a man comfortable with teasing. "You must have sisters."

"Sisters?"

"You seem relaxed in the presence of women." Heat returned to her cheeks. And why wouldn't he be? A fool could see he was a man who could easily charm a woman into his bed. Mortified, she shook her head. "I did not mean—"

"I know what you meant." A smile tugged at his mouth, deepening his dimples. "And I do have sisters. Three of them, to be exact, and a brother. If you would want to be knowing," he gently teased, "my name is Colyne."

"Thank you." Before she uttered something else humiliating, Marie hurried out, the soft rumble of his laughter trailing in her wake.

Colyne shook his head as the lass all but fled the cave. As she stepped into the sunlight, hints of gold teased by the sun shimmered through her hair like a majestic fire.

He sucked in his breath. For a moment he'd almost lost his good sense and agreed to escort the comely lass to the coast. With a curse, Colyne rubbed his throbbing temple. What was he thinking? Since

Elizabet had married another and broken his heart, he'd nae been drawn to another lass. *Elizabet.* His chest tightened as he thought of the woman he loved, a lass he'd known since his youth, a woman who he would forever hold in his heart.

Nay, Alesia inspired naught. 'Twas the woman's beauty that intrigued him. He must focus on reaching France and of learning what she knew of the writ, nae more.

A wave of dizziness swept over him as he knelt. Bracing a hand on his knee, he took several deep breaths until his vision cleared. Aye, his travel would be slowed by his injury, but it couldna be helped. He reached for his gambeson.

"What do you think you are doing?"

At Alesia's reproach, Colyne's grip eased. The thick padding plopped upon the dirt. He shot her a quelling look as she stood in the entry, herbs piled in her palm. With a muttered oath, he snatched the gambeson. "I am donning my mail." Dizziness threatened his balance as nausea gnawed in his gut. Irritation slammed through him when his fingers quivered from the effort to hold his gear.

"You are too weak to be moving about," she snapped, "much less entertain ideas of travel."

"You brought me in here?" he asked.

She arched a cool brow as she walked toward him and then deposited the handful of leaves on the flat surface of a nearby rock. "*Oui.* I am stronger than I look."

Mayhap, but with her slender frame and without help, the task of moving him hadna been easy. He was at least a hand's length taller than her.

"And you removed the arrow?" Her head made a slight tilt, but he noted that with each question, her expression grew more guarded. "How long have we been here?"

"Two days."

A sword's wrath. Two days of much-needed travel lost.

"You had a fever," she explained. "You will be weak and needing food and rest, not moving about."

He ignored her rebuke and donned the gambeson. His wounded shoulder burned from the effort. "What I will be needing or nae is my decision."

She scoffed. "If you had half as much wit as charm, you would be—"

"Charming, am I?" Colyne challenged, pleased by her spirit.

Coolness flickered in her eyes as she stalked over and shoved the water pouch in his hand. "Drink this."

Nay, he wasna about to be thrown off topic so easily. He waggled the leather vessel at her. "You said I was charming. I heard you."

Her eyes narrowed. "I also think you are——"

"Hold, lass," he interrupted, assured by the fire in her eyes that her comparison would be far from flattering. His lips twitched with amusement at her heated reply. He took a gulp. "But I will be thanking you for the water."

Alesia snatched the leather sack from his hand and secured the top. "Save your charms for those who will be swayed by them."

At the coolness of her tone, he chuckled, and then Colyne sobered at how easily he'd flustered her by his teasing. As a missionary, how had she handled those who vied for her attention? Given her beauty, numerous men would have tried.

She withdrew a flat round made of oats from the bag and handed him the baked good.

"My thanks."

With a cool nod, she removed an oatcake for herself and then sat on the ground.

Out of reach, he noted. Intrigued, Colyne studied her. Even irritated, Alesia moved with a natural grace as if life had dictated such. Yet, the worsted wool of her dress indicated a simpler existence, which prior to their speaking he'd believed. Nay longer. Now he suspected the simple garb a ruse, one tied to the reason she'd found him here.

"I am surprised to find someone of your class in the Highlands," he said, phrasing it more as an observation than a question, in hopes she'd open up to him. "Even voluntarily."

She focused on her biscuit and then took a dainty bite. "I explained why I am here."

"Aye, you did." But the hesitation before her reply assured him something about her story was untrue.

Moss green eyes locked with his. "And what brings you to an end where I find you unconscious with an arrow in your shoulder?" She tore off a piece of her flat round, but he didna miss the worry hidden within her question, or the subtle cut that she knew little of him as well and had her own suspicions.

"I am nae an outlaw."

She regarded him like a queen weighing sentence on one of her subjects. "You would not be."

"You know little about me to draw such an opinion," he said, curious as to how, in fact, she had come to such an accurate conclusion in such a brief time. As if she had lived a life where her judgment of those around her was a necessity.

"Your actions speak clearly of your character," she explained, drawing him from his musings. "If you were a scoundrel, you would not have cared a wit about my misfortune."

"You have discerned more about me than most would in our short acquaintance."

For the first time since he'd regained consciousness, her mouth curved in a smile, one that briefly grazed her full lips. A look hinting of passion. One Colyne found himself wishing to taste.

Caught off guard by his thought, he stared at her. Except for Elizabet, never had a woman roused his interest.

Until now.

What was it about Alesia that intrigued him? He knew little about her, and he had misgivings that what she'd disclosed was the truth. A sword's wrath. France was his sole objective. Until he delivered the document to King Philip, he could trust nay one.

Including her.

"Learning to deduce a person's motives is a necessity with the life I have been given," she explained.

"And exactly what has life offered you?"

Alesia stood. "You must be thirsty. I will refill the water pouch."

The silky ease with which she guided the conversation away from herself assured Colyne she had done the same many times over. "It can wait."

Without glancing back, she picked up the sewn leather and started toward the exit.

"Who are you?" At his quiet command she halted, neither did he miss how her body tensed. "I can believe you are a missionary, but there is something more that you are hiding."

She faced him. Her fingers clutching the leather grew white.

"Your words. The graceful manner in which you move," he said as he studied her, "have given you away. And your hands are soft and unblemished, those of a well-bred lady, nae of a commoner."

Though slowly given, she nodded her assent. "I once traveled in those circles," she replied, her words rich with distaste. "I do so no longer."

"You are nae fond of nobility?" he asked, curious as to how she would react if she learned he was an earl. Would his status repel her? The thought disheartened him.

"Nobility?" she repeated, her words wielded with cold precision. "'Tis an insult on the word. Many who bear powerful titles are often a pathetic reflection of the noble personage they strive to personify. So caught up in their own worth, they see naught of the self-serving fools they have become."

"Is that why you traveled to Scotland?"

With a sharp tug, she secured the sack. "Monsieur, what I chose to do or not do is my concern."

"Indeed." He chose his next words with care so as nae to raise her suspicions. "'Tis only that I find your appearance here—"

"I have explained my reason."

At the rebuff in her voice, he refrained from further questions, but before they parted, he would have his answers. A stiff silence fell between them as he pondered a subtler approach. "I will be taking a second oatcake."

Suspicion flashed on her face.

He offered her a roguish smile. "Because I am hungry."

She arched a doubtful brow, but she walked over, reopened the sack, and removed another round. "You need several more days of rest before you begin moving about." Alesia nodded toward the armor near his thigh. "Without bearing the weight of your mail," she added with emphasis. "If you are not careful, you will reopen the wound I have bound. I need not inform you of your outcome should your injury putrefy." She stepped closer, and then tossed the oatcake onto his lap.

Colyne caught her hand before she could move away.

Her eyes narrowed with warning.

"I want to thank you." But a part of him had wanted to touch her. And he'd guessed right. Her skin did remind him of silk.

Ire flashed in her eyes as she tugged to free herself from his hold.

He let go, but nae without regret. "And I am nae thirsty."

After a moment's hesitation, Alesia sat on the other side of the blackened remnants of their small fire, her expression wary. "As you are awake and without fever, on the morrow I shall leave."

"You will go alone?"

She angled her head in a regal tilt. "Monsieur, I will do what I must."

Instead of admiring her sheer determination, anger ignited at her foolishness. "With the unrest between England and Scotland, travel will be dangerous."

"I am well aware of the challenges I face." She lifted a curious brow. "Unless you have changed your mind and have decided to escort me to the coast."

A sword's wrath, 'twas nae a luxury he could offer. "'Tis impossible."

The fragile hope in her eyes vanished. "I see."

Nay, she didna! He was a hunted man. For all he knew, Renard's men scoured the woods within a league of their position. Without wanting to, he had placed her life in jeopardy.

If caught, his life was forfeit.

But if they found Alesia with him, he doubted their actions would be those of honor. Grizzly visions of the men taking liberties with her ravaged his mind, of their thirst for their own base needs.

He wanted to help her, but for her safety they needed to part. As long as she remained with him, the risk to her life increased. "You do nae understand."

Her face softened with concern. "Then make me."

Tiredness washed over him. Colyne wished he could explain, but too much lay at stake to take such a risk. "Nay, 'tis better if you know naught."

"But . . . why?"

The concern in her voice had him again damning the situation. With a curse, Colyne stood. His legs trembled, as if mocking his weakness. He couldna escort Alesia to the coast; she was a stranger, a woman whose presence here raised numerous questions. Still, how could he allow her to travel unprotected? Neither could he forget that she'd saved his life.

Bedamned this entire situation.

"Fine," Colyne snapped. "I will take you eastward to a trusted friend. But nay farther. He will make arrangements for you to reach France."

She paused as if mulling over his offer.

"I would nae hesitate if I were you," he warned. "I might change my mind."

"Then I accept your gracious offer," she replied, her voice somber, but a wisp of laughter danced in her eyes.

A sword's wrath, the lass toyed with him! And as much as he should be irritated, Colyne found appreciation at her daring, a tactic he'd employed himself moments before.

The hard, steady cadence of hooves echoed in the distance.

Colyne turned toward the entrance. Renard's men!

Alesia's face paled. "They have returned! We must keep quiet until they have passed."

Returned? Guilt collided with suspicion. Why hadna she told him the men had searched the area while he was unconscious? Whatever the reason, thank God she had kept them hidden. He unsheathed his sword, biting back the pain in his wounded shoulder. "Move behind me."

Frustration flashed in her eyes. She rushed over and tried to pull the blade from his grip.

"Ale—"

What do you think you are doing?" she demanded.

The rumble of hooves increased.

In disbelief, Colyne stared at her hand clasped above his own. "Release my weapon!"

She gave a hard tug. "You are too weak to be wielding a sword."

"If we are discovered, you had best pray for my strength."

"Why?"

"Because," Colyne snarled, "the men want me dead."

Chapter 3

Colyne hadna thought her face could whiten further but it did. "My lady?"

Panic streaked through her eyes as she stared up at him. "They want you dead?"

A sword's wrath! "Hide behind the boulder."

She didn't move.

"Now!"

With a start, Alesia ran to the large rock near the back of the cave, and he followed.

The thrum of hoofbeats halted near the entrance.

Sword readied, Colyne tensed.

"She is not out here," a rough English voice grumbled.

"Our orders are to find her," another man snapped.

"We have searched for three bloody days now," a man farther away stated. "She is long gone."

A man close to the entry grunted. "If you want to keep your head, you best pray that we find her."

A horse squealed, another snorted, and leather and mail clanked as the men rode off.

The rumble of horses faded.

Colyne exhaled a relieved sigh as he stepped from behind the boulder. Whoever the men were, they were nae searching for him. With the threat over, weariness swept him. He needed to rest. He sheathed his blade and turned toward Alesia.

And stopped.

Eyes widened with guilt watched him.

And he understood. "The men are after you."

She stepped back.

Irritated that he'd nae suspected they sought Alesia at their mention of a woman, he stepped closer. When she made to move farther away, he caught her shoulder. "Tell me!" Sweat trickled down his face at the effort, but anger gave him strength.

"*Ou—oui.*"

He cursed beneath his breath. "Before you end up getting us both killed, tell me what in blazes is going on!"

At the Scot's furious glare, Marie trembled. Though she believed he was a man of honor, what did she truly know about him? His Christian name? His belief that men were after him? However tempted to admit the truth, Scotland's freedom was too big a risk for her to offer him her trust.

Colyne's grip on her shoulder tightened.

She winced. "Please, you are hurting me."

His hold gentled, but he didn't release her. "Why do the men want you?"

The lie of gold or some other viable reason as to why the men pursued her came to mind. No, she couldn't tell him another untruth.

She shook her head. "I cannot."

"Canna or willna?"

She'd not believed it possible for him to appear more dangerous, but with his eyes darkening like an incoming storm and his body tensed as if prepared for battle and towering over her, he appeared every inch the warrior. "The reasons are mine alone."

Blue eyes narrowed. "'Tis nae only your life that is at risk."

"I know," she quietly replied.

"Do you?" A muscle worked in his jaw as he studied her, and with an exasperated sigh, he let her go.

Marie didn't move back but stood before him humbled. He was wounded. How could she have been so selfish as to have asked him to jeopardize his life further by escorting her to the coast? "Monsieur—"

"Colyne," he said between gritted teeth. "I think we can agree to bypass the formalities."

She nodded. "Colyne, I have decided to take my chances."

His nostrils flared with annoyance. "Pray tell, lass, what does that mean?"

Marie shifted, uncomfortable beneath his all-too-seeing glare. "It means I will continue my journey alone. You need rest, time to heal. You are in no condition to travel, much less further endanger your life by escorting me to your friend's home."

"Is it a man?"

"What do you mean?" she asked with caution, barely controlling her rising panic.

He glanced toward the cave's entry. "Is it a man who sent his knights in search of you?"

The tension in her body ebbed. "*Oui.*" Let him believe her reasons for running were personal. It would simplify everything. Neither was it a lie.

"Who is he?"

He far from understood the importance of the question he asked. "What does it matter who it is or the reason his men are searching for me?"

Colyne shot her a wry grin. "If I am going to risk my life escorting you, I need to know what I dangers I face."

Hope stumbled through her. "You will escort me? But—"

The Scot held up his hand, any trace of humor gone. "To my friend's home, as I offered before. Nay more. Once you are in safe hands, I must go. I have my own business to attend to."

Colyne's reaction to the knights who'd ridden by flickered through her mind. Uneasy, she cleared her throat. "You believed the men were after you?"

His expression grew shuttered.

Marie tensed. Was this Scot a threat? She didn't want to believe she'd miscalculated to such a degree. But if she was wrong . . .

Long seconds passed as he stared at her, his deep gaze assessing. "Aye, they are."

"Why?"

A grim smile touched his mouth. "Well now, lass, I have my own reasons. Ones I will nae be sharing. And," he paused, "you will have to trust me as well."

Marie disliked this turn of events. "It seems I will."

Humor softened the stern angles of his face. "A fair trade, would you nae agree?"

At his teasing, she looked away, unable to find anything light-hearted about the situation. Though men pursued him with deadly intent, he didn't hold a country's fate in his hands.

If he was in better health, she would accept his offer. As a woman who enjoyed quick wit, 'twould be interesting to remain with Colyne for a while longer, for their discussions if naught else. Except his pallor betrayed his weakened state. Neither could she forget how the sword had trembled in his hands as the knights had ridden by. He was in no condition to protect her, much less travel.

"My thanks for your offer of escort, but I must decline."

Colyne's mouth tilted into a half smile that sent her pulse racing.

Flustered by her reaction, she dropped her gaze. At his soft chuckle, she looked up. "What?"

"Only you would debate this."

"I am not—"

His smile widened. "You are."

"I was," she amended, finding herself hopelessly charmed. 'Twas foolish to entertain agreeing to his offer. He was too weak to travel. But if she didn't agree, then she'd be alone, a stranger in a war-torn land. Though she far from trusted him, despite his cautious manner, he treated her with courtesy and respect without the knowledge of her royal ties. "Thank you. If you insist, I will accept your offer. But we must remain here another day to allow you time to heal before you travel."

He nodded, but Colyne's eyes scoured hers, his wariness easy to read. With his intelligence, she'd expected nothing less.

"They say when you share your worries, the choices you need to make become so much more clear."

Sadness filled her at the sincerity in his voice. "I cannot." And sadly, never could.

Canna? She could, but the lass was afraid of whoever sought her. Colyne took in the bruise on her cheek, disgusted by men who found strength in battering women. If the scoundrel who'd struck her stood before him, he would serve the bastard his own brand of justice. "You are exhausted and need to try to sleep."

Alesia glanced toward the cave's entry. "The men—"

"I will keep watch."

She scraped her teeth across her lower lip. "Only for a short while."

"Go to sleep," he said, evading any agreement to her request. Unless absolutely necessary, he would allow her to rest until she awoke on her own.

With a yawn, she walked toward the back of the cave, lost in shadows.

"Where are you going?"

"Behind this ledge is a small chamber. While you slept, I crafted a bed from dry grass and leaves." Pink crept up her cheeks in a flattering hue. "For you to use once I had left. If the men did a quick search of the cave while you were asleep, you had the chance of being overlooked."

"And why have you nae slept there?" he asked, impressed by her tactical measure. "It would have offered you more comfort than on the cold, hard ground."

"While you were asleep, you developed a fever, one that thankfully went away before you awoke. I could not risk leaving you alone."

Moved by her sacrifice, he stepped toward her. "So you slept by my side until the fever broke?"

Her blush deepened. "*Oui.*"

Caught off guard by her sudden shyness, he halted, too easily picturing her moss-colored eyes dark with passion. "Go to sleep," he whispered. Before he did something foolish like kiss her.

With a blush on her cheeks, she slipped from view. Dried grass and leaves rustled as she settled behind the wall of uneven rock.

Colyne blew out a rough breath and walked outside. Alesia's genuine nature bespoke a nurturer, a woman given to helping others. How had he wondered if she was King Philip's bastard daughter? Nae that she couldn't be as giving, but raised beneath a royal hand and without ever having a need, he had his doubts.

After a quick survey of the surroundings, he leaned against a boulder at an angle, where he could spot riders in the distance, but close enough to the entry so he could hear her if she called.

He rubbed his temple and tried to ignore the throbbing in his left shoulder and the dizziness he couldna shake. He needed to deliver the missive to King Philip, nae ponder the thoughts Alesia inspired. A sword's wrath! The only reason he'd agreed to escort her to his friend was that 'twas too dangerous for her to be in the Highlands alone.

Disgusted with that lie, he shot a cool look to where he knew she lay. Aye, and so what if she intrigued him? 'Twas nae the same feelings he had had for Elizabet. Pain lanced his heart at the thought of the woman he loved. With a grimace, he scanned the surroundings. She was happy now. He should be happy for her. And he would be. When was another matter.

Two days later, Colyne strode through the forest with Alesia at his side. Though his body hadna fully recovered and against her objections, he'd announced it was time for them to leave.

A grim smile touched his lips. For his sanity, he couldna remain trapped within the cave with her another day. It had taken every ounce of his willpower nae to satisfy his question of how her mouth would feel beneath his.

"How is your shoulder?" she asked, her tone crisp.

"Am I slowing you?"

Impatience simmered in her eyes. "Not at the moment."

Colyne laughed. He should have found disapproval in her outspoken manner. Instead, he was fascinated by her intelligence, impressed by her ability to debate him on the most insignificant of issues and, on occasion, to reason a point to where he conceded to her view.

He didna have the heart to inform the lass that he'd kept his pace slow more out of concern for her than his injury. He'd dealt with worse discomfort in his life, but traveling afoot through the Highlands proved an arduous trek for a knight familiar with such demands, much less a gentlewoman. And the slippers she wore offered her little protection against the sticks and rocks strewn about the forest floor.

At the break in the trees, a glen lay before them, thick with rich blades of grass scattered with heather. He scanned the familiar, narrowed tract of land. Soon they would arrive at Stephano's home. His friend would secure her safe passage to France. With a fresh mount and Alesia in trusted hands, he would be on his way.

And he would miss her.

Greatly.

"You said you had three sisters and a brother?" She glanced over, her eyes bright with interest. "Are you close?"

"Aye. And what of your family? Are you close as well?"

She looked away and kept walking. "Are you the eldest?"

"You have nae answered my question," he said, remembering her avoidance of speaking about herself before.

"I have many relatives," she finally replied, "many of whom disagreed with my decision to live on my own or to aid those who are less fortunate." She shrugged. "I should not pry into your private life."

A smile touched his mouth. "I wish to pry into yours."

Alesia stared straight ahead, nae allowing Colyne the luxury of discerning her reaction. "I have led a very boring life."

"I doubt that," she said.

When she didna respond further, his smile grew. "Your silence will only make me more curious."

She halted and turned with a scowl. "This is not a game we play. There are men out there who, for various reasons, want both of us dead. What difference does it make if you know of my family, or if I have chosen to live a simpler life without the false pageantry of nobility?"

"Is that what you have chosen?" Colyne caught her hand as she started to turn away. "I did nae mean to upset you."

"The fault is mine. I was the one who asked about your family. I will not do so again." She shot a cool look at his hand. "Now release me."

"What are you afraid of?"

"We both have secrets neither of us are willing to share. In a day, two at most, we will never see each other again." Her voice began to break.

Colyne stepped closer, but she shook her head.

As if erecting an impenetrable wall between them, she moved back. "You are a stranger to me," she whispered. "A fact I have no wish to change."

"Is it so wrong to offer friendship?"

"Monsieur, can we not go?"

"Answer me. Please."

Sadness shadowed her face. "And if I did, will you answer any questions I have about you as well?"

"A sword's wrath!"

Alesia's eyes narrowed. "How dare you expect answers when you will give me none!"

At her regal tone, Colyne started to laugh, helpless to do otherwise.

Red slashed her cheeks. "'Tis good one of us finds humor in this situation."

"Och, lass." He caught her hand and pressed a tender kiss upon her knuckles, pleased when she didna try to pull away. "I was only seeking friendship, naught more. 'Tis the request too much to ask?"

Except when her gaze moved to where his lips had touched her skin, he knew he lied.

As if reading his mind, she trembled. "Do not."

He released her hand, shaken. By the desire darkening her gaze, she wasna as immune to him as she would like, which helped naught. "Come." The tall grass brushed against his legs as Colyne strode forward. At his side, her soft steps matched his, but he didna turn. If she hadna stopped him moments before, he would have kissed her.

A mistake. What did he know about the lass? Little, a fact she ensured. Though born within the ranks of the gentry, for whatever her reasons, she had discarded the status her nobility offered and worked to help those less fortunate.

Her choice.

One that changed nothing.

He should be pleased by her withdrawal. At least she didna have the brain of an ass. That honor belonged to him.

"Mon Dieu!"

Colyne turned, startled by the fear in her gaze. "What is wrong?"

Her hand shook as she pointed in the direction in which they were heading. "Look!"

Beyond the next hill, a thick, black column of smoke billowed into the sky.

Dread ripped through Colyne. Stephano! Please, God, nae them. "Wait here!"

She caught his arm. "I am coming with you."

Furious she'd defy him, he tore her hand free. "You will stay!"

Alesia's face paled. "What is it?"

He refused to admit his suspicions. If he was right, she didna need to witness the carnage spewed upon the other side of the glen.

She stared at him, her troubled expression breaking down his resistance.

"I will be back." Before she could offer further objections, he bolted toward the black churning cloud at a dead run.

And prayed he was wrong.

Chapter 4

Marie raced after Colyne, the stench of smoke growing with each step. As she crested a mound, she broke through the trees. Stopped. The horror before her stealing her breath.

Near the base of the angled slope, Colyne knelt amidst the blackened rubble. Bodies lay scattered around him, some butchered, others with arrows protruding from their backs. The cloying stench of charred flesh almost drove her to her knees.

A sob tore free.

Colyne's gaze riveted on her. His face a mask of outrage and grief, he shoved to his feet.

But his eyes.

Merciful Lord. His eyes held the horrors of a man who'd witnessed too much death.

She wrapped her arms across her chest as her body began to shake.

He stormed toward her, his mail smeared by blood. "I told you to stay!"

"I . . ." The crofter's hut was engulfed in flames. Livestock lay mutilated in a twisted mass of hides and horror. Not even a lamb was left unscathed. And the people. Her chest tightened with pain. "Who could have—"

"The English." Condemnation carved through his words like an angry blade. He caught her shoulders.

Instead of shaking her as she'd expected, Colyne drew her against his chest and turned her away from the barbaric slaughter. His body trembled against hers.

"The bastards think they can quell us into subservience," he rasped, "but they are wrong. Their butchery fuels our hatred."

Tears rolled down her cheeks as Marie cried, grieving for those slaughtered, for his country under merciless assault, but mostly for him. However much her own despair, Colyne's must be doubly so.

This travesty underscored her urgent need to reach France. Until she explained that the Duke of Renard was behind her abduction, her father would believe rebel Scots were guilty of the inflammatory act. And Scotland's future would be in grave danger. Without France's monetary support, Scotland's forces would wither.

His hold eased, and then he began to whisper in Gaelic. By their soft flow, they were words meant to soothe, but they spilled out raw with heartache. On a shudder he grew quiet.

Mon Dieu, she must not fail. "I am so sorry," she whispered, her voice thick with tears.

"You need to go back to where I asked you to stay and wait. Once I am finished here, I will come for you."

"I will not leave you here alone."

Colyne lifted his head. Tears filled his eyes and anguish carved his face. "You will—"

"*Non*," she interrupted, furious Renard had used her as a pawn to put Scotland's freedom at risk. "You will not face this alone. Do you think this does not affect me?"

He released a raw breath. "You should have stayed beyond the knoll."

"Why?"

"These are my people."

"They were slaughtered! Innocent people cut down in cold blood." She caught his hands, needing him to understand this act of savagery was as devastating to her as it was to him. "If you think I will stand by and not help you bury them, you know little of me."

He drew her forward, his eyes burning into hers. "I have tried to . . . I am sorry. I am so sorry." Colyne claimed her mouth, demanding, taking, shattering her with the intensity of his kiss. But beneath the anger, she tasted his grief. This wasn't about passion but need. To know there was still good left within the world.

Without warning he released her, and she stumbled back. "Colyne," she said, breathless, her lips still tingling.

He held up his hands, his face pale with shock. "I should nae have touched you."

"You—"

Anger stormed his eyes. "I had nay right!" He dropped his hands and stalked off.

Grief swept her. All he could see was his wrong, not the man devastated by loss. Marie ran in front of him, forcing him to halt. He glared at her, but she held her ground. "I understand," she said, her mind still warring against the horrors around her. She pressed her fingers on the side of his face, his tears warm against her hand.

Colyne flinched, but he didn't move away. "You understand naught."

"I believe you are a man of great compassion. People you love have been murdered. You grieve. How could you not?" Marie stroked the back of her hand against his cheek as tears streamed down her face. She'd not believed the situation could worsen, but it had. "You knew them."

He turned away, but not before she witnessed him wiping away his tears.

"Oh, Colyne." She stepped closer, unsure how to console this compassionate warrior, or if she even could.

"I would never hurt you."

"I know."

"Let me help you."

His gaze searched hers. "Why is it you are never what I expect to find?" He closed his eyes and then drew her against him.

For a long while he held her, with their hearts torn, their grief a living thing, but in their unity they found strength.

And within his embrace, Marie understood that the situation between them had changed. After this moment, no matter how much each wished to remain distant from the other, they could never be strangers.

However much the thought of leaving him hurt, she found solace in the memories she would have of this gallant man, a man of honor, determination, and great compassion. He protected those he loved. Wept for those he lost. Compared to Colyne, those who had pursued her in the past, men whose greed dictated their lives, were but empty shells of humanity.

He brushed a tear from her face. "Come." He turned toward the devastation.

Without question, she followed.

* * *

For the next several hours they worked to bury his friends, the crackle and hissing of burning wood as the fire raged, a macabre backdrop.

With a blackened shovel, Colyne heaved the next pile of dirt atop the shallow grave. Emotions choking him, he forced himself to continue. By God, his friends would be buried with honor.

A short distance away, Alesia walked toward the gutted crofter's hut, now a charred skeleton consumed by flames. She halted. A gasp escaped her as she collapsed to her knees, and her hand closed around the shredded remains of a doll. She clutched the doll against her chest, great heaving sobs wracking her slender frame.

Understanding her grief, fighting his own demons, Colyne dropped the shovel and strode to her. He knelt at her side.

Without hesitation she turned into his arms. "This is all so senseless."

"Aye, 'tis." The bloody bastards. There were nay reasons good enough for this senseless slaughter. But that wouldna stop King Edward in his quest to conquer Scotland.

"There now, lass." Colyne rocked her in his arms, her tears warm upon his neck, and he found comfort in holding her, a comfort he'd nae experienced since Elizabet.

An ache washed through him at thoughts of Elizabet, and he shoved them aside. She was out of his life, forever. As for Alesia, through the sharing of a tragedy, they'd formed the beginnings of a friendship, one that would last days at most.

She sniffed. "I am sorry."

The path of tears trailing through the dirt and soot on her face made his heart ache, but the determination in her eyes left him in awe. Surrounded by death, like a beacon in the night, this one woman offered hope that he could push aside his anger and grief over losing those he loved, including Elizabet.

Mayhap he'd been correct when he'd first seen Alesia and thought her a fairy from the Otherworld. "You have naught but earned my pride," he said, humbled by this woman who could give so much of herself for a country nae her own.

Another tremor shook her, but she didna turn away beneath his probing gaze.

Colyne stroked his thumb across a smudge on her cheek. *Who are you?* he wanted to ask. He believed she had nae walked into his life without reason. Whatever the cause, fate's hand had played a role. More so as this was the second time she'd aided him. He looked down.

Her fingers clutched the ragged doll. Her breath hitched. "This must have belonged to the little girl. I—"

"Shh." His hand trembled as he withdrew the battered toy and laid it within an unscathed bowl. He wrapped her fingers within his own. "Come." He stood and drew her with him. "Little more remains to be done. Gather your belongings and then refill the water pouch. I will take care of the rest."

She hesitated, her expression grief-stricken, but the resolve to continue as strong.

"There is an outcrop of rocks at the edge of the forest. Once I am through, I will meet you there. Please, I must finish this alone." Their burial a final farewell to friends whom he'd loved.

Alesia nodded. Her breath hitched as she turned and walked away.

As she neared the forest, Colyne reached down and picked up the blackened doll. With the scorched shreds of the child's toy in his hand, he stared at the woman who for the first in a long time had made him think of another besides Elizabet. Why? When Alesia slipped from view, on a rough sigh he set the doll in the bowl and then immersed himself in finishing the last of the grisly tasks.

Marie scanned the forest as Colyne led her through the thick weave of trees. She inhaled the clean, sweet scent of the earth, rich with a blend of bracken, mint, sorrel, and other familiar herbs. After the stench of death, she savored every untainted breath.

She stepped over a stone, and then glanced toward Colyne. His skin was pale and his face taut with grief. With how close he'd been to the deceased, it would be a long while before the scars of this day could begin to heal. She couldn't ease his burden, but mayhap she could take his mind from his pain. Or at least try. "Where are we going?"

He stared straight ahead.

She continued on, hoping to strike up a conversation. "You grew up within these woods?"

Colyne looked over, his eyes clearing a degree, but sorrow lingered. "Aye. At times we would sneak out when we were supposed to be practicing with our swords."

"We?"

"My sisters, my brother, and I."

"Your sisters were allowed to practice with swords?" She could envision her father's fury if she dared such. Not to mention the commotion among the gentry such a brazen act would incite.

A shimmer of a smile curved his mouth, then faltered. "Do you find the idea of a woman learning to defend herself provincial?"

"Not at all." The idea of wielding a blade held its own appeal. "It is only that I have never met a man who would let his daughters train with weapons."

"You never met my father." Pride reflected in his eyes. "He was an unconventional man."

Indeed, if anything like his son. "Your mother approved of this activity?" she asked, curious to learn more about his family.

Grief shadowed his face. "She never had a say. While giving birth to my youngest sister, she died."

Her chest squeezed. "I am sorry."

" 'Twas a long time ago. I barely remember her."

"But you loved her."

A stick snapped beneath his boot. He glanced toward the leaves trembling overhead in the late-afternoon breeze. "Aye."

The trees began to thin, and she hurried forward and fell into step at his side. "My mother died in a fever when I was young. I have no memory of her, not even the faintest gesture or the tenderness of her voice. Only the whimsical memories my father shares when he speaks of her. Yet, I find myself missing her greatly."

Tenderness softened the sadness in his eyes. " 'Twould seem we have something in common." The rush of water drew his attention. "We are almost there."

As she walked, the churn of water intensified; around her, a bed of moss cushioned the ground. The downy softness gave beneath her slippers.

"Watch out." Colyne caught a broken limb bent low before her and moved the branch aside. He gestured her forward.

"My thanks." Marie stepped from beneath the branch's shadow and halted. With reverence, she took in her surroundings.

Illuminated by the golden rays of the late afternoon sun, a stream spilled over a shallow ledge and poured into the small loch. On the far bank, where the current slowed, a bed of reeds peeked up, while lilies, along with the moss and yellow flowers, nestled amidst a cloud of heather to rim the water's edge.

Emotion welled in her throat as she turned. "'Tis wondrous."

As he watched her, Colyne's eyes softened, then he gave a rough sigh. "'Tis. And necessary. After this day, we both need to bathe." He strode to a plant thick with pink flowers and tore off several leaves, returned, and handed them to her. "'Tis soapwort. Crush them as you wash. They will produce a lather and help remove this day's grime." A hint of a dimple touched his mouth. "As a healer, I believe you would be knowing that."

Touched by his chagrin, she gave him a gentle smile. "I do, but it does not take away from your thoughtfulness."

For a long moment he stared at her. Desire trickled through his gaze, then resignation. He stepped back. "Do nae take too long. Though we have seen nay one, 'tis possible English knights are about."

Though soft, his cloaked warning shattered the illusion of peace around her. Marie scanned the rugged hills framing the gentle setting with a wary eye. Though embraced by serenity, danger existed, a fact underscored by this day's carnage.

He pointed toward where a shallow ledge extended from the top of the knoll. "I will be over there, keeping watch for anything suspect." With the stealth of a predator, he slipped into the woods and out of sight.

Thankful for his guard, she turned her attention to her disheveled state. With a grimace, she peeled off her stained garments and then stepped into the water, appreciating the cool slide after working through the rancid heat of the afternoon.

Taking a gulp of air, she dove deep. When Marie surfaced, she burst from the water, then swam with long, sure strokes toward shallow ground.

Halfway to shore, she tread water. She made out Colyne's outline as he stood on an outcrop overlooking the loch, which allowed him a clear view of the surrounding area as well.

Heat spread over her face. If he glanced in her direction, he would see her naked. Her body tingled with awareness, and the cool temperature of the water did little to douse the warmth sliding through her body.

Unsettled by the desire Colyne aroused, she swam toward shore. For the first time in her life she'd met a man who knew neither her title nor her role in life, and yet he'd offered her not only his protection but his friendship.

No tricks. No schemes designed to charm her into a marriage for personal gain, even when she refused to tell him of her reason for traveling to France.

Or was his easiness a cover to shield his own secrets? Did he believe if she viewed him as nonthreatening, she wouldn't question him further about the men who sought him?

On edge, she dove deep and then resurfaced. Exactly what was he hiding from her? What fate had befallen him to the point where men chased him with lethal intent?

Marie dismissed any thoughts of villainy on his part. Since he'd first awoken in the cave, he'd demonstrated over and again that he was a man who valued fairness. Somehow, for reasons he refused to share, he'd become embroiled in a dangerous situation.

As much as she wanted to believe he was loyal to Scotland's cause, without knowing for sure, in matters of trust she must proceed with caution.

"Alesia?"

Colyne's use of her second name was a blunt reminder of her deception. Neither could he discover her father was King Philip.

And if he did? Enticed by the promise of a royal tie and wealth, would greed flare in his eyes, as with most men when they learned of her station? Or would respect and honor remain there instead?

Marie hated her doubts, but life had taught her to be wary of men. Except for her maid and the knights assigned to guard her, she lived alone in a coastal village, far from her father and the court crowded with false smiles given only for self-gain.

She preferred her simple life in a small house by the sea, found satisfaction in working alongside the healer to aid those with simple means.

Until she'd met Colyne.

Now, an emptiness she'd never experienced unraveled inside. He made her want, not only physically but with a yearning to share more than a few days of her life with him.

"Alesia?" Colyne called again.

Frustrated with the unwanted emotions he made her feel, she swam until her feet brushed against the smoothed rock. "I am going to wash out my clothes," she said, thankful for the distance. "'Twill take but a trice."

"Nay, lass. I have set a clean gown behind the rocks near where you entered. It was spared from the fire, so I brought it along."

She glanced toward where his voice echoed, surprised by his kind gesture. How many men would have done the same?

Or cared?

Not that it mattered. They each had their own lives. Even if she longed to know more about him, to grow closer, time, as fate, stood against them.

Chapter 5

Colyne stood near the edge of the cliff, the air alive with the vibrant song of crickets and a gentle breeze sliding across the land. Yet he found little peace.

A short distance away, embraced by moonbeams, Alesia stared at the sky. From her solemn expression, she too was lost in thought. How could she nae be? The horrors of finding Stephano and his family murdered earlier this day haunted him still. Bedamned the English bastards.

"Colyne?"

The rawness within her voice nursed his guilt. He should have ensured she'd remained shielded from the carnage the English troops had left in their wake. Though horrified by the gruesome sight, she'd lent a hand, helping to bury those he'd loved.

"You are tired. Go to sleep. I shall keep watch." His voice broke at the last. With a hard swallow, he stared at the hills of the Highlands he so loved, a home he would die to keep free.

The light scrape of slippers upon stone alerted him of her approach.

"I have made a bed for you against the cliff." A part of him yearned to offer her succor, while another wished to seek comfort in her arms. He frowned. Either would be an unwise decision. Secrets shadowed her eyes, guided her response when he asked questions of her past, or of those who pursued her.

She halted at his side.

Her warm scent of woman and lavender melded with the freshness of the night, and his body hummed with awareness. God help him, he wanted her. But to turn to her now, to take advantage of the loss still haunting them both would be wrong. "You need to try and rest."

A long moment passed. "I am sorry for your loss. It is hard to lose someone you love."

"My thanks." Through half-lowered lashes, Colyne watched her kneel and pick up a weathered rock.

On an unsteady sigh, Alesia stood. She rolled the stone within her palm. "Will you tell me about the girl who owned the doll?" she asked, her question unraveling in a fragile whisper.

Moonlight shimmered through tears trailing down her cheeks.

"I am sorry," she whispered. "I only wanted to talk to you, to try to find a way to help you, as I know the family we buried were your friends. Sometimes it eases the pain when you . . . But I know you want to be alone." She turned and cast the stone.

A splash echoed from below.

A sword's wrath. Though he grieved for those he loved, she hurt and needed his strength. And damn the circumstance, he would be there for her. "Alesia?"

With a sob, she stepped into the circle of his arms.

Colyne drew her close, finding solace in her touch, hope in her presence, and a rightness he'd never expected, more so than he'd ever experienced with Elizabet. Confused, he held her, unsure what to make of this realization.

Her tears dampened his neck.

"'Tis fine, lass." Murmuring words to calm her in Gaelic, he cradled her against his chest until her sobs stilled, her breathing calmed, and tremors nay longer shook her body. He stroked her hair, unbound from its earlier braid.

"Her name was Katherine." The happiness of the child's memories flooded him. "A wee lass. Hair black as midnight. Green eyes that danced with devilment. But a heart—" his throat tightened— "a heart filled with love."

Colyne struggled against the fact that he would never again hear the wee one's laughter. Or watch her eyes widen with childish delight as he told her tales of the fairies who would whisk away even the stoutest man if he held their fancy.

"Whenever I would visit their home," he continued, "I would hear of her latest antics. Once when I rode up 'twas to find the lass lodged within a rowan tree and refusing to come down. When I asked why, she claimed to have stolen a tart. In her most serious tone, Katherine made me swear her location to secrecy."

Alesia sniffed. "What happened?"

"'Twould seem the lass had stolen nae one but the entire lot. Before long, her stomach began to ache and she ended up calling for me to help her down." A sad warmth embraced his heart as the poignant memory replayed in his mind. "I remember her vowing to her da to never be stealing so many tarts again. But, when he was nae looking, she winked at me, and I could tell her mind already had strayed in that direction."

Alesia looked up at him, her tear-filled eyes hazed with sorrow. "A very special girl."

His hand stilled. "She was." He lifted a lock of Alesia's honey-colored hair and secured it behind her ear. "I always wished one day, when I was blessed with a child, that she would have the same spirit." Emotion swelled in his throat as he shook his head. "I canna believe she is gone."

"At times there is no reasoning for the why of it," she said with a rough whisper. "Sadly, life's cruelty touches us all."

The chirp of crickets spilled through the night as she lifted her head and surveyed the land, slowly consumed by darkness. She turned.

The solemn appeal of her expression he expected but nae the glimmer of hope.

"You will always have her." Alesia pressed her palm over his heart. "Here."

Colyne laced his fingers through her own, humbled by her strength, amazed at her belief in goodness when her own journey had delivered her into her own personal nightmare.

"After a while the pain will give way to the warmth of memories, to times when laughter will fill your life." She paused, her gaze intense. "Life is too short to dwell upon what we cannot change."

"What challenges have you endured to gift you with such wisdom, my lady?" he asked, unsure how to deal with the feelings she stirred within him.

"Naught more than you yourself have faced."

Her reply perplexed him. As a noble as well as a knight, he'd witnessed more than his share of death and the tragedies wrought of war.

With each brutality, his mind had dulled in frustrated acceptance that however much he tried, he could save but so many.

Alesia was obviously a woman of rank. Imagining her protected within castle walls, he doubted her ability to understand the tragedies of war. Or the wisdom garnered. Yet her sage words, and the lingering sadness in her eyes, were traits he'd witnessed only in people who'd suffered greatly.

Another contradiction.

He wanted to press her to reveal her secret. Except he refused to risk her withdrawal. "You are weary," Colyne said, reluctant to release her but aware he must.

"As if you are rested?" she said in quiet challenge.

What a lass. She'd argue with a saint. He couldna help but admire her spirit. "Go." He released her hand. "Try to sleep. I will be standing guard."

"You have not answered my question."

A fleeting smile grazed his mouth. "Have I mentioned you are stubborn?"

Her lower lip trembled, reminding him all too clearly of her fragile state.

"Could you sleep this night?"

At her solemn words, the lightness of the moment faded. "Nay."

"Neither can I." She gestured toward the bed of leaves. "If I lay there, I will only stare at the sky and think of everything. Could I stay beside you this night? I . . ."

Need you, his mind finished. She didna say the words, but in the moonlight, her eyes whispered the request.

"Please?" she whispered.

Tenderness curled through him. If for only a few hours, being with her would help him as well as he battled the painful memories of this day. He gestured toward an area of smooth rock. "Bring your blanket over there. You can sit with me."

Thankful he'd granted her request, Marie retrieved the tattered wool throw. When she returned, Colyne had settled into a sitting position that allowed him a clear view of their surroundings.

At her approach, he motioned for her to sit before him.

She spread the blanket on the stone and then sat. As she settled against the solid warmth of his chest, the steady beat of his heart pulsed against her.

Drawing a deep breath, she stared into the sky. A trace of clouds edged the western horizon, and the moon, outlined by a ring of silver, hung over the treetops. "When I gaze into the heavens and see such beauty, it makes me wonder how anyone can revel in hatred."

"Too often people focus only on their own gain, nae on what is right."

The soft rumble of his voice was a balm to her bruised nerves. She nodded, thinking of the strife Scotland faced. "As King Edward?" He stiffened against her, and she knew she'd hit upon a concern uppermost in his mind.

"He believes his harsh actions are warranted," Colyne said, anger pouring through his words.

"Though I disagree with his method, he is overlord of Scotland."

"Earned through treachery," he spat. "After Margaret, the Maid of Norway's death, King Edward stated his good intent was in helping Scotland choose a king during their time of unrest. But, as many Scots suspected, his offer was naught but a guise in his efforts to claim Scotland."

Marie hesitated. She couldn't reveal her royal connection, but she needed to warn Colyne that King Edward would stop at nothing to seize a country he already considered his. "He is a determined man," she said carefully, "and will not halt his aggressions until all of Scotland has thrown down its weapons and sworn fealty to him."

His body tensed. "He can try."

"I know." The slaughter they'd witnessed today was but a taste of the butchery to come if the English king was allowed to release his full wrath upon Scotland.

"With France's backing," Colyne continued, "we have nae only the means but another force for King Edward to face."

By the grace of Mary, he had no idea of how precarious Scotland's ties were at this moment with France. If Renard had reached her father and convinced him that the Scottish rebels were behind her abduction, her father may have already severed the much-needed support for Scotland's bid for freedom. "You are cold?"

She frowned. "What?"

"You are shivering." Colyne wrapped the woven wool over her shoulders, then slid his arm around her waist and drew her closer. "Better?"

Until she spoke with her father, naught could make the situation better. She nodded, not trusting herself to speak.

He pointed east. "Over there."

A flicker of white raced through the sky and then faded into the night.

His warm breath sifted across her cheek. "They say when a star falls, 'tis a gift bestowed from the fairies."

Emotions tightened her throat and she nodded, unable to speak.

Silence stretched between them, his concern all but spoken in the whispers of the night.

She nestled against his muscled chest and laid her cheek against the hollow of his throat. "I shall try to rest."

"Aye, you do that."

Weary, Marie struggled to sleep. But only after hours of tormented thoughts about what would happen if she failed to reach her father, and with Colyne still holding her safe in his arms, did she finally fall into an exhausted slumber.

A battering of cool wind against his face woke Colyne. He grimaced. Somewhere during the dawn, he'd drifted off. Rubbing the sleep from his eyes, he took in the angry clouds rolling overhead. The gentle wind of last night now railed across the landscape with a harsh slap.

A storm was moving in.

Alesia shifted in his arms. Her thick mane of honey-colored hair framed her face and her lips were turned upward in a soft pout.

A yearning curled tight inside. What would it be like if he kissed her?

Thunder rolled in the heavens.

He grimaced as he scanned the darkening sky. It appeared a higher authority than he would remind him of the folly of such a thought.

Concern edged through him at the dark circles visible beneath her eyes. However much he hated to wake her, they needed to put as many miles between them and their pursuers as possible. And, from the look of the black clouds, find shelter before the storm broke.

"Alesia?"

Her lips twitched into an endearing frown.

"Alesia," he whispered again.

She continued to sleep.

"Ah, lass. What am I going to do with you?" he whispered, charmed and a wee bit envious that she'd fallen into such a deep slumber. Many a battle ago, he'd nurtured the ability to awaken at the lightest sound.

The first drop of rain splattered against his brow. Then another.

Colyne squinted toward the threatening sky and then gave her a gentle shake. "Time to be up with you."

Moss-green eyes fluttered open and stared up at him in sleepy confusion.

A pure shot of lust pumped through his blood.

Another splatter of rain hit his hand.

On a muttered curse, Colyne gently set her away from himself and stood, his body sluggish from lack of sleep. "We need to find shelter before it begins to pour."

"What?" she asked, her voice groggy. She started to stand and stumbled.

He caught her shoulders. Warm rain had started to fall, soaking her garb and outlining Alesia's full breasts. He gritted his teeth. He had to think of something else. The miles they must travel this day. The misery of trudging in this damp and treacherous weather. The men who chased them.

Nay matter how hard he tried, his every thought came back to wanting her. "Wake up now, lass."

A tired smile curved her mouth. "I am awake." As if a trick of the fairies, desire wove through her gaze in a devastating slide.

He swallowed hard, his hands trembling from the effort to keep his distance. If she kept looking at him that way . . . God help him, he wasna a saint. "Can you stand alone?" She nodded, but he didna let her go.

Alesia watched him, her full lips tempting, threatening to destroy his will.

Nay, he wasna going to kiss her. He would be a fool to consider such. Hadna he spent the last several minutes reasoning the harm in doing exactly that?

"Colyne?"

The raw yearning within her words ripped through his good intention like a well-honed blade. With a curse, he cupped her face.

Alesia's eyes darkened with understanding—a split second before Colyne claimed her mouth.

Chapter 6

Heat. It washed through Marie, overwhelmed her until all she could do was cling. Though she'd been kissed before, never had it been this potent, this intense, or this exquisite. Colyne's mouth moved over hers with deft sureness, giving, taking, luring her to respond until her blood flowed wild. Though their bodies were snug, she wanted more.

With his eyes locked on hers, he began to touch her, caress her as if he knew her every secret place, and her body burned until she thought she would ignite. On a rough breath, his fingers skimmed along the curve of her neck and then began to loosen the ties of her gown.

A shiver of anticipation slid through her.

This moment.

This day.

This man . . . everything was perfect.

As he inched the delicate fabric past her shoulders, night-dampened air whispered across her exposed breast and mingled with the heat of Colyne's touch. A low groan rumbled in his chest as he caught her nipple between his lips.

Sensation shattered her every thought.

"Elizabet."

Marie froze.

Elizabet?

She plunged to realty with a sickening lurch.

Colyne's eyes widened at the realization of what he'd said, the fire within shattering to panicked disbelief. "Oh, God. I am sorry."

She shoved away from him as her cheeks burned with mortification and jerked up her gown. The entire time he'd been kissing her, touching her, he'd been thinking of another!

He reached toward her. "Alesia, I—"

"Stay away from me!" Her words trembled, filled with the shame of what she'd allowed. Memories of how the Earl of Archerbeck, a man she'd loved in her past, and a man who had used her for his own gain, had tainted her senses like bile in her throat. An ache built inside. She knew better than to trust a man, a lesson Archerbeck had taught her all too well.

"How dare you!" Shaking with disbelief at her own weakness, Marie took another step back. How could she have allowed a stranger past her barriers? Have responded to him with complete abandon?

Or wanted him even now?

A ruddy hue swept across his cheeks. He shook his head. "You do nae understand."

"You are wrong," she replied with as much dignity as she could muster. "I understand completely."

He caught her shoulders as she turned to run.

Marie glared at him, unsure if anger or humiliation guided her actions. Or both. "Release me!"

As he stared at her, his eyes darkened with sorrow, and she remembered him mumbling Elizabet's name during his fever. "You love her?" At his silence, she wrenched free. She was a fool to punish herself this way, but she needed to hear him admit the truth.

He watched her a moment longer, the regret in his eyes matching her own.

"Colyne," she urged.

A muscle worked in his jaw, and then his expression grew unreadable. "'Tis nae a subject I will be wanting to discuss."

The quiet calm of his voice stoked her ire. How could he retreat with such stoic efficiency while her emotions still roiled? "I did not ask for your kiss."

"You did nae," he rasped.

"After what has passed between us, do you not think I deserve an explanation?"

Apology burned in his deep blue eyes. He swallowed hard. "Elizabet is someone I once cared about. She chose another."

Cared about? From the heartache in his words, he loved Elizabet still. "Why did you kiss me?"

"When I awoke with you in my arms . . . God help me, I wanted you."

"*Non*," she charged, angry he'd used her in place of another woman. "You wanted Elizabet. Deny it."

Anger clouded his face. As quick, defeat. "You are wrong, 'twas you who drew me."

Marie opened her mouth to disagree and then refrained. As if her own actions were proper? She was promised to Gaston de Croix, Duke of Vocette. A marriage that would take place before summer's end. Yet she had returned Colyne's kisses, shivered at his touch, as if she had the right to give her favors to another man.

Her guilt grew.

How could she condemn Colyne for saying the name of a woman he obviously loved? He had his own life, one that didn't include her.

Rain pattered against her skin.

Marie brushed several wet strands of hair from her face as she composed herself, drawing on the diplomacy she'd honed over the years. She needed to focus on reaching her father and telling him the truth of her abduction, not yearn for a man in love with another.

"We must find shelter," she said, thankful for the calmness of her voice.

"Nae, we must continue on."

She frowned. "We?"

"I will be taking you to the coast. There I shall speak with a friend who will offer you protection and arrange passage for you to France."

He didn't add more; she didn't need him to. His solemn tone said everything. Once she was in safe hands, they'd part ways forever.

Hours later, Colyne studied the turbulent skies. Since they'd started out that morning, it had continued to rain, at times so hard they were forced to seek temporary shelter beneath trees or rocks.

Guilt knifed him as he glanced toward Alesia, walking at his side. How could he have spoken Elizabet's name? In the few kisses he and Elizabet had shared, never had she inspired a fragment of the feelings Alesia evoked.

The full impact of his musings left him stunned. For the first time since Elizabet had wed, the woman he'd loved since his youth hadna been on his mind. Nay, she'd been there, buried beneath conscious thought, where memories of her lingered and would continue to haunt him. Exhaustion had allowed Elizabet's name to escape from the recesses of his mind.

Nae desire.

The reasoning should have left him satisfied, but if he loved Elizabet, how could he be so drawn to this elusive enchantress? Or were his longings those of a man desperate to find relief from the pain of losing the woman he loved?

His steps faltered. Mayhap with the secret Alesia kept, he found her safe in that he could never trust her enough to fall in love with her?

Colyne glanced toward her. Though she masked her hurt with a noble front, he saw the confusion she fought to disguise.

The pain he had caused.

Damn him, he'd taken liberties where he'd had nay right. From this moment on, he'd nae touch her again, would keep his focus on delivering the writ to King Philip—where it should have remained from the start.

To make amends for hurting her, he would escort her to Glasgow and procure arrangements for her continued travel, and then secure his own passage to France.

Thunder echoed through the darkened skies. The warm rain of this morning had grown cool. Now, it pounded the earth, creating a layer of mist swirling inches above the ground in a blur of white.

He silently cursed the weather as they walked, their steps muted by the damp earth. They were both soaked to the bone. Though clumps of rock jutted out from shallow cliffs around them, he'd yet to find shelter large enough to offer adequate protection.

Colyne stepped over a log, and the writ secured within its hidden compartment rubbed against his side. He frowned. King Philip's bastard daughter was still hidden somewhere in the Highlands.

Or had the other Scots searching for the lass found her? *Please, let her be safe.* God help them if they found her dead.

In the misty silence, Alesia's stomach growled.

Colyne took in her cool expression as she stared straight ahead. They walked beneath an old oak, its leaves sheltering them from most of the rain. He halted. "We will stop here and eat."

The lass kept walking.

"Alesia—"

She whirled. "I have changed my mind, monsieur." Each icy word issued emphasized her regal control. "It is best if we separate. I will find my own way to France." With her head held high and the rain pelting her body, she strode off in a different direction.

Colyne stared, amazed at her defiance. The stubborn fool. Did she think she could travel through the Highlands without a care? Had she forgotten men intent on killing her prowled the woods? Or did she despise him so much that she preferred risking her life rather than enduring his company? "Alesia!"

She didna look back.

A crushing weight settled over his chest. *Let her go.* 'Twas best to be rid of the lass, of the complications she brought, the unwanted emotions she aroused. As her outline blurred in the downpour, Colyne cursed, then broke into a run. He'd vowed to protect her, and by God, he would keep his word whether she liked it or nae. "Alesia, stop!"

She broke into a run.

A sword's wrath! With long, ground-eating strides, he caught her arm as she started down a steep hill. She whirled on him like a wildcat, all claws and fury. "Leave me alone!"

"Alesia—"

"Non." She yanked her arm back and lost her footing. The combination of the sharp decline and their awkward stance threw them both off-balance.

Colyne slammed against the ground, with Alesia landing on his chest. Leaves squished beneath them as they started to slide down the muddied bank. She tried to shove free, but he held her tight. As they shuddered to a halt, in a quick move, he rolled on top of her and pinned her to the ground.

Flecks of moss and pine wove through her damp, honey-colored hair as she glared up at him.

A face that would haunt him with its beauty, a woman whose spirit lured him until it was hard to breath. He would have let her go, should have, but beneath her anger he saw the passion still burning hot. And all his good intentions fled.

He leaned closer.

Alesia's eyes widened with panic. "Get—"

Colyne claimed her mouth in a fierce kiss, his lips moving across hers with relentless possession. After a moment's hesitation, she buried her fingers in his wet hair and pulled him closer.

Thunder boomed nearby.

Blood pounding, he broke free and stared at her mouth, swollen with his kisses, her eyes dark with passion. "This time when I kissed you, Alesia," he rasped, "I was thinking only of you!"

Red scorched her cheeks. Her chest heaved. "And that is supposed to make me forgive your actions?"

"Nay." He released her. Curses. He'd only meant to . . .

She scrambled to her feet and took a shaky step back. "Do not," she ordered when he started to rise.

Colyne stood, the warrior in him demanding her complete surrender, the strategist understanding that if he pushed her now, he could destroy any remaining trust between them.

Trust.

As if, after his actions this day, he deserved any from her?

"What do you want from me?" she asked, the quiver in her voice blurring his objectivity.

For the first time in his life, he wasna sure. "I do nae know."

Eyes fragile with pain watched him. "At least you are honest."

"You understand naught. I—" *What? Want you? Need to explain how, for some reason, you are able to make me forget the pain of losing the woman I loved?*

He fisted his hands at his sides and then slowly released them. Somehow he had to repair the breech he'd constructed between them. Or at least try. "Let me take you to the coast. Please."

Moss-green eyes narrowed. "I can make it there by myself."

He would have smiled at her stubbornness if the situation wasna so dire. "Alesia," he said gently, "you are traveling north."

"I—" She glanced toward the direction in which she was headed, then back toward him, her blush darkening a shade deeper. "I was upset. I would have realized my error and corrected my direction." Her cold glare dared him to disprove her claim.

"You will be needing my guidance. Besides the arduous travel, predators live within these woods. Neither can you forget the men searching for us."

At the reminder, her face paled, but determination creased her jaw as well.

She didna like it. He didna expect her to. From the short time he'd known her, if nothing else, he'd learned she wasna a foolish woman.

Alesia tilted her chin. "I could make it."

He suppressed the smile warring to break free. "Of that I have nay doubt."

* * *

Marie nodded, appeased by Colyne's agreement. "We shall travel together, but only if you keep your distance."

"In the future, I will take naught that you do nae offer freely."

A grumble of disgust fell from her lips. "As if I would let you touch me again." But even as she said the words, she knew she'd lied. Her skin still tingled where his fingers had caressed her, and her body ached where he had not. She might as well admit it: when it came to him, she wasn't immune.

"Are you hungry?"

Thankful he'd changed the subject, she shook her head. "We should keep traveling." Marie didn't want the quiet solitude of sharing a meal with him. She needed to keep in mind her upcoming marriage to the Duke of Vocette.

Lightning shattered overhead. Thunder rumbled in its wake. Large drops of rain splattered in the puddles.

Colyne grumbled an oath and held out his hand. "'Tis dangerous enough to make our way down this slope when it is dry. This storm has made it worse." When she hesitated, he caught her fingers and started down the decline toward where a jagged sheet of rock fell straight to the earth, severed by the stream meandering below.

As she started to protest, another blast of thunder shattered nearby. Then it began to pour until she could barely see.

Conceding, she allowed Colyne to guide her around the sharp wall of rock, then down the steep slope. Even with his assistance, she half-fell, half-slid the rest of the way down.

At the bottom, the ground leveled out near the stream. He gestured toward a small cave beneath a shallow overhang. "Let us hope 'twill be large enough for us both."

Exhausted and thankful for the refuge, Marie climbed over the few rocks necessary and ducked into the opening. The recess was deep enough for the two of them to fit inside.

Barely.

Colyne moved in beside her and her relief fled.

Too aware of him, she tried to shift away.

His mouth twitched with laughter. "Unless you feel like standing outside in this mess, you will be finding nay more room."

Marie remained silent. There was naught humorous about this situation.

He glanced over. "I promise, you are safe with me."

Safe. Awareness tingled through her at the roll of his gentle burr. After their last kiss, when he'd cut through her defenses with pathetic ease, doubts lingered if there was anything safe about him. And wedged beneath this layer of rock, snug against his muscled frame, did little to douse her desire.

No, there was naught safe about this situation.

Clothing rustled. "Here."

She tensed.

Colyne held out an oatcake.

Marie hesitated and then accepted the fare. "My thanks." She edged toward the cave's entrance.

"Alesia—"

At the use of her second name, guilt swept her. "I have to—"

The shouts of angry men echoed nearby.

Chapter 7

A sword's wrath, Renard's men! Colyne pulled back, cursing as a sharp rock protruding from the cave wall jabbed into his wounded shoulder.

"Who is out there?"

Terror filled Alesia's eyes as she watched him, and his guilt grew. "A band of knights." Bedamned, he should have kept alert during their travels. "We must remain hidden until they are gone."

With the way the riders huddled their mounts together against the storm, he suspected they would soon seek shelter.

The squish of hooves sinking into the soft bank sounded.

That Renard's men continued their search in such foul weather spoke volumes; they would stop at nothing to find him.

"Do you know them?" she whispered, pressing against him to peer over his shoulder.

Pain tightened in his chest. How could he nae? The bastards were the knights who'd slain his friend Douglas, the reason he now carried the writ. "Aye."

"Who are they?"

He fisted his hands, tamping down the need for revenge.

"Colyne?"

A muscle worked in his jaw. "Men who want me dead."

Thick, honey-colored lashes dropped to shield her eyes. "I . . ."

"What?" he asked, irritated by the reminder of her secrets.

"How did they find us?"

He made a quick survey of the knights, irritated by her avoidance of his question. After their kiss, he'd . . . What? Believed it would change their relationship to something deeper? If so, he was a fool.

After Elizabet had married another, he'd understood too well how a kiss, nay matter the heat, guaranteed little.

"It has been raining too hard for them to have trailed us." Colyne shrugged. "I doubt they know we are here."

Above the ledge, a knight cantered past, then several more.

A fall of rocks clattered near the entrance. Through the curtain of rain spilling over the stone above, Colyne watched as the legs of a knight's mount flashed by.

Alesia gasped.

"Steady now." Mail scraped stone as Colyne reached for his dagger.

More rocks thunked down the muddied slope near the cave's entrance. Through the blur of rain, another knight came into view. Mud sucked at his mount's hooves as he rode toward the group of men a short distance away who had also started to descend the embankment.

Alesia inched closer. "What are we going to do?"

He counted twenty riders. Too many to take on alone, especially injured. "Hopefully they will leave in search of shelter."

Several men cantering across the upper rim of the slope joined the main group.

With a sigh, Colyne relaxed his grip on his dagger. The rain streaming over the cave's narrow opening had concealed their presence. In an effort to ease his throbbing shoulder, he shifted. As he turned, another sharp rock dug into his wound. He muttered a foul curse.

"What is wrong?"

"Naught." They had more important things to worry about than his injuries.

A burly man, who appeared to be in charge of the horsemen, rode to the stream's edge. "Wherever they are," he shouted above the roll of thunder, "they could not have traveled past here."

"They?" Alesia whispered. "How do they know we are traveling together?"

"Perhaps they stumbled upon the cave where you tended me," he replied. "Or discovered the burials or other signs of us being together."

"'Tis too dangerous to cross," the lead man shouted back.

Alesia's hand tightened on Colyne's shoulder. "Look at the stream!"

The knight in charge scanned the angry torrent of churning water rushing past. Massive tree limbs bobbed in the current as if they were fallen twigs. "They must find another place to cross."

"So must we," Colyne whispered as he faced her.

A frown wedged across her brow. "What direction will we take?"

With a grimace, he surveyed their surroundings. A wall of rock on their left removed the decision to travel north. With the steep banks slick and treacherous, retracing their steps wasna possible.

One choice remained.

"After the riders leave, we will head downstream."

The burly leader scowled at the blackened sky and then faced his horsemen. "We will set up camp here. Guards will be posted. If they try to pass this way, we will catch them."

Her eyes widened. "They are staying?"

A muscle worked in Colyne's jaw. "'Twould seem so."

"Over there," the leader called. One hand shielded his face from the driving rain as the other motioned toward a stand of trees crowded on the top of the embankment, a short distance down the burn.

An outlook allowed them a fair view of their surroundings and, unknowingly, the ability to see any move he and Alesia would make.

The knights secured their horses in the nearby trees and hurried to construct a makeshift shelter.

"What are we going to do?" she whispered. "We cannot stay here."

As if he didna realize that. He curbed his temper. Circumstance, nay her, instigated their plight. The small cave offered them protection from the weather, but with their bodies wedged in the confines and his wound aching, they couldna remain much longer. Having Alesia's body pressed against him, and his wanting her, helped naught.

They must find a larger shelter if he was to keep his sanity. Colyne gave her hand a squeeze. "Wait here."

As he started to pull away, Alesia tightened her grip. "What are you going to do?"

"At the next rumble of thunder, I will release the horses. With luck, they will believe the blasts frightened their mounts. Once the men give chase, I will return. Then we can leave."

Her face paled. "You cannot go out there alone. Your arm is not fully—"

"'Tis too dangerous for us to remain. Our only hope of escape is to create a diversion."

"Even so, they will keep the horses guarded. And what if you do not—"

"I will be back," he said, his words nae as steady as he would have liked. The possibility he wouldna return was all too real. Wanting to divert her concern, he gave her a teasing smile. "You are nae worried about me, are you?"

Eyes rimmed with concern, she scowled at him. "This is not a matter to make light of."

"That it is nae." He cupped her face, swept his thumb over her bottom lip. "If I do nae return, you are to remain here until 'tis safe, then leave."

"Colyne—"

"Promise me!"

"I . . ." She closed her eyes for a long moment before opening them, the fear within easy to read, as well as anger. "*Oui*, but you must promise that you will return."

He'd meant to make the parting simple, but with her impassioned demand, she'd made it impossible. Aching for her, he claimed her mouth, his kiss turbulent, filled with unchecked desire.

A horse whinnied in the distance.

He broke the kiss, pressed his brow to hers, and banked his desires.

He needed to go.

The writ!

When he'd sworn to Douglas as he lay dying that he'd deliver the writ to King Philip, never had he imagined he'd entrust Robert Bruce's missive to another, especially to an unknown woman embraced by danger.

Colyne studied Alesia. However much the risk, he believed she was a woman of her word. Now, in the ultimate act of faith, he would test that belief.

With unwavering trust in her, he withdrew the writ from the hidden fold of his undershirt. "Here."

Wariness flickered on her face as she stared at the bound leather. "Why are you giving this to me?"

Thunder crashed into the rain-dampened silence, a stark reminder that he must go. "If I do nae return, stay hidden until the English knights have gone." Colyne shook his head when she made to speak.

"Travel north for a day, two at most. I know 'tis well out of your way, but seek a man named Blar MacTavish of Clan Fraser. Give him this." He laid the bound leather in her palm.

"Who is Blar MacTavish?"

At the fear rattling her voice, he cupped her face. "A friend," he said with soft assurance. "Someone you can trust." He didna reveal the contents of the document. If someone captured her, she could truthfully claim she didna know what message was secured inside, and might be allowed to live. "Tell him . . . Tell him Douglas is dead. That this needs to be delivered immediately. MacTavish will know what to do."

Her eyes searched his. The shimmer of unshed tears spoke of her desperation. "Who is Douglas?"

"Douglas was a knight who . . ." Colyne fought back the crush of grief. "He was my friend."

Sadness darkened her eyes. "I am sorry."

He nodded, the time to leave long past. "Remember, if I do nae return, take this to MacTavish. He shall ensure you receive safe escort to France."

A tear wove down her cheek.

Shaken, he wiped away the moisture with the pad of his thumb. How could he leave her? He stared at the leather bound writ and sobered. How could he stay? Somewhere in the Highlands, King Philip's bastard daughter was being held against her will, her abduction blamed upon rebel Scots. An accusation Renard might already have conveyed to the French king.

Unless this writ from Robert Bruce, explaining the English noble's contemptible ploy, reached King Philip, Scotland's support from France might be lost.

Neither could Colyne forget that more than his country's freedom lay at stake. The threat now included Alesia's life.

Desperation had Marie reaching out for him. "I . . ." What? Need you? She stared at Colyne, her cheeks burning from her near revelation. She couldn't need or want him. That he'd entrusted her with an important missive had deeply moved her, how could it not? "Be safe."

Only his smile answered, a look so tender it made her ache.

His mouth claimed hers in rushed desperation, and then he broke the kiss. "I will return." Stone scraped beneath his feet as he slipped into the downpour.

Trembling, Marie settled against the stone wall. She stared at the raindrops collecting in the puddle left by his footprints. Never could she think of Colyne as anything more than a friend, but shamefully, she'd already overstepped boundaries she had no right to ignore.

Why couldn't she have met him before agreeing to the betrothal with the duke? But she had, and 'twas a promise to her father she could not break. She released a sigh into the misted silence and drew the writ against her chest. "Please come back to me, Colyne."

The monotonous batter of rain continued. She traced her finger along the sewn edge of the bound leather.

A writ.

Her father often sent messages of import through similar means. Was this the secret Colyne kept hidden from her? If so, why hadn't she discovered the document when she'd removed his mail and garb to tend to him back at the cave? She frowned. He must have hidden it within the thick folds of his undershirt, and with her nerves on edge she'd missed it.

Curiosity bade her to untie the damp straps and discover the contents, or at least view the sender's seal. Honor stilled her hand. Whatever message lay secured within belonged to another. She'd promised Colyne she would deliver the writ into safe hands if he didn't return. If his brave act cost him his life, then so help her, she would follow through on her vow.

The wind-whipped rain increased. Lightning flashed overhead. Thunder shuddered with another ferocious blast.

Squeals of frightened horses rent the air. Moments later, the knights' mounts galloped past.

Shouts rose above the fury of the storm. Blurs of angry men appeared on the hilltop, running after their steeds. Then, they too, disappeared into the forest.

Time passed with an ominous hand.

Marie edged to the entry of her small haven, her face inches from the lash of rain. With a shiver against the damp air, she searched the steep hills, scanning past the rain-soaked trees, their limbs and leaves caught in a macabre dance.

Every distant shout of the outraged knights left her further unsettled. Had they spotted Colyne among the horses?

Was he caught?

Or dead?

She hugged herself and prayed.

Rumbles of thunder shattered around her. The rain fell faster.

Still, Colyne didn't return.

She refused to give up hope. He *was* alive. But each passing second added doubts to his fate.

At the slap of leather against stone outside the entrance, Marie
withdrew her dagger.

"'Tis Colyne," he said, his breath coming fast as he slipped inside, his clothing soaking wet, his face haggard.

With a cry of relief, she sheathed her weapon and threw herself
into his arms. He hauled her against him and moved deeper into their
cramped shelter. Then he was kissing her as if she were his entire
world, his mouth hungrily stealing her every moan.

Colyne broke the kiss and held her tight, the rapid rise and fall of
his chest a potent reminder of the risk he'd taken. "We must leave," he
said, his smoldering gaze assuring her that his words were at odds
with his wishes.

"I know." She took a calming breath. "I was so scared. When you
did not come back, I . . ." She paused. "You are here now. That is all
that matters."

"I didna mean to be gone so long. To avoid being seen, I was
forced to hang on to the side of a saddle and ride out with one of the
panicked horses. I doubled back as soon as I could."

Her fingers trembled as she held out the writ, her emotions too
volatile for her to speak further.

"My thanks," he said, his tone grave. He stowed the dispatch in
what she now knew was a hidden pouch within his undershirt. "We
must leave before they return."

Mud oozed beneath her slippers as Marie followed Colyne into
the tempest, her thoughts as tumbled as the storm-tossed leaves
whipping past.

The image of her betrothed flooded her mind. Gaston de Croix, a
duke, a man with enormous wealth and power. Duty demanded she

follow a path already made, except now the idea of marriage to another man left her empty.

And what of Colyne's whispering Elizabet's name?

Colyne was a man who loved passionately, Marie reasoned. He wanted her. But could his desire for her compare with his feelings for the woman he'd loved in the past?

She reined in her musings. Decorum must guide her decisions, not emotions. She would put all thoughts of Colyne out of her mind.

Besides, he believed she was a missionary. How would he react if he learned that she was King Philip's bastard daughter? Would he be angry? Or would greed sway his thoughts instead? She hated these doubts but had learned the price of trusting with her heart.

The weight of her responsibilities sat heavy on her mind. However wrong, she cared for Colyne. He had risked his life to protect her. And when faced with possible death, he had entrusted her with the writ.

If thrown into danger, would she have dared tell him the truth of her heritage and why she must return to France? She stole a glance at the cavalier knight who traveled at her side.

"Alesia, the cliff is collapsing to your right!"

Lost to her troubling thoughts, Colyne's shout gave her a second's warning. Marie tried to turn away, but the ground beneath her began to split.

Then gave way to emptiness.

Chapter 8

On a curse, Colyne lunged for Alesia as she slipped over the ledge. His hand caught hers.

Barely.

With their fingers linked, she slammed against the mud-soaked bank. Her eyes locked on his, widened with terror. "Help!"

"Hang on!" Pain knifed through his wounded shoulder and his body began to shudder. He gritted his teeth. A sword's wrath, he would nae lose her! He inched back.

Pieces of the waterlogged bank beneath them continued to break free.

Alesia twisted in his hold as the churning torrent rumbled far below. "Colyne!"

"Stay calm," he rasped. The ground beneath them began to tremble. A large slab of earth tore free, slamming into the raging waters below. Beneath him, fissures split open and widened.

Her body shifted as she dangled over the edge, wrenching his shoulder.

"Alesia, use both hands to hold my right one."

On a sob, she wrapped her fingers around his.

With his other hand, Colyne caught the bush to his left. The branch bent as, inch by grueling inch, he pulled her up. At his next tug, her head came into view. "When I tell you to," he shouted, "use your feet to climb out."

Alesia nodded.

"Now!" he called and pulled with all his might. Another burst of pain shot down his left shoulder. Blackness threatened. Colyne gulped a breath, then another as he gritted his teeth and continued to pull.

Deep lines wedged her brow as she dug her feet into the muck and slowly climbed.

As her slipper came into view, he yanked her over the ledge.

With a gasp, she tumbled against his chest, and they collapsed on the soggy ground, their breathing labored, her body trembling with fear.

He glanced behind her.

Cracked slabs of rock and earth widened.

"We must move farther back!"

The ground beneath them shook, and the bush he clung to tore free.

Colyne shoved Alesia ahead of him and scrambled after her. "Go!" His boot hit air as the bank disintegrated beneath him, but his other foot found purchase on the slick earth. He lunged forward, hit solid ground.

They ran.

Several paces away, a muted roar built in their wake.

"Faster!" he shouted.

The land beneath them heaved.

A sword's wrath! Colyne grabbed her and dove. A huge tremor rocked the ground as they rolled to a stop. With his heart pounding, his brow soaked with rain and sweat, Colyne held her in his arms as, several feet away, the remainder of the cliff collapsed.

Trembling, he laid his brow against hers. A sword's wrath! He'd almost lost her.

Eyes wide with fear watched him. "Y—you saved me."

Emotion tightened his throat as he stared at her, wondered if he could ever let her go. "I would never leave you." Her eyes searched his with such gratitude that his heart tightened in his chest.

She shook her head. "*Non*, you would not."

Desperate for her touch, he slammed his mouth over hers, tasting rain and fear and another emotion he refused to identify.

Lightning flashed.

Colyne broke the kiss. With a rough sigh, he stroked her wet hair, wishing everything was different.

The time.

The place.

The circumstance.

Loud splatters of cold rain continued to pound the earth, a potent reminder that naught had changed. They needed to leave before the knights returned. "Lass, we must somehow make our way across."

"Will we use the fallen tree?"

He followed her nervous gaze toward a large oak caught in the churning torrent that straddled the banks. Though it extended the entire width of the burn, its angle, along with the amount of water spilling over the trunk, made using the downed tree too treacherous. "Nay. We will have to go back, find another shelter, and wait until—"

Loud shouts had Colyne glancing over his shoulder. With a curse, he shoved his way into the protective cover of bushes, pulling Alesia with him. As he peered through the tangle of branches, two mounted knights rode into view. Both shielded their faces against the wind and rain as they followed the water's edge.

"They have caught their horses!" she whispered.

"Aye." He unsheathed his dagger.

The men rode closer until they were almost upon them. "'Tis a fool's lot," the nearest rider shouted as he guided his steed around the jagged remains of a barren stump.

"It is," the second knight agreed, riding at his side. "A braying ass would not be out in this foul weather." He guided his mount toward the collapsed portion of the bank, gave a quick look down, and then reined him away. "Unlike us, they have probably fled south and are sheltered from this misery."

"It matters not if they are on the run or have taken refuge," the other man stated. "We will be doing our duty and keeping to our rounds." His horse whinnied as they rode up the incline, the whip of wind stealing away any further bits of their conversation.

Once the guards rode out of sight, Colyne sheathed his dagger. *So much for retracing their steps.* The coldness of the ground seeped into his throbbing shoulder as he glared at the fallen tree. "We are going to have to try to cross using the oak." He laced his fingers through hers. "Ready?"

Though fear clouded her eyes, she gave him a fragile smile. *"Oui."*

Pride at her bravado surged through him. Aye, she was a rare lass indeed, especially one cut from the gentry. He stood, pulling her with him, and ran toward the rush of water.

* * *

Her body trembling with exhaustion, Marie kept pace with Colyne. Frustrated by the turn of events, questions of her kidnapping resurfaced. How had the English duke known her whereabouts or executed her abduction with such seamless accuracy? Of the many scenarios she'd considered, the only thing that made sense was that someone within her father's trusted circle was involved.

"We will climb on the tree here," Colyne said, breaking into her thoughts. "I will go first." He grasped a root and made his way to the top of the trunk. Frustration lined his brow as he helped her up. "I am sorry. If we could go another—"

"But we cannot" she interrupted, "so let us cross."

"Aye." He edged along the tree's gnarled length.

With the raging water filling the air, she followed.

Halfway across, as if by a miracle, the rain ceased, but the strong winds continued. Waves broke over the surface, the foam-edged tips spewed by the gusts.

"Be careful," Colyne warned as he moved steadily forward.

Nerves prickled along her skin as she forged through the surge of water spilling over the trunk. Careful to keep her balance, Marie scoured the woods in their wake.

No guards.

When Colyne reached the end of the trunk where thinning, leaf-filled branches remained, his troubled gaze met hers. "The limbs are too weak to hold us. We must wade to shore."

The strong current tugged at her legs. She nodded.

He bent a limb back for her to grab, and she noticed his wince of pain. "Hold on to this."

Marie clasped the branch.

As he slid in, water rose to his chest. He clung to one of the thicker branches and then reached up. "Interlock your fingers with mine."

She wedged her foot against a limb. As she leaned toward him, debris caught within the powerful current and plowed into the trunk.

The tree shuddered.

Marie stumbled forward. "Help!"

Colyne caught her and hauled her against his chest.

"I am fine," she hurried out, the roar of water rushing past.

"Are you sure?" he asked, sounding far from convinced.

"Oui." But she wasn't. Her pulse still raced at how close she'd come to being swept away.

A horse's whinny echoed from across the stream.

On a gasp she turned, caught the outline of the guards making their rounds in the darkening night. *Mon Dieu!* "They are coming back!"

He tugged her with him as he headed toward the dense branches.

"Do you think they saw me?"

"Nay." The current shoved her against his side as he waded deeper into the tangle of leaves. "If they had, they would have called to alert the others." After settling them behind a thick bough, he grimaced. "We must remain here until they pass."

She nodded. Cold, Marie pressed closer. If they remained in the icy water much longer, they were both going to freeze.

"Put your arms around my neck and lean against me. It will allow you to rest." At her hesitation, subtle humor flashed in his gaze as he lifted her arms to his bidding. "Lass, why are you always so stubborn?"

"You need to rest as well, more so with your injuries." But she couldn't deny the refuge found within his powerful embrace.

Tenderness warmed his expression. "I am a seasoned warrior. I will rest when time allows. Nae until."

Mayhap, but he was still a man, and an injured one at that. With a sigh, she leaned against his solid strength and waited.

After a long while, the men on the opposite bank rode past them into the forest.

Once they'd disappeared from sight, Colyne lifted her in his arms and started forward.

"What are you doing, carrying me? Put me down."

Water sloshed around them as he trudged toward shore. "Nae until we are nearer to dry land."

With an exasperated sigh, she glared at him. "And you call me stubborn?" Without the water supporting her weight, the pain in his shoulder had to be excruciating. "I can walk from here."

Colyne hesitated and then complied. Together, they splashed up the bank.

With each step, her legs rebelled. Determined to hold her own, she slogged forward.

Once they'd pushed their way through the shield of brush, Colyne halted. "Wait here." He returned to the shoreline and filled their tracks in the softened earth. Then he grabbed a branch and erased the last signs of their passage. Weary eyes studied her as he walked back. "Are you able to travel?"

"*Oui.*" Even if she wasn't, for him she'd try.

He tossed the limb aside.

Taking her hand, they walked in silence. Naught but the muffled crunch of their steps upon soaked leaves and twigs betrayed their presence, their movements shielded from the river by a dense wall of brambles and the night.

With the storm having passed, the air held the rich scent of cleansed earth. Except for errant splatters tossed to the ground as gusts continued to shake the canopy overhead, the wind no longer assaulted the woods.

"The sky is beginning to clear," Colyne said.

She scanned the angry clouds racing past, leaving the heavens unblemished in their wake.

As if conjured, moonbeams sliced through the darkness, edging the clouds with wisps of silver. Throughout the forest, shimmers of light played amongst the rain-slicked leaves and danced across the shadows with magical delight.

But the coldness of her body, along with thoughts of the men who searched for her and Colyne, stole any fragment of peace. They were safe, but for how long? At some point the knights would deduce they'd crossed the stream. She prayed they'd be long gone before then.

As she started up another steep incline, her body began to shake. Marie paused, trying to catch her breath.

Colyne halted and studied her face in the moonlight, his own marked by strain. "Are you injured?"

"*Non,* I am . . ."

"Exhausted." A scowl marred his brow as he scanned the forest. "However much I wish we could stop to rest, 'tis too risky."

"I know." If allowed, she could fall asleep right here on the damp ground, and no doubt with his fatigue, he could do the same in a trice.

"I know of a shelter. 'Tis several more hours of travel, but it should be safe for the night."

Regret weighted his voice, and she damned the entire situation. "You are from the Highlands. Could we not travel to one of your friends or family and rest there?"

"Nay."

The fierceness of his tone caught her off guard. "Why not?"

"The men know we are traveling together. They would expect me to contact those I trust." His expression darkened. "Nay doubt they have guards watching their homes, and I will nae jeopardize the lives of those I love or further endanger yours."

His concern brought back turbulent memories of her secrets. And his. "They are after what is in the writ?"

Colyne turned away.

"Look at me," she demanded, hurt that he continued to hide the truth. "After what we have been through, can you not at least answer that?"

He shook his head.

"What does—"

He rounded on her, the anger in his eyes making her breath catch. "If we are caught and you are ignorant of the content, there is a chance you will be allowed to live."

Allowed to live? She glanced to where he'd hidden the document. What information could be so important that men would kill for it? Gold? Rebel plans for an assault against the English? The location of hidden arms to fuel Scotland's effort for independence?

"If the threat is so great," she asked, temper seeping into her voice, "should I remain with you?"

"Aye," he said, his words laden with regret. "With the men aware you are with me, you are already involved. At least while you travel at my side, I can protect you."

Protect her? He was all but weaving on his feet. After the strain on him this day, his shoulder had to be near useless from the pain. If the knights had discovered them before they'd safely crossed the stream, how long would he have held his own? An ache built in her throat.

By the grace of Mary, as much as she wanted him to guide her to the nearest port to seek passage to France, he needed the freedom to travel unimpeded more. She ignored the weariness filling her limbs, the residing chill from crossing the frigid water. She could make it on her own. Hadn't she been doing so until she'd come across him? "Go on without me. I am only slowing you down."

The corner of his mouth quirked into a weary smile. "You are. And if I was wise, I would leave you with the first person I knew I could trust."

Her heart ached. "It is not a matter to make light of."

"Nay, far from it." He scrubbed his face, the tiredness of his expression wiping away any lingering traces of humor. "From the first, I have found myself torn over what to do about you. " Desire kindled in his eyes, warming her blood. "As wise as it would be to let you go, I canna."

At his admission, Marie couldn't help but embrace the thrill in knowing he wanted her—a woman he believed to be a noble. Not the king's daughter. She sobered. Intimacy with Colyne would not be a trifling matter. She sighed. For now, she would cherish each moment they shared. "Then let us go." Marie shot him a teasing glance as she forced her feet to move. "That is, if you are able to travel."

"Is that the way of it, then?"

"*Oui.*" Pushing herself, she kept pace as they started up another incline.

"I think I misjudged you," Colyne said after they'd traveled a distance.

"Misjudged me?" She tensed. Had she done something? Said something to give away her birthright?

"I thought you were stubborn. Now I understand; 'tis determination."

Heat crept up her cheeks. She'd allowed her fears to make her jump to a false conclusion. "I have been called both."

In the moonlight, he glanced toward her. "I have nay doubt. 'Tis your determination that amazes me. Who are you, Alesia?"

The softness of his words did naught to ease the question's unnerving impact. "A woman who is bound to duty, monsieur," she said, her words more formal than she'd intended.

"Monsieur?" At her silence he arched a speculative brow. "'Tis more than duty."

She longed to tell him the truth, but doing so would solve nothing and change everything. For once she wanted to be seen not as a king's daughter but as a woman. She hungered to know a man without questioning the sincerity of his words.

"Do not," she said when he made to speak. The simple command severed the air between them like a dagger in the night.

Colyne's eyes darkened with desire as he stepped toward her.

Tempted to retreat, Marie stood her ground. But she couldn't dismiss the potency of his nearness or the need his presence inspired.

"Why do you withdraw when I mention your past? I care for you, wish to know you better. And, from the way you return my kisses, you have feelings for me as well."

She started to turn away, but he cupped her chin. Fissures of warmth seeped through her where his fingers touched. His gaze seemed to penetrate her, to search her mind for answers. "Tell me what you are thinking."

Shaken by the unsteadiness of her own voice, Marie turned away. "Does it matter?"

"I do nae want it to, but when it comes to you, aye." Colyne breathed. "You make me feel desires I had believed lost."

Did he speak of Elizabet?

"Alesia?"

Though whispered, his use of her second name screamed her deception. How could she care for Colyne and offer him lies? But she had no choice. Scotland's fate depended on her reaching her father. "I find myself drawn to you as well." She would give him that but naught more. To admit her growing feelings would add more heartache to an already painful separation.

"Drawn to me?" he asked, his annoyance clear.

"We must go. We have tarried here overlong."

His jaw tightened. "You feel naught for me but mere attraction?"

She struggled to quell her frustration. "We are cold, wet, and tired from our journey. Now is not the place to discuss the depth of how we feel for the other." His gaze fell to her mouth and heat slid through her body, unleashing words she'd meant to withhold. "You make me want you when I have no right."

Desire flamed hot in his eyes and her heart ached. All her life she'd wanted a man who made her desire him. Now she'd found a man who'd given her that.

Was she wrong to want Colyne? To yearn for a man who wasn't hers to have? And if she walked away without knowing true passion, would she regret her decision in the empty years ahead, married to a man she didn't love?

Colyne skimmed the pad of his thumb against her lower lip. "At times, our emotions are nae something we can dictate."

"As with Elizabet?" she threw out, ashamed but desperate to create much-needed distance between them.

Chapter 9

At the mention of Elizabet, Colyne braced himself for a barrage of emotions. With Alesia aware of his first love, he should have anticipated the question. Truth be told, with his heart broken since her marriage, he'd smothered his feelings and tried to avoid having time to think, or to feel.

Except, as he stared at her, the storm of expected grief never came. A sword's wrath, how did the emotions he'd struggled to banish since she'd married suddenly vanish? Why did he nae ache at the mere thought of her?

Confused, he exhaled. "I have known Elizabet's family since my youth. Somehow, over the years and without expecting to, I fell in love," he said, surprised at the ease at which his thoughts unfurled. "Before I told her of my feelings, she married another."

"I am sorry."

At Alesia's quiet words, his body began to hum a soft warmth. As if blasted from a catapult, he understood. 'Twas she who had allowed him to heal.

But it made little sense. Aye, she was beautiful and he desired her, but he didna love her. Within days they would part and he would . . .

Miss her.

Greatly.

He dismissed the pull of emotions, the ache inside him at the thought of her leaving that refused to go away. 'Twas fatigue that muddled his thoughts, nae more.

Unsettled, Colyne began walking east. "We must keep traveling." However much he wanted her, 'twas imperative to keep his focus on delivering the writ. And he needed to remember how little he knew about the lass.

Regardless of much he wished otherwise, he must use caution.

Shielding the afternoon sunlight with his hand, Colyne scanned the heather-strewn field.

"What is wrong?"

At the nervousness in her voice, he glanced over. "Naught, I was but searching for any sign of English troops." He refused to admit that part of his unrest came from his wanting her, as well as his bewilderment at how she'd made the pain of losing Elizabet fade.

Alesia scoured their surroundings with a tight frown. "You think we are in danger?"

As much as he wished to reassure her of their safety, he could nae. "Though we have spotted nay sign of our pursuers for two days, 'tis unwise to tarry in a field where we could be easily seen."

After one last sweep to ensure 'twas safe, he led her into the distant woods. From there they crossed several fields thick with brambles, the air rich with the smell of grass and a blend of wild herbs, as well as the potent scent of a distant moor. Every so often, he picked up the faintest trace of the sea.

Colyne took in the familiar rolling fields and the sweep of the distant forest, pain twisting his gut.

"Are we close?"

"Aye. We will arrive at the outskirts of Glasgow this night." There, he would check for any ships preparing to depart. The possibility existed that he could sail on the morrow.

And leave Alesia.

Forever.

His chest tightened at the thought. As if he had a blasted choice? He needed to reach King Philip posthaste. He didna have the luxury to remain with her until a ship arrived equipped with cabins befitting a lady.

But she would be safe.

Robert Wishart, the Bishop of Glasgow, a friend he'd known since his youth, resided here and would ensure her safe passage to France. And sadly, he was a man to whom Colyne needed to break the news of Douglas's death.

Colyne smothered his melancholy thoughts. Though close to Glasgow, danger surrounded them. 'Twas unwise to mull over leaving her for fear of letting down his guard on any front.

"Except for a crofter's hut," she said, "I have seen no sign of a village, much less a glimpse of the sea."

"I have kept our path off those normally traveled."

"A wise choice."

At the fatigue in her voice, he glanced over. Though she kept pace, her body had begun to tremble. He'd planned on traveling straight through to meet with the Bishop of Glasgow, which would take several more hours. But she was exhausted. He needed to find a place closer for her to rest.

'Twas nae as if he was delaying their parting. Tiredness etched the lass's face and weighed her every step. That he could never quite push the questions of what about her drew him had little to do with his change of plans. Their delay would give them a few extra hours together, naught more. And what of her secrets? After the past days of fighting for their lives, had he nae earned a degree of her trust? With the possibility of his sailing on the morrow, he should leave the subject untouched. However much wisdom guided him to remain silent, considering how important she was becoming to him, Colyne found it imperative to know. "Alesia?"

A tired smile tugged at her mouth. *"Oui?"*

"Why are there men after you?"

The tender warmth of her expression chilled. "Do not."

She started to turn away, but he caught her shoulder, annoyed by her immediate withdrawal. "After all we have gone through, everything we have confided in each other, what could you possibly nae be able to tell me?"

She yanked free, her stance regal. "And can you share the reason why 'tis crucial that you deliver the writ?"

With Scotland's freedom at risk, 'twas nae a choice he could make. "Nay, but my reasons are bound by honor."

"Are they?" Her eyes blazed with anger. "I have your word that the message you carry is of great importance, yet you refuse to tell me its contents or your destination."

"As I explained, if we were ever caught, your ignorance of my goal could save your life."

"I understand duty, monsieur," she said, her words crisp. "The weight of its responsibilities, the hard decisions it can bring."

Monsieur! Blast this entire situation. And what right did he have to demand anything from her when he couldna reveal the reason he traveled to France? With Alesia already wary, he should have allowed their conversation to move onto safer ground.

But she intrigued him—and frustrated him—like no lass had done. Ever.

Including Elizabet.

A muscle worked in his jaw. Fine, she wanted him nae to ask, he wouldn't. He had his own life and she had hers. Colyne walked beneath a tall pine and then into the warmth of the sun. Was part of her secret that she was married?

The light spring breeze sifted through the blades of grass as the rays of the sun warmed his face. Inside, his bones had chilled to ice. He halted. "Do you love someone else?"

Regret etched her face as she stopped before him. "*Non*," she breathed, "I swear it."

Thank God. Though his mission prevented him from remaining with her, he couldna bear thinking of her being in love with another.

Her eyes searched his with soft desperation. "If we only have a short while left, let the time be filled with good memories."

Sadness swamped him at her grief-stricken words, and then he paused. Their separation was one of choice. Excitement pouring through him, he caught her shoulders and gave her a hard kiss. "Once I have delivered the writ, I will come back for you."

The happiness in her eyes faded to caution. "With so much danger ahead, 'twould be unwise to make any future plans."

"I want to see you again," Colyne said, perplexed by her reply. After his heartbreak over Elizabet, Alesia had made him feel more than he'd ever believed possible. And with their growing friendship, as well as the heat of their kisses, he found it difficult to believe her feelings for him didna go deeper as well.

Mayhap her hesitation came from nae wanting to involve him further in her troubles. A needless worry. "Lass, when this is over, I will find you."

At Colyne's passionate declaration, Marie stepped back. *Mon Dieu*, however much she wished it, once they parted, she could never see him again. Heart aching, she swallowed hard. She must tell him of her betrothal to Gaston de Croix. And when Colyne learned of her impending marriage, would he glare at her in disgust? Curse her deception?

Or hate her?

Tears burned her eyes at the latter. She'd made a mess of this.

On the morrow they would part and she would never see him again. Shattered by the thought, she struggled for composure. Though she'd known him but days, somehow, he'd come to matter.

Matter? A pitiful word considering the emotions he made her feel. With Colyne, she felt whole, complete. The bond they'd forged would be with her forever. To add to the torment, never before had a man made her want his touch.

Colyne had.

Desperately.

Through lowered lids she studied him, memories of him half-naked leaving her body tingling with awareness. Too easily she could envision him taking her to his bed.

From the intensity of his kisses, he must desire her. If he asked, could she give herself to him, aware she was promised to another? More, was she wrong to make love with a man who wanted her for the woman she was, not for the royal tie she could bring him?

Thoughts of the upcoming marriage brought naught but visions of a cold, empty life, one void of a man who truly cared for her. Saddened, she fell into step beside him as Colyne started walking.

They had this one night. If they made love, she would savor the rightness of it. Any consequences would be hers to bear. And on the morrow she would tell him of her betrothal.

"Tonight we shall stay at an inn where I doubt anyone chasing us would search," he said. "Tomorrow I will make arrangements for your stay until you sail."

Marie nodded, half-listening, and walked in silence. She would have this night on which to build memories to cherish for a lifetime. After she'd told him of her promise to wed the duke, she prayed that one day Colyne would find forgiveness toward her for her deception.

By the time Colyne led Alesia to the outskirts of Glasgow, darkness had claimed the sky. In the shadows of the forest, he helped her don a servant's robe he'd procured from a crofter's hut they'd passed.

"We will nae attract attention dressed in this garb." He drew another robe over his own head, wishing they were already inside the safety of the inn. After securing the tie, he led her toward the city. "Keep near my side."

Fear flickered on her face, but she took his hand. "I will."

They moved deeper into Glasgow. Horses drawing rickety wagons stumbled over the rut-battered streets. Men dressed in the same nondescript servants' garb quietly passed.

" 'Tis not as I expected," Alesia said, a tremor in her voice.

"What?"

She nodded toward the decaying buildings, the squalor as far as the eye could see. "I had expected to find well-kept homes or businesses."

"In a better part of the city, aye, you would."

Unease swept her. "A better part?"

Colyne led her through the ill-tended streets cluttered with debris. "After weighing the risks, I decided traveling through this shabby part of town would be for the best. In the company of a noblewoman, the men searching for us would believe I would choose a safer route."

"I see."

Colyne gently squeezed her hand. "I will keep you safe."

"I know."

Humbled by her belief in him, he continued on. At the next corner, he stole a glance behind them. "This way." Confident they were nae being followed, he guided her into a darkened alley.

The stench hit first. A putrid mix of decaying food, stale mead, and a hint of something morbid. He didna pause to decipher the latter. He'd slipped through this part of the city too many times to linger. Desperation governed those who lived in this squalid area, thieves who killed without hesitation for something as simple as a loaf of bread.

A curse, then the sound of the slam of fists exploded nearby.

Alesia's fingers tightened on his.

"Keep moving." He increased their pace. After maneuvering through the dismal streets, a weathered stone building pleading neglect came into view. He led her into the shadow near the front door. "Wait here."

Her breaths came in short, rapid bursts as she scanned the darkened alleys around them. "But—"

"Go along with whatever I say."

She caught his sleeve. "What are you going to do?"

"If all goes well, secure us a room."

A scattering of people shuffled past, their varying degrees of inebriation evident by their boisterous tones. None appeared to notice them. Satisfied they'd drawn nay attention, Colyne walked up and knocked on the door.

Footsteps sounded on the other side, and then the heavy panel swung open with a rusty squeak. The aroma of cooking meat filled the air as yellowed candlelight illuminated a plump man sporting a scar stretching from his ear to his throat.

Iohne reminded Colyne of a cross between a brigand and the homeless roaming the streets. But he'd dealt with the innkeeper before. The Scot believed him to be the servant of an English lord who had sent Colyne to buy stolen goods from reavers, a cover that had served him well in the past and would do so now. "I shall be needing a room," he said, speaking the King's English, as this man would expect.

Iohne scowled. "I have none to offer ye."

Familiar with his ploy, Colyne held out several coins.

The man spied the flash of silver and greed lit his face. He wiped his arm across his mouth, slick with grease. "I might be having a room, but it will cost ye an extra pence."

Colyne nodded toward Alesia. "My wife is with child," he said with exasperation to add another layer of believability. "I have naught but another pence."

Iohne scowled at Alesia. "She is nay my worry." He started to close the door.

Colyne wedged his boot against the weathered panel. "Wait!"

The man's scowl deepened. "Will ye be wanting the room or nae?"

Colyne muttered a curse, which earned a satisfied gleam from the proprietor. "I shall give you my last pence, but I will be asking for a loaf of bread, cheese, wine, and a bath in return."

The innkeeper grunted and then opened the door wider. "I will be seeing the coin first."

He searched his garb, as if he indeed had little to spare. After several seconds, Colyne handed over the coin.

"Pàdraig," the gruff man called over his shoulder.

Moments later, a young boy stumbled into view, his tousled hair and swollen eyes a testament to the fact he'd been asleep.

Iohne gestured toward Colyne. "Take 'em to a back room, then, bring 'em drink and food and a bath. Be quick about it." With a warning glare at the lad, he turned and left.

Once the innkeeper disappeared from sight, the boy studied Colyne with distrust, his brown eyes too old for his years.

Regret filled Colyne as he took in the lad he'd nae seen before. With the English armies raiding, burning, and destroying many of the towns and villages under King Edward's decree, this boy, like many, fended for himself. At least he had a roof over his head. For now. Until the rebels ended King Edward's bid to claim Scotland, little chance existed that the lad's future would change.

Or hold hope.

Pàdraig retrieved a candle from a corner table and waved them forward. "Follow me."

Colyne held out his hand to Alesia.

She stepped into the light and entwined her fingers through his.

As they followed the lad down the hallway, he peeked back several times, as if ensuring they kept their distance. From his wary expression, sadly, Colyne could imagine the depraved reasons why.

They reached the farthest door, and Pàdraig opened it and ducked back, giving them wide berth.

"My thanks," Colyne said.

"I will return with your food and water for a bath." The wary youngster edged past them and hurried off.

Colyne led Alesia inside. After he'd closed the door, she faced him. "Why were you speaking like an Englishman?"

Candlelight illuminated her face as she slid the hood back, her suspicions easy to read, doubts that rankled him. "I am nae a traitor to Scotland," he all but growled. But why shouldna she wonder? He hadna explained that he'd intended to use a false cover or speak with an English tongue.

With a grimace, he crossed the small room to where another candle sat. After lighting the wick, he set the taper he'd carried by its side. "If anyone comes around asking about a Highland Scot, the innkeeper would be reporting none, especially nae an Englishman and his wife."

A rosy hue crept up her cheeks. "His pregnant wife."

The image of her round with their child moved him. He shoved aside the thought. "I—"

The sharp rap on the door interrupted his reply, but he didna miss her wistful expression. A sword's wrath. Colyne raised her hood to shield her face and then held his finger to his lips.

She nodded.

He answered the door.

Pàdraig lifted a basket. "Your bread and wine."

"My thanks." Colyne accepted the fare, and the lad quickly stepped back.

A shuffling echoed from the hallway. Two burly men carrying a tub came into view. "Ye wanted a bath?" the closest man asked.

"Indeed." Colyne stepped aside.

With several grunts, the two men lugged the wooden tub into the far corner of the chamber, then left.

Pàdraig returned, hefting a steaming bucket of water. It took the lad several trips, but he finally filled the tub. Sweat streaked the boy's face. "If you need anything else, I will be in the outer room." He laid out several clean towels along with a bar of soap near the tub, and then started toward the door.

"Lad," Colyne said.

Pàdraig turned, his feet planted as if he might bolt.

Colyne handed him a coin. "My thanks."

Surprise widened the boy's eyes as he stared at the half pence. "Thanks, me lord."

"I am a servant as you," he said, immediately correcting the lad. "We must watch out for our own."

A timid smile touched the lad's face, and then he nodded toward Alesia. "And if your wife is needing anything more, I will be seeing she has it."

After the lad departed, Colyne closed and barred the door. He would have to be more careful. A servant would have little extra coin to share. A slip such as the one he'd just made to the wrong person could cost them their lives.

The scent of the warm bread and wine filled the air as he set the food, the goblets, and the bottle of wine near the candles on the crude table. Colyne turned.

Paused.

Embraced within the fragile light, Alesia stole his breath. The enormity of how truly secluded they were hit him with a stunning force. Though secrets existed between them, at this moment the men who chased them were far away. Hidden in this inn under the guise of an Englishman and his wife, at least for the upcoming night they should be safe.

And alone.

She pushed her hood back and watched him through half-closed eyes, but he didna miss the interest warming her gaze, a sensual look that invited erotic thoughts.

Traitorously, his glance strayed toward the sturdy bed. His blood flowed hot. Too easily, he imagined Alesia naked upon it. His fingers trembled as he poured a goblet of wine and handed it to her. "We need to eat, bathe, and then rest as much as possible this night." A safe plan.

A becoming blush stole up her cheeks.

"What is wrong?" he asked, aware as he spoke of the foolishness of his question. The reasons for her concern could be numerous.

She shook her head. "'Tis unwise to admit."

"You can tell me."

"'Twas that you looked upon me with such pride."

Once again he was surprised by her complexity—a blend of innocence and sage worldliness. He stepped toward her, intrigued. "Has nay one ever told you how beautiful you are, discovered your inner strength that leaves me in awe?" Her chin tilted in a regal slant, reminding him of the first time he'd seen her.

"There are many motivations for a man's flattery," she replied, her voice growing cool. She stepped back. "Words are as easily given as forgotten."

Sadness slid through him. "Who hurt you, Alesia?"

Her expression grew guarded. "No one. I refuse to let them."

Apparently, someone had, deeply. "What happened to make you distrust people so?"

"You would not understand."

"Because you would nae allow me to?" he gently prodded.

Fire flashed in her eyes. "It is complicated."

"I expected nothing less from you." The truth. From the start he'd found her a tempting challenge. Except, as he'd grown to know Alesia, the way she made him care, to want to protect her, surpassed any emotion he'd ever expected or, after Elizabet, ever believed he could experience.

With longing, Alesia glanced toward the steaming tub. "Must we speak of my past now? I have told you that I find those of the nobility self-serving. Is that not enough?"

Colyne hesitated. "Will you reveal what you are keeping from me before we part?"

The immediate pain in her eyes had him moving closer. "What is it?" he asked, his voice firmer than he'd intended.

"Colyne, I—"

At the denial in her eyes, he caught her shoulders. "Trust me, Alesia. For God's sake, I would never harm you."

Her eyes silently pleaded with him. "It is not that simple."

Colyne cupped her face. "I care for you deeply. Whatever secrets torment you, they shall nae change how I feel."

A silent battle raged in her eyes, and then she gave a slight nod. "I will tell you," she finally conceded. "But first, can we not have this one night?"

Need darkened her gaze and his throat grew dry. A sword's wrath. However much he wanted her, she couldna begin to fathom the reality of living as a fallen woman. He shook his head. "You are a virgin and I will nae—"

She laid her finger on his mouth. "I am, but you said you cared for me. I feel the same for you. I want you as a woman does a man."

Bloody, merciful God! His entire body burned as he struggled to maintain control. Intimacy with her would offer more than pleasure but invite responsibility.

Neither could he forget that if her unchaste state were learned of by the gentry, she would be shunned. He remembered the harsh treatment served to a baron's daughter when others learned of her indiscretion. In the end, she'd withdrawn from society and remained in seclusion. A fate he'd never wish upon Alesia.

"What I wish and what is right," Colyne rasped, "are two different things."

Moss-green eyes narrowed. "To the devil with propriety."

Sweat beaded on his brow as he fought to keep from plundering the sweetness of her lips, to take her as his body demanded. "Once I finish delivering the missive—"

"No one can guarantee my safety or yours. For tomorrow, the next day, much less for several weeks from now." She paused, her gaze intent. "Give me this one night."

"Alesia," he rasped, his breathing ragged, his body aching with wanting her, "do nae ask me to do this."

She leaned close and pressed her mouth intimately against his. "It is too late, I already have."

Chapter 10

As Alesia's taste filled him, Colyne's heart slammed against his chest and his body hardened to a fierce ache. A sword's wrath! He caught her by the shoulders and, with regret, held her away. "I want you, but if the gentry should learn of this indiscretion—"

Moss-green eyes flashed with heated determination. She stepped back and began to loosen her cloak. "You yourself said each day is filled with danger. Who knows if we shall ever have this time alone again? Time that we can be with each other."

His body trembled beneath his restraint. "You do nae know what you are saying," he forced out, giving her a chance to walk away.

Her fingers trembled on the hood of her cloak. "You do not want me?" she whispered, a catch in her voice.

Do nae want her? That such an interpretation would ever occur to Alesia left Colyne dumbstruck. He exhaled a rough breath. "I want you more than is right."

She tugged the cloak free and it tumbled to the floor. With her gaze locked on his, her fingers moved to the ties of her gown.

"Do nae." Colyne's body trembled as he stared at her, wanting her, needing her more than he'd ever believed. He damned decorum, damned propriety, and damned his weakness when it came to her. On a groan, he gave into his longings and stepped forward. "Let me."

His blood heated as he freed her gown, inch by glorious inch. She inspired feelings in him he'd believed lost, and he found it incomprehensible how anyone could have hurt her. Alesia's past may have offered her the belief that she wasna wanted, but he would show her differently. He would teach her to understand the beauty and depth he saw in her.

With the flick of his wrist, the last tie fell away. On an unsteady breath, he edged the dress from her shoulders. The gown puddled atop her cloak.

Illuminated within the candle's golden glow, she stood before him wearing her chemise, a simple yet elegant shift. The dusky tips of her breasts jutted proudly against the creamy fabric, taut, beckoning.

Without hesitation, she moved into his embrace, warm and willing, and liquid heat slid through him to melt the last of his reserve. "God help me," Colyne whispered as he claimed her mouth. He'd meant for the kiss to be gentle, but she pressed her sweet body against him, threaded her hands through his hair and dragged him closer. Their mouths entwined in a greedy kiss.

Hard.

Fast.

Desperate.

With his mind spinning from her taste, he took the kiss deeper, teasing, seducing, until she moaned from the onslaught of sensations.

Like a fantasy, she met his every demand.

His breath coming fast, his body screaming with need, Colyne slowed his pace and broke away, refusing to take her with such untamed intensity.

"What is wrong?" she asked, her eyes wide with questions, her lips swollen from his kisses.

"You have never been with a man. Your first time. Our first time," he added, his words thick with emotion, "will nae be a fast coupling to sate our desire." He stroked his finger along the soft curve of her neck.

Her eyes softened. "Our first time." She laid her palm upon his cheek. "'Tis a blessing to share such a special moment with you."

He dismissed the unease her words stirred. Tomorrow would come soon enough, as would the time to unravel the worries plaguing him.

She started to remove the chemise, but he stayed her fingers. "Nay."

Alesia lowered her hands and gave him complete access.

Colyne stepped back to admire her beauty, to cherish her every curve, each tempting swell. "Do nae move." Tremors rocked him as he tugged off his garb until he stood in his undershirt and braies. Catching his breath, he skimmed his fingers over the fabric of her chemise. "It feels like silk."

Heat stole up her face. *"Oui."*

He slid his fingers up her arms and then cupped the curve of her shoulders. "As long as 'twas nae a gift from a suitor."

Alesia's blush deepened and she shook her head.

He laughed. "I am but teasing you."

"I know." Her cheeks continued to flush in an inviting contrast.

With tenderness, Colyne brushed a kiss upon her mouth, pausing, savoring, before moving to the curve of her jaw.

On a quiet moan she arched her neck, and he gently took, her taste potent as he skimmed along the velvet length. "We shall learn many things together," he murmured against the base of her throat where her pulse raced warm and inviting. "But first—" he drew away, pleased by the desire in her eyes—"I will help you bathe."

She frowned. "I can—"

"Nay." He cupped her face pressed a soft kiss upon her mouth. "I assure you, you have never experienced anything like this before. Do nae move." Colyne retrieved the heather soap, along with a cloth. After soaking the linen with water from the tub, he returned. "Come here."

Alesia walked toward him as if a nervous queen, regal, elegant, but with a freshness nae found in any royalty he'd ever beheld. A hand's length away, she stopped, her gaze confused.

Heated images of what this night would bring singed his mind as Colyne lifted the dampened cloth and laid it upon her nipple.

She gasped, and a shiver swept her body. Warm, caressing drops rolled down the delicate silk, saturating the chemise until it clung to her magnificent curves.

With reverence, he skimmed the wet linen in provocative circles over the silk and kept his every movement slow to relish her sensual awakening. Like a fairy's magic, wherever he drew the sodden cloth, her soft curves became visible beneath the translucent material.

Need seared him, and he grazed his teeth along her throat. Like honey, her taste sweetened his tongue, beckoned him to fulfill his every fantasy. On a moan, he caught her silk-covered nub between his teeth and nipped.

"Colyne!"

As she arched beneath him, his body shook with the effort nae to take her now. A sword's wrath! He'd but touched her and she'd come apart.

Thrilled by her sensitivity to his every touch, he lifted his gaze to hers. Colyne flicked his tongue against her taut bud.

Her eyes glazed with need.

He clenched his teeth. *Keep it slow.* He would, if it took every last ounce of his strength.

Sweat broke out on his brow as he again skimmed the cloth over the soft swells of her breasts. Then he caressed the soapy linen over her most sensitive place and whorls of downy hair became exposed beneath the glistening sheen.

Tempted, needing to taste her, he drew the tip of her silk-covered breast into his mouth and began to suckle.

Her head tilted back on a wanton sigh. "Colyne."

On a maddening growl, he dropped the cloth and skimmed his hand up her thighs, her shivers at his touch offering their own sweet torture. "Open for me, Alesia."

"I—"

He drew a steadying breath. "Trust me." As her legs relaxed, he skimmed his hand over her dewy flesh in slow, smooth strokes, savoring the way her body responded at his every touch.

As her pulse raced, Colyne knelt before her, skimming kisses through the wet silk as he moved lower. He glanced up to find her eyes watching him, her breath unsteady, and his body went up in flames.

Swallowing hard, he pressed his brow against the flat of her stomach and regained control.

Barely.

Fingers trembling, he slid her shift up until she lay exposed to him, completely, totally.

His heart pounded against his chest at her pure perfection. "Now your bath, as promised."

Confusion clouded her eyes. "But I—"

"Watch me," he commanded softly.

His senses hummed as with sinful slowness he eased the moistened cloth to her thighs, enjoying her gasps of pleasure. Once he'd washed and rinsed her with gentle thoroughness, he set the cloth aside. "I am going to kiss you—" he cupped her, as if the most exquisite fare—"here." Keeping his gaze on hers, Colyne leaned forward and slid his tongue along her slick folds.

Alesia's gasp ended on a moan. She lay her head back.

Her taste intoxicating, he blew lightly across her swollen flesh, and then recaptured her nub and gently began to suckle.

Her legs began to tremble.

Pleased by her sensitivity, wanting her quaking against him, he used his fingers and tongue to drive her over the edge. As her body began to convulse, Alesia caught his shoulders. "Colyne!"

With her cries of release surrounding him, he drew her against him and absorbed her every quiver.

"I . . . This . . ." She shook her head. "I never knew . . ."

Her breathy words, her soft moans, tore at his fragile control. "'Tis you who are amazing." Lifting her in his arms, Colyne claimed her mouth as he walked to the tub, drinking in her heady response. He lowered to one knee and then set her into the water. On a groan, he ran his hands along her entire length. "You are perfect," he whispered. "Everything a man could desire and more."

A sultry smile caressed her mouth. "You are beautiful as well."

Colyne chuckled. "I am nae sure I am flattered by such a laud."

"Handsome, then," she said as she scanned him from head to toe; he hardened further beneath her gaze. "And breathtaking."

"Am I now?" Pleased, he stood. With slow movements, he began stripping away his tunic and braies. She watched him as he removed each garment, her gaze becoming more daring, leaving him further aroused.

Naked before her, Colyne reveled in the boldness of her gaze roaming his muscled frame. As her eyes lowered past his hips, she paused. A frown creased her brow. "I—"

"I shall be gentle. If I could remove the pain of the first time, I would."

Hesitant, her gaze lifted to his. "I know." She tried to turn away, but he caught her face.

"You are untouched. You are allowed to be nervous." He lifted her chin. However much he wanted to make love with her, she needed to be sure. "And," he paused, gathering strength, "if you have changed your mind, I will stop."

Moss-green eyes softened. "I want you, Colyne. More than my next breath."

He swallowed hard, aching for her, nae wanting to hurt her . . .

ever. "There will be pain with your first time. After, you will feel only pleasure. That I promise. Now," he said as he picked up the cloth and moved into the tub behind her, "I will finish washing you. Lean back against me." Alesia settled against him, the softness of her skin a comfortable fit against his body's throbbing demand. As his erection grazed her silky curves, he gritted his teeth.

His body burned as he built a thick lather in his hands and slathered soap over her every inch.

"Mmm, this feels wonderful," she whispered.

"For me as well, lass." Aye, 'twas heaven itself.

"I have decided," she said on a slow breath, "that you will bathe me from now on."

"Will I now?" Pleased, Colyne skimmed his finger over her triangle of downy hair, then slid into her slick warmth and slowly withdrew. As he continued his erotic massage, her pulse raced beneath his touch, and her body began to tremble. Aware of the tension building within her, a pressure he fought himself, he stopped.

"I shall be rinsing you off."

"*Non*," she said, her plea deep and throaty. "It is my turn to wash you."

He caught her hand as she reached for the soap, all too easily imagining her fingers wrapped around his full length. "Do nae," he strangled out. Genuine surprise flashed on her face and he smothered a groan. "You can bathe me later. I promise."

She tucked an impish grin into the corner of her mouth. "I have done this to you, have I not?"

"Aye," he muttered, grabbing the soap. "A fact you are proud of, are you nae, lass?"

Delight sparkled in her eyes. "I am."

She was going to be the death of him yet, but he'd die a happy man. Quickly working the soap into a frothy cloud, he lathered himself, then reached over for the bucket and rinsed them both.

His body hummed with anticipation as he carried her to the bed. The air of the hot spring night warmed their chamber, but it was naught compared to the scalding heat where their flesh merged.

With care, he lay her upon the sheets. Like a green lad, he trembled as he knelt over her, shuddered as he pressed his length against the velvet of her slick warmth. "Say you want me."

She reached toward him in invitation. "*Oui*, I want you."

Slow, he reminded himself, warring against the overwhelming desire to thrust deep.

"Colyne?" Alesia shifted beneath him, and he almost lost control.

"Lie still." He rested his brow against hers and drew in a slow breath. "I need a moment longer."

Instead of heeding his quiet command, she pressed her mouth over his.

A low growl swirled in his throat, but she only laughed, a rich, smoky sound, which assured him that she was enjoying her advantage. Thrilled by her growing confidence, he deepened his kiss and eased himself inside her until he wedged against her thin barrier.

Alesia stiffened.

"Trust me," he said, her sweet tightness threatening to drive him over the edge. Holding himself still, he slowly nipped along the soft fullness of her mouth. Once she relaxed against him, he caressed her until she moaned, and her body arched against his. Pleased, he started moving in a steady rhythm. When she matched his pace, on his next stroke, Colyne surged deep.

Stilled.

Eyes illuminated with hurt watched him.

Aching that he'd hurt her to any degree, Colyne brushed away several strands of hair from her face. "'Twill only feel good from now on. I swear it."

Slowly, the fragments of pain on her face faded until only desire glowed. "The discomfort has gone."

"Just feel," he whispered, nuzzling the curve of her neck, then easing up to savor her mouth. With slow, tender strokes to show her what she meant to him, he set the pace. With his next stroke, her body began to quake.

"Colyne!"

"That is it," he urged and quickened the pace. As she arched against him and her body began to convulse, he drove deep and found his own release.

Sated, he rolled to his side and drew her with him, never having felt so complete. Sadness tightened his chest. "If I could," he whispered, aching at the thought of letting her go, "I would wish this moment forever."

Alesia tensed and then tried to pull away.

Her flash of guilt reminded him of her request to wait until the morning to tell him what she was hiding. A sword's wrath, he needed to know. "What is wrong?" When she would have turned away, he caught her chin.

Her eyes pleaded with his. "Do not ask me now."

"How can I nae? We made love, have given ourselves to each other in the ultimate act of trust."

Silence echoed between them, warm with the scents of their lovemaking.

She didna reply.

Hurt, Colyne searched her face, trying to understand why she hesitated. "A few hours will change naught."

Tears glistened in her eyes. "I know that far too well."

Fear, hard and cold, raked through him. The last time he'd seen her cry had been when they'd buried his friends murdered by the English. By the grace of God, could her secret begin to match such a travesty?

Then, as if impaled by a sword's blow, he understood what drove her guilt, what had her pulling away from him even now. Colyne didna want to believe she'd lied to him. "Tell me."

Red rimmed her eyes. "Whatever happens between us from this moment, I shall cherish the love we made this night. Neither will I forget you. Please remember that."

"Who is he?" Colyne demanded, praying he was wrong.

Her breath hitched. "My betrothed."

Chapter 11

"Betrothed?" Colyne boomed.

Marie flinched. The true depth of her betrayal weighed heavy on her soul.

Fear that Renard's men would find her as she traveled through the unfamiliar Highlands had convinced her to ask Colyne for his help in reaching Glasgow. But it offered no excuse for their intimacy.

Eyes narrowed, Colyne released her and stood. He stalked the chamber. The candlelight, which had cast a golden glow over his body as they'd lain entwined, gleamed upon his nakedness, accentuating each taut stride. Now he looked more like a confined beast than her lover.

Shame filled her. However wrong her actions, she could not forget the feel of his hands upon her skin, their fine-tuned strength that could wield a blade as well as make love to her with infinite tenderness.

Each step he took expanded the emotional distance between them, his silence far more unnerving than if he'd spoken. She couldn't just sit here. She had to say something. Anything.

With the sheet secured around her, she slid her legs over the edge of the bed.

His eyes cut to her. "Stay away."

Marie swallowed hard. Damn her selfishness. She'd never meant to hurt him. She needed to make him understand that she'd wanted this time with him to take with her, for once they parted they couldn't see each other again.

Her hand trembled as she fisted the sheet. How had she allowed the situation to unravel to such disrepair? "I only wanted to—"

Colyne rounded on her. "We made love, Alesia. Does that nae mean anything to you?" At her hesitation, he stormed over. "Answer me!"

"*Oui*," she whispered, her heart breaking. She'd allowed her desires to guide her. Her self-serving decisions were no better than those of the gentry she abhorred.

With a curse, he prowled the chamber, pausing where a small table held their uneaten fare. Colyne turned. Deep lines dredged his face, but his eyes . . . Her breath faltered. *Mon Dieu*, his eyes were raw with hurt.

"How could you allow me to take what by right belongs to another?"

Marie straightened her shoulders. She deserved his wrath. "I never believed I would experience what you have made me feel. When I did . . ." She shook her head. "I am sorry."

His eyelids narrowed as he stepped closer, his body towering over hers. "Sorry? You kept me ignorant of your betrothal because you wanted me? Bedamned! My feelings are nae something to be used on a whim!"

She swallowed hard. Except for not revealing the contents of the missive he carried, Colyne had been nothing but truthful. "I never meant to—"

"How can you dismiss your pledge to another man and nae understand the gravity of such a decision?"

"I was desperate." Her reason sounded weak even to herself.

He scoffed. "Desperate?"

His gaze burned into hers, and then he shook his head with a frustrated sigh. "Are you nae aware that your betrothed will realize that you have been with another man when you go to his bed?"

"It will matter not to him." A sad fact she'd long since come to accept. She could have been hideous, crippled, or a harlot having known the favors of numerous men, and for the royal connection, they still would have sought her hand.

"Your betrothed will nae care?" Colyne arched a skeptical brow. "I find that hard to believe."

"It is difficult to explain."

He crossed his arms over his chest. "Try."

What should she tell him? That he'd been the first man who'd cared for who she was and not for her birthright? Or that for the first time in her life, she had grown to cherish every moment spent with a man who was not her father?

And as horrible as her actions in giving herself to Colyne were, a part of her, however wrong, would savor the love they'd made. If he walked away and never spoke to her again, at least she would have the memory of this night.

"My father . . ." So caught up in the passion flaring between them, she'd not considered her father's reaction if he learned of the loss of her innocence. He would be furious with her, more so in light of her betrothal. And what would he do to Colyne?

Have him imprisoned?

Killed?

She couldn't allow Colyne to bear punishment for her sins. He'd only taken what she'd freely offered. Any wrong was hers to bear, but would her father view it as such?

Marie stared at him, unsure, hurting, and afraid. With his life possibly in danger, she couldn't reveal her father's title. But Colyne deserved some explanation. Neither would she expect forgiveness.

"Your father?" he prodded.

Taking a deep breath, she scraped together her composure as taught by the years of being a king's daughter. She found it heartbreaking at how calm and poised she could be when her entire life lay crumpled at her feet. "My father arranged the marriage."

He gave a curt nod. "'Tis common."

"It would be, except he gave me the right to choose the man I wed." She hesitated, damning what she must say, words he deserved to hear but would never truly understand. "I do not love him, nor have we met."

He unfolded his arms from his chest. "Your father gave you a choice to marry for love, yet you promised yourself to a stranger?"

The heat of his words and the disbelief made her want to curl into a ball and weep. "I never expected to meet someone like you."

A muscle worked in his jaw. "After my time spent with you, I find it hard to believe you would have settled for anything in your life."

She exhaled. "I was tired of men falsely trying to gain my attention, and treating me as if I were a simpleton. Though I do not love my betrothed, my father assured me he shall treat me with respect. The other men . . ."

"The other men!"

Marie interlaced her hands so he wouldn't see them shake. "They sought to bind themselves to me to gain an alliance with my father. He is a powerful lord," she finished on a whisper.

Colyne watched her, his gaze shrewd. "A strong allegiance is often part of arranged marriages. You are a beautiful woman, Alesia. Could they nae see that as well as your intelligence?"

"Men driven to gain power see not the beauty in a well-crafted sword, only the lethal bite of the blade."

"If they bid for your affections with anything but sincerity, they were fools."

Fools or not, if Colyne knew the truth, it would change how he viewed her. "I should have told you before of my betrothal. I meant to, but the days passed so quickly and there was so much on my mind." She drew a calming breath. "Tonight, I was afraid if I told you, you would leave me untouched. I wanted this night with you to cherish. But my fears of a lonely life are little excuse for my actions." She paused, gathered her courage. "I was selfish. It is just that . . ."

"What?"

That I love you. The unexpected revelation shocked her to the core. She must be wrong. She cared for him deeply, but love?

Mary's will, with her future already pledged to another, she could never contemplate a life with Colyne. And as much as she wanted to, she didn't dare inform Colyne of her royal tie.

She stared up at him, wanting him to see the truth in her eyes as she spoke. "You make me feel what no other man has. When you kiss me, touch me, you make me want what is forbidden." Shame filled her at her words, but she forced herself to continue. If not her pledge, she could give him this. "You made me understand what it is like to be truly wanted—for me, not for the prestige I can bring a man." Her breath hitched. "I was wrong. I am sorry."

He stared at her for a long moment and his anger fell away to frustration. On a rough sigh, he stepped forward and cupped her chin. "I am sorry as well."

She'd prepared herself for his condemnation but not his empathy.

A tense second passed.

Then another.

The pain she witnessed in his expression stole her breath. Marie lay her head upon his chest. "I beg of you, do not hate me."

"I canna. Even after . . ." He stroked his thumb against her cheek. "God help me, I still want you." Colyne drew back and studied her. "There may be a way."

"A way?"

"Aye. I shall speak with your father on your behalf."

Panic swept her as she thought of Colyne approaching her father. "Do you not think if I believed there was a way to stop my wedding I would?"

"If you were given the option to choose your betrothed," he continued, " 'twould seem that your father will understand it would be a mistake to allow you to marry a man you do nae love?"

"It is impossible," she said, her words cool as she struggled for calm. Duty weighed heavy on her shoulders, concerns she could not dismiss.

Even for Colyne.

But a part of her wished for his intervention because his heart was involved. A wish. Though he cared for her deeply, it was far from love. Aching, she started to turn away.

He caught her hand. "I will meet with your father. Mayhap ending your betrothal will be as simple as paying the promised dowry."

However much she wished it, nothing he could say would alter her destiny. She shook her head. "My vow has been given. My father will not change his mind."

A smile touched his mouth. "Your father may dismiss a common knight, but there is something I have nae told you."

She remained silent. Whatever he was about to share would change nothing.

He laced his fingers through hers. "I am a knight, aye, but as well, the Earl of Strathcliff."

"A Scottish lord?" Marie wasn't sure whether to laugh or cry. Loving Colyne, had she met him before her betrothal, given his title and status, her father would have happily granted her permission to wed him.

"Alesia—"

Colyne's use of her second name was a blunt reminder of his ignorance of her royal tie.

And the danger.

"I am sorry, but your nobility changes naught." He stared at her, his confusion tearing her apart. By the grace of Mary, she'd made what should have been a beautiful bonding a disaster. She needed to put distance between them; it would be wise. Sensible. And she would, with the oncoming dawn, but hours remained until then, precious time she would savor. "Make love to me again, Colyne. Give me this one night with you."

"How can I—"

"I know it is wrong," she rushed out. "More than I have the right to ask."

Blue eyes narrowed. "On the morrow I will make arrangements for us both to sail."

"And for that I give you thanks." Trembling at the thought of letting him go, she stood. "You must accept that once you depart, we cannot see each other again. Ever. Please, lay with me until dawn." She struggled to swallow. "But if you choose otherwise, I understand."

"If I spoke with your fa—"

"My father will not change his mind."

Alesia might be convinced that he couldna sway her father to end her betrothal, but Colyne believed otherwise. "Who is you father?"

Silence.

So be it. Once he'd delivered the writ to King Philip, he would seek the noble out and speak with him in private. 'Twould nae be difficult to find an influential lord who had a beautiful daughter named Alesia who had journeyed to Scotland as a missionary. And a woman who had served her people as a healer. Whatever the price to release her from her betrothal, he would pay.

She believed her decisions took away his responsibilities toward her; he disagreed. Though unaware of her betrothal, he'd known of her chaste state.

Still, he'd allowed intimacy.

Aye, he could blame his actions on her impassioned request, of how she'd pressed against him and destroyed his will, but he refused to use excuses for a choice he'd made. With his every intimate touch, he'd known his decision, had accepted its consequences.

After experiencing her untutored passion, the guileless sensuality of her every move, he'd wanted more than what one night would give them.

"I need you, Colyne." Desire-filled eyes searched his with desperation. "If it is within you to forgive me for what I now ask, make love to me."

Her desperate plea cut through his musings. His body hardened as his mind relieved images of her beneath him. "Alesia—"

She unbound the sheet and stood naked before him. Illuminated within the golden candlelight, her breasts, full, round, and tempting, lured him. "Do you still want me?"

He silently groaned. Want her? Colyne's gaze feasted on her tempting curves, at how the shimmering light slid over her as he wanted his hands to, and doubted he'd ever get his fill.

A sword's wrath! He should walk away. He wasna a green lad unused to joining with a woman or the pleasures the act inspired. But as her scent of woman and lavender teased his senses, never had he wanted anyone as much as he wanted her. If he were to be damned, then so be it.

Pulse racing, he crossed to her, claimed her mouth in a fierce kiss. He would find a way to right this wrong.

Dust-streaked sunlight stole through the aged window to expose the room in a dim glow. For a selfish moment, Colyne held Alesia, who slept in his arms, and enjoyed the hazy peace. It didna matter that he lay within a downtrodden inn or that, somewhere in the city, Renard's men searched for him and wanted him dead.

For this one instant, he was content.

Though caution had advised him nae to touch her again after their heated discussion, his body had burned at how throughout the night she'd reached for him over and again.

Colyne pressed a kiss upon her brow. In sleep, the lines of worry that had marred her face since they'd first met had smoothed. She was beautiful. 'Twas as if the fairies had delivered him a princess.

The princess.

King Philip's daughter.

She was still out there. And he prayed his kinsmen had found her. Odds were, even if she had been rescued, Renard had long since sailed to France and would have begun planting seeds of doubt about the Scottish rebel's treachery in the king's ear. Until King Philip's bastard daughter was returned or the sovereign read the writ, the French king wouldna learn the truth.

However much he wished to linger, responsibility dictated otherwise. Aware he tempted fate, Colyne nibbled his way across the soft curve of her lips, then slowly claimed her mouth in a deep kiss.

A frown draped her brow, and then thick, honey-blond lashes raised. Through half-closed lids groggy with sleep, a smile, warm and sated, curved her mouth. "Make love with me."

At her breathy request, he was lost. Colyne touched her with infinite care, amazed at the feelings she evoked. Would the passion she aroused always be so strong? He found himself believing 'twould be so.

A while later, with her body trembling from release, Colyne lifted himself on his elbows and stared at her.

"Good morning, my lord," she said.

The husky purr of her words lured him back. He promised himself he'd only take a wee taste of her lips. Colyne leaned closer. Their lips touched. Melded. Heat stormed him and his mind hazed.

With regret, he pulled away. "I must leave to speak with my friend in Glasgow." Then he made the mistake of glancing down. Beneath him, her breasts pressed against his chest, their bodies merged to where her warmth brushed against his hardness.

Her eyes, warm from their lovemaking, watched him, their invitation clear.

Colyne swallowed hard. "You are making it difficult to leave you."

After a soft kiss upon his mouth, Alesia leaned back. "Can you not stay a while longer?"

"If possible, I would remain here forever." He glanced through the grimy window to where the sun slowly rose into the sky and grimaced. He couldna delay his departure further. With a grumble, Colyne sat up, and then retrieved his braies.

She rolled onto her stomach. Naked, she watched him with sinful invitation. "How long will it be until you return?"

He silently lauded his stamina, comparing it to a saint's as he tugged on his trews. "I should return before midday."

"Do you think the men searching for us will be in Glasgow?"

"Aye. We have been lucky nae to have crossed paths with them over the past several days." He resigned himself with one last glance over her tempting body. "Stay within the room until I return."

Alesia's mouth softened into a sensual pout. "I will miss you."

"Aye, you will," he said, with a boldness she aroused. Her laughter trickled through him, reminding him of all the reasons he wished to remain.

After he'd donned his garb and topped it with his cloak, Colyne gave in to one last kiss, slow and deep, until her hands wove around the back of his neck and she tried to pull him into bed. The chains of his forged mail clinked as he broke free.

She gave a frustrated groan. "You did that on purpose," she softly accused.

He winked. "Indeed. But I am a man who never starts anything he canna finish."

A wanton smile on her face, she sat up, her breasts jutting proudly, as if beckoning his return. "You could—"

"I must go," he interrupted, too familiar with where his tarrying would lead. He shifted the tie of his trews, his teasing leaving more than her frustrated. "Upon my return, we shall finish this . . . discussion."

"Colyne," she called when he'd reached the door.

"Aye?"

Her hand slid to cup her breast as her gaze held his. "I shall be waiting."

He clenched the handle of the door. A sword's wrath, the lass was a temptress. He'd faced many an adversary on the battlefield with the odds against him. Surely he could resist the lass's charms until his return. "Stay here," he ordered. "Do nae go anywhere until my return, nay matter the cause."

At his reminder of the danger, she lowered her hands and her face paled. "What if you do not return?"

"I will be back." Even if he had to crawl.

"Be careful."

Colyne shot her a smile, wanting to ease her worries. "I will."

A cool breeze greeted him as he stepped from the ramshackle inn. The early morning light exposed the poverty of the streets, the air ripe with dank smells oozing from the crumbling buildings shoved against one another.

Well familiar with the dangers of Glasgow, he made a slow sweep around him. Several people were out, but they kept their gazes averted as they passed. Confident he wasna being watched, he hurried toward a narrow side street.

Three streets away, as he rounded a curve, he spied several knights halting travelers and questioning them. With a curse he drew back and then peered around the corner.

One of the men turned.

He flattened himself against the wall. 'Twas the man who'd shot him with the bolt. He glanced down the alley. If he backtracked, 'twould make his journey twice as long. He grimaced. Alesia would worry at his being late, but he dared nae take the street.

Several hours later, the bells announcing the arrival of midday tolled as Colyne reached the Glasgow Cathedral. He grimaced. Alesia would be expecting him. At least she was safe where at the inn. But what if the men had discovered her whereabouts? Nay, he'd hidden their identities well.

He slipped into a side entrance. The scent of frankincense and myrrh hung in the air. Having visited the cathedral many times before, he moved with sure steps through the solemn hallways adorned with intricately woven tapestries.

At the end of the corridor, he gently pushed open a thick oak door. Stained-glass windows encased by sturdy, handcrafted frames arched toward the ceiling, designed with various finely crafted pictures of Jesus, Mary, and several biblical settings. With his every entry into this chamber, the enormous sense of spirituality filled him. 'Twas as if he could feel God's presence.

The murmurings of a deep voice in Latin had Colyne glancing toward the front of the room.

On his knees, a bishop with his head bowed, adorned in long flowing robes, flanked by two priests, continued with their prayers.

Colyne walked forward, the thick woolen rug muting his steps. Several paces from the altar, he halted.

Melodic chants filled the chamber.

Familiar with the prayer, he silently followed along, saddened by his dual purpose here. He'd come to request aid in ensuring Alesia's safety and future travel to France. But he also needed to break the news of the loss of their mutual friend, a man who had saved the bishop's life.

Over the years he'd always anticipated his visits and enjoyed their time together. But he'd never considered that he'd offer Robert Wishart, a man who'd acted as his mentor throughout the years, such heartbreaking news. Though his friend wore the robe of a bishop, it wouldna protect him against the grief of learning about Douglas's death.

With a heavy heart, Colyne brushed his hand against the place where the document lay hidden. Nay, he wouldna fail their friend. The writ would be delivered to King Philip.

The murmurs ended. Whispered strains of the prayer faded.

"Leave us," Bishop Wishart said to the two members of the clergy without turning.

Colyne smiled at his friend's ability to sense the presence of others: Another reason he'd chosen Robert to watch over Alesia. His innate sense would add another layer of safety against those who sought her. And though a bishop, with his broad shoulders and sturdy frame, his friend appeared more as if a knight.

Both priests rose. As they noticed Colyne, surprise, then recognition flashed on their faces. They nodded and then walked past. Moments later, the door closed with a soft swish behind them.

Robert made the sign of the cross. He stood and turned, his wizened face wrought with concern. "I am surprised to see you. The last I had heard, you were attending a secret meeting of Parliament in the Highlands."

"Aye," Colyne replied, nae shocked his friend would be so well informed. His station provided him with many venues in which to gather news of importance to Scotland's fight for freedom. "You have heard about the abduction of King Philip's bastard daughter?"

The bishop gave a solemn nod.

Hope filled Colyne. "Have they found her?"

Thick, shaggy brows dipped in worry. "Nay. Wherever the Duke of Renard has hidden her, 'twas with a crafty hand."

"I had hoped they would have found her by now." Colyne paused, hating the sad news he brought.

He frowned. "What is wrong?"

"Douglas is dead."

The warmth in Robert's eyes shattered to sorrow. "How?"

"By Robert Bruce, Earl of Carrick, Guardian of the Realm of Scotland's dictate, Douglas was carrying a writ to King Philip, explaining the English duke's treachery," Colyne replied. "En route to the coast to sail to France, Renard's knights attacked him."

His friend's face paled. "God in heaven! Renard has the writ Robert Bruce intended for King Philip?"

With a hard swallow, Colyne touched his cloak. "Nay, I have it. I came upon Douglas wounded and dying. I swore to him that I would deliver the writ." He stepped forward and clasped a firm hand upon the bishop's shoulder. "I give you my oath that his death will nae be in vain."

Wishart's fingers trembled as they touched the cross hanging from his neck. "I thank God you made it here safely."

Silence hung between them.

Colyne stared at the crucifix secured behind the altar, at the blood weeping down Christ's body. "I need to ask three favors of you."

"Anything."

A muscle worked in his jaw as he held Robert's anguished gaze. "The only way the English duke could have known of the missive was if one of his informants were seated in the private meeting."

"A traitor?" Though a whisper, the bishop's question cut through the room like a curse.

"Aye," Colyne replied, his own anger as fierce at deducing the reason. "I mention it as Robert Bruce needs to be informed of this news."

"Consider it done."

"My thanks."

"Would your second request be to secure passage for you aboard a ship to France?"

"Aye, but if possible, I would sail with someone trustworthy instead of an unknown merchant."

"The writ is too important to risk falling into untrustworthy hands," Robert agreed, his voice trembling, evidence he struggled to contain his grief. "I shall send a runner to learn who is in port. If any captain's ship we trust is moored at the pier, once he learns of the graveness of this matter, I am confident he will adjust his itinerary and sail to France posthaste." He rubbed his thumb over the cross. "And the last?"

"There is a woman."

Robert's brow lifted. "A woman?"

"During my escape with the writ, I was wounded," Colyne explained. "A French missionary named Alesia found and cared for me. Her party was attacked while traveling in the Highlands. She said they were returning from Beauly Priory."

With a frown, the bishop rubbed his jaw. "I was nae aware of missionaries visiting from France."

Unease swept him. "You did nae know?"

The bishop shook his head. "I have heard naught of such an arrangement."

That didna make sense. One would think with the strife between England and Scotland, Alesia's party would have taken every precaution to ensure their safety. So why hadn't they informed the bishop of their arrival?

Chapter 12

Late afternoon bells tolled, sending nerve-shattering bongs through the waning spring day. The strong tang of the sea and the stench of the city invaded the confines of the chamber. Marie's stomach churned.

She wrung her hands and again looked at the door. "Where are you, Colyne?" Hours had passed since he'd left. Had he reached his destination? Had his pursuers seized him? Or had they killed him, and his body now lay on the street?

Stop it!

There could be many explanations for his delay. She searched her soul for reassurance, found naught but ominous reasons.

On a sigh, she turned toward the bed, and images of Colyne flooded her. The way he'd loved her, how he had ignited feelings she'd never imagined. With memories of him making her body tingle, the dankness of the chamber seemed less threatening. Marie released a calming breath. He would return.

And then what?

His fierce possessiveness as he'd loved her staked its own claim.

Mon Dieu. How could she have been foolish enough to believe that news of her betrothal would deter such a strong-willed Scot? He was an earl, a man used to wielding power.

Footsteps echoed outside.

Withdrawing her dagger, Marie flattened herself against the cool wood adjacent to the barred door.

The pad of firm steps halted.

Please let it be Colyne.

Pulse racing, she strained to hear the murmurs of other men, grumbles to alert her if they were English. Seconds dragged, each one stretching her nerves tighter.

"Alesia?"

At Colyne's whisper, she sagged back.

The door thunked against the wooden bar as he tried to enter. "Alesia?" he whispered, this time louder.

Relief sweeping through her, she sheathed her dagger, tugged the barrier free, and flung open the door.

Colyne stepped inside.

She ran into his arms and poured herself into a kiss, erasing the hours of uncertainty.

The door shut against his body's weight as Colyne turned with her and pressed her against the wood, his mouth taking hers as desperately.

A long moment later he drew back, his eyes dark with desire. "Had I known of your hearty welcome, I would have spent time away before."

Heat stroked her face at his playful taunt, but when she made to turn away, he caught her chin. "You must think me foolish."

"Alesia, I was but teasing."

She floundered for a second. "I missed you."

Laughter simmered in his eyes. "Is that what you would be calling launching yourself in my arms and sweeping my breath away?"

He was enjoying himself, she mused, feeling even more foolish. As her pulse slowed, she studied him. An earl. How had she missed his aristocratic mien when his every act, the very chivalry of his decisions, stated the obvious?

But she knew. Since her youth she'd seen too many within the gentry who used their powerful positions for their own benefit. And with each selfish act she'd witnessed, her views on nobility had grown jaded.

Marie tried to pull free, but he held her snug in his arms.

"I have missed you as well," Colyne said, his mouth covering her own with ferocious heat.

Lost in the tumble of sensations, she wasn't sure at what moment he carried her to the bed. He quickly relieved her of her gown and himself of his mail and the remainder of his garb. With his mouth skimming over her flesh, nothing else mattered.

"I want you," he murmured as he caressed her breasts as his tongue teased hers, driving her blissfully insane.

She tried to maintain her grasp on sanity, but as he continued to kiss her, touch her, he shattered her hold on that as well.

Until it was only him.

Only her.

As if the dangers beyond their chamber didn't exist.

Her cries entwined with his husky murmurs. She arched as he sank deep within her over and again. And with his every stroke, she ascended higher. Until her world exploded with a rain of purple mist and swirls of lavender.

Then she was floating, drifting back to find herself in Colyne's arms, his mouth claiming her every cry, his body's trembling matching her own.

The rightness of the moment made her yearn for all she could never have. Shifting in his arms, she settled against his chest. How did one's heart ache and swell in the same instant? But hers did, painfully so. She truly loved Colyne, and the acknowledgment made the pain of leaving him all the more unbearable. "Colyne?"

At Alesia's sated whisper, a breath of male satisfaction slid through him. "Aye?"

"Why were you so late in returning?"

He lay his head against the curve of her neck and allowed himself this moment of peace. But as he listened to her slowing heartbeat, he couldna dispel the disquiet Robert's ignorance of her or her party's journey to Beauly Priory had caused. "I took another route back."

She caressed his cheek. "Why?"

"I was recognized by the men searching for me."

"What?" She tried to sit up, but he drew her back for a soothing kiss.

"Nay worry," he said against her mouth. "I know the streets and hid in an alley until they'd passed."

Worry flickered in her eyes. "I was hoping you were wrong when you suspected the men following you had made it to Glasgow."

He nodded. "As much as I wish we could make love again, we need to travel to safer quarters this night."

"Is that why you dragged me to bed upon your return?" she teased.

"Dragged you, did I?" He nuzzled lower and kissed his way to her breast. "As I remember, 'twas you who launched herself into my arms." And kissed him with such intensity, logic had hazed his mind.

Now, with his body sated, his doubts concerning her reason for being in the Highlands resurfaced. A sword's wrath! He hated this not knowing. When he'd first arrived, he should have asked her about Robert's ignorance of any French missionaries visiting Scotland. His questions would be answered and his doubts gone.

Or would they?

She had withheld the fact of her betrothal. Even if she confessed her true reason for traveling to England, could he trust that she was telling him everything?

Torn, he drew her to his side. He wished these secrets between them didna exist, but until he'd delivered the writ and could tell her the reason for his own mission, wasna he just as guilty of withholding information?

At his silence, Alesia lifted her head, and the desire in her eyes flickered out.

A sword's wrath! He should never have allowed them to make love again until he learned the truth.

"What is wrong?" she asked.

Though encased in control, he heard the fragility of a woman who'd suffered too many of life's blows, a woman who could erect emotional barriers with lethal effectiveness and shut out everyone.

Including him.

Colyne despised tainting their last moments of intimacy, but for his own peace of mind, he needed an explanation. "While I spoke to my friend of our need for safe lodging and passage to France, he informed me that he had heard naught about French missionaries in Scotland."

"A friend?" she whispered, her voice growing cold.

Nay, she wasna going to avoid his question this time. "Why did you come here?"

She tried to roll away, but he stopped her.

Her gaze grew guarded. "You believe I lied to you?"

"Did you?"

"Why ask me when it is obvious you believe I have?"

Damn her evasion. "Trust me with the truth."

"Trust." Though she breathed the word, he heard the catch in her voice, proof she struggled against whatever boundaries prevented her from telling him. "*Oui*, I trust you. More than is wise."

"Are you a missionary?"

Honey lashes lowered. "I have told you all I can."

"Have you?" The regret in her eyes left his heart aching, but the surge of guilt haunting her face spurred his anger. Colyne caught her wrists when she would have moved away. "Why—"

"They are nearby," a man's deep voice called from outside.

Renard's men! Colyne motioned for her to be silent.

Eyes wide with fear, she nodded.

With honed stealth, he slipped from the bed, crept to the window, and peered out.

"What do you see?" Alesia whispered.

He turned, finding irony in the fact that he would still want her in light of the imminent danger. "Our pursuers are outside."

She grabbed her garments. "We must slip away before they search the inn."

"Aye," he replied as he dragged on his garb and then hurried to don his mail.

Marie tugged on her chemise, the muted voices of the men outside the window leaving her shaken. But that was far from her only concern. How had Colyne's friend known that no French missionaries had traveled to Scotland? Who exactly was this man?

With them having to flee the inn, she'd evaded answering, but Colyne wouldn't rest until he had received a satisfactory reply. Somehow she must avoid the issue until they parted. His ignorance of her royal tie was the only way to keep him safe.

He peered out the window and then turned. "Are you ready?"

"*Oui*." She donned her cape. Her heart squeezed as she took in the chamber one last time. At least they'd had a few hours of intimacy. Once he'd sailed to France and delivered the writ, he would never find her.

After securing his sword, Colyne pulled on his cloak. Tenderness touched his face. "All will be resolved."

It wouldn't. It never could.

In silence, he cracked open the door, peeked out. "Nay one is outside at the moment. We can leave." Taking her hand, he led her from the inn.

As they traveled, she took in the growing night. A murky haze shielding the moon, casting the city in a bloody hue. Dread curled tight within her. Was it a premonition? Did it forebode Colyne's death?

Or hers?

He slowed as they reached the end of the alley, scoured the busy corner. In the shrouded light, the hard angles of his face were carved into a frown. "Are you well?"

An ache began to pound in the back of her head. "I am fine. We need to hurry." Enough danger lay around them without her hindering their pace.

"We are almost there and then you can rest."

The concern in his voice touched her. Though angry with her, even though she'd hurt him, he still found compassion. And, regrettably, she would cause him further upset.

He moved ahead of her with catlike grace, his steps sure, his body tensed, prepared to react.

The warrior.

"What is wrong?" he whispered, studying her with unnerving intensity.

"Naught." But there was. Colyne had never told her who he'd met with earlier. His friend was clearly a knowledgeable man who apparently knew the comings or goings of missionaries and could destroy her story.

"We canna linger." He started forward.

She followed, her mind spinning through the possibilities. Was Colyne so determined to find out her secrets that he might inadvertently ruin any chance she had of returning to France?

Panicking, she slowed. She couldn't risk facing whoever they were going to meet. Marie glanced around at streets that offered anything but safety. Neither could she risk leaving Colyne's protection.

Mon Dieu, what was she going to do?

Chapter 13

Marie kept pace with Colyne as he wove through the darkened streets. At the next corner he drew to a halt, peered down the alley. After a moment, he faced her, his brows drawn in a worried frown. He waved her to follow and started forward.

A feeble light spilled ahead of them, weaving into the dismal shadows that engulfed the streets. Each darkened passageway held the promise of danger.

Or possible death.

A shiver rippled through her. She couldn't allow anyone to recognize her; neither could she risk slipping away from Colyne and traveling through this dangerous part of the city alone. Until she met whoever he led her to, neither would she know whether her identity had been compromised. Fighting for calm, Marie glanced at Colyne. He reminded her of her father, of his love for an unpopular cause, and then of his proving how an unthinkable goal could be achieved. In his offering support to the Scots, her father dared to confront King Edward, aware his actions could incite war. Like Colyne, he valued freedom.

Surely her father would find favor in this courageous Scot. She exhaled a rough sigh. Unless he learned she had given Colyne her innocence.

And what of her betrothed? She'd convinced herself that Gaston de Croix wouldn't care if she came to him unchaste. But what if she'd erred? What if, furious at her unfaithfulness, her betrothed insisted in her incarceration in a nunnery for the rest of her life? Or would he demand Colyne's death? Icy fear cut through her. No, whatever restitution necessary would be hers alone to bear.

Colyne pulled her deeper into the shadows, and then halted. He gently squeezed her hand. "My regrets for the numerous alleys we have traveled, but I believe this is the safest route." With a gentle caress, he brushed his mouth against hers, then broke the kiss. "You are trembling."

"I am tired." Not a lie, but far from the truth.

With a sigh, he brushed back a lock of her hair and tucked it behind her ear. "We must continue."

He led her through the alley, but the aged walls blurred through her tears. Worse, because she'd withheld her identity, Colyne hadn't a clue as to the perilous boundaries he had crossed.

As they stole past a corner illuminated by an oil lamp, Colyne caught a glimpse of Alesia's face. Her pallor worried him. If the bishop's report hadna indicated the strong presence of the English duke's knights within Glasgow, he would have accepted Robert's offer to use his coach.

But he'd nae risk a connection between him and the bishop. Such a link would end his ability to transmit vital communications for the rebel cause. That didna ease his guilt at how his ties kept him from giving Alesia respite from her exhaustion.

The echo of bells tolled nearby.

"Where are we going?" she asked.

"Look ahead."

In the decaying light, an enormous structure rose from the earth. With hard angles of stone that arched to frame windows of elaborate design, the architecture appeared as if crafted for royalty.

"Glasgow Cathedral," she breathed. "That is our destination?"

"Aye." The relief in her expression eased his misgivings of her having lied about being a missionary. A muscle worked in his jaw as Colyne scanned the streets. He hated his doubts. Why couldna he erase his suspicions?

Confident nay one was watching them, he guided her toward the rear of the church. Clusters of vines thick with leaves shielded them as they hurried down a path of stone steps embraced by moss that curved to a thick oak door.

He rapped twice on the solid wood. Paused. Then knocked again three times in rapid succession.

Soundlessly, the door swung open. Robert's shadowed form filled the somber light. He gestured them inside. "Hurry."

After Alesia entered, Colyne followed and secured the door. The coolness of the earth below was a sharp contrast to the warmth outside. Robert gave her hooded form a cursory glance before meeting Colyne's gaze. "You were gone overly long. I grew worried."

Colyne shoved back his hood. "It was necessary to evade the knights searching for us."

The bishop gave an understanding nod. "I suspected as much. Though I doubt anyone will visit the cathedral's cellars at this late hour, we must nae tarry. Follow me." He lifted a taper, turned, and started down a narrow hall.

The scent of age, oak, and myrrh surrounded them as they moved deeper inside. Wine casks stacked on either side boasted of the cathedral's wealth. Ahead, the hallway curved and then opened to a set of sturdy steps that led to the chamber Colyne had visited hours before.

Instead of starting up, the bishop moved behind the stairs to a hidden door. He motioned them inside.

Colyne noted Alesia's surprise as she entered the concealed chamber. Several candles on a small table illuminated the room, its musty scent confirmation of its infrequent use. The dirt floor lay bare, the walls were unadorned, and a large cloth covered an indiscernible heap in the corner. The room also contained a bed and food stores.

He remembered the first time Robert had brought him here. Carried him, he corrected. He'd had the misfortune of running across drunken English troops. Under their interpretation of King Edward's orders to quell any Scot they met into submission, he'd almost died. Safe from prying eyes, he'd recuperated in this room.

Alesia pushed back her hood as she turned to Colyne, her gaze apprehensive.

He took her hand. "My Lord Bishop, may I present to you Lady Alesia, the noblewoman I spoke of earlier."

Robert gave her a courtly bow. "My lady."

"Lady Alesia, may I introduce you to My Lord Robert Wishart, Bishop of Glasgow." Because Alesia was a missionary, Colyne had expected recognition once he'd revealed Robert's name, but nae fear. Why would she be afraid? It made nay sense. On a religious journey, wouldna she find relief in the sanctity of the church? Or at least comfort in landing beneath the bishop's protection?

"My Lord Bishop, 'tis an honor," she replied.

Her mien again struck Colyne as regal, her voice tailored in cool discretion, as if she was used to meeting dignitaries. Which, as a prominent noble's daughter, she would be. So why did he sense something far more important was being played out before him? The bishop's brows furrowed deeply as he studied her. "Have we met before?"

Alesia paled. *"Non."*

Colyne believed her, more because his friend would never forget a woman presented to him within the ranks of nobility, especially one as beautiful as Alesia. So why would the bishop's presence unnerve her?

"I need to speak with you in private. I have important news that canna wait," Robert said, cutting through Colyne's musings.

"I will be there in a moment," he replied, frustrated. Instead of finding answers about her, he encountered more questions.

The bishop swept a discerning glance toward Alesia and then left. Her breath unsteady, she stared at the door as it settled in his wake, her fingers clenched tight.

Confused, Colyne watched her. Did she fear that Robert had recognized her? *Demand the truth!* Jaw tight, he glanced toward the door. A sword's wrath, Robert was waiting for him. He leveled his gaze on her.

Her eyes flared and then grew cold.

She'd gained a brief reprieve. From her unease, they both knew it. On a silent curse, he strode to the entry, jerked the door open, and looked back. "I shall return soon."

With a frustrated sigh, he secured the aged panel. As he started up the stairs, he found Robert waiting for him at the top. Colyne paused. "Do you know her?"

The bishop studied Colyne with solemn regard. "I have never met Lady Alesia before. Has she told you her full name?"

The breath he'd held rushed out between clenched teeth. "When I asked, she refused." Nor had she told him after she'd given herself to him in the most intimate of ways.

"Has she spoken of from which region of France she hails?" At Colyne's hesitation, Robert's brows lifted. "You do nae even know that?"

"We have traveled hard," he replied, embarrassed he could have made love to her and nae known the location of her home, much less her full name.

"You carry the writ," Robert said with a frown. "'Tis nae like you to jeopardize a document of import by entertaining the presence of a stranger, much less risk offering one escort through the Highlands."

Colyne nodded, heat slashing his cheeks at the more than deserving chastisement. With Alesia, he'd acted like a green lad tasting his first kiss. "As I escaped Renard's men, I was hit in the shoulder with an arrow. Alesia found me unconscious and saved my life. I couldna leave her. Nae to mention that after the attack on her party, she needed comfort and understanding, nae for me to pry."

"Given the situation, I can understand your helping her and respecting her privacy. But after the days you have traveled together, especially considering the importance of your reaching King Philip, I would have expected you to take every precaution in learning as much about her as possible. Dangers often come from the seemingly innocent."

He tensed. "You believe Alesia is a threat?"

"Nae to your mission." The bishop worried the cross he wore around his neck. "'Tis nae like you to leave so much unanswered."

He agreed. Never before had he allowed his emotions to overrule his common sense. A reason he was sought out for the most difficult missions for the rebels, and why he was often called upon by Robert Bruce, when the Guardian of Scotland needed a man he could trust. Shamefully, since he'd met Alesia, 'twould seem his logic had fled.

"But then," the bishop continued, his voice gentling, "except for Elizabet, I have never seen you so entranced by a woman."

Caught off guard, Colyne stared at his friend. "What do you mean?"

Robert laid his hand on Colyne's shoulder. "We have known each other too many years for me nae to see the warmth within your eyes when you look upon her. But I advise you, before you become involved with the lass, learn more about her, I would. . . ." He studied Colyne and then dropped his hand. "Or am I already too late?"

Memories of himself and Alesia making love flooded Colyne's mind. "I care for her deeply."

"You know little about her," Robert cautioned.

"Mayhap, but I have learned she is genuine and caring." He paused. "After I have delivered the writ, I wish to return for her."

A frown deepened the bishop's brow. "Do you think that is wise?"

"Nay," Colyne replied with complete honestly. Besides her betrothal, she didna trust him enough to tell him the secret she hid, both solid reasons why he should let her go. "But I care too much about Alesia to forget her."

"From one friend to another, all I ask is that you weigh your future decisions in her regard with care before you act. I would nae wish to see either of you hurt."

"What news have you learned?" Colyne asked, changing the subject, understanding Robert's concern.

"I have received word that three ships are moored at the pier, one of them the Kincaid. Your friend, Lord Thomas Kirketon, Earl of Logan, is the captain."

Relief swept him. "Which will be my transport to France." Once his childhood friend learned of his destination, along with the reason, he would offer him passage.

"He is planning to sail to Portugal on the morning tide."

An urgent pull flooded Colyne. "Then I shall leave for the docks immediately."

"What of Lady Alesia?"

"I ask that you keep her in your care until you can secure passage for her to sail to France. I refuse to subject a lady to the Kincaid. Though Logan sails for profit, we both know that more often than nae, he and his men scour the seas to relieve the English ships of supplies meant for their troops."

Robert nodded. "I am pleased Logan's loyalties lie with the Scots. With regards to Alesia, I will ensure she is kept safe."

With the time to leave her having arrived, he found himself far from ready to depart. "My thanks for watching over her." Sadness lurked in his friend's eyes, and Colyne understood. He placed his hand on the bishop's shoulder. "My heart is heavy at the loss of Douglas. I still grieve."

"He is in God's hands, a thought that offers me great comfort." Robert released a sad sigh. "Take care, my friend. May God bless your path and see you safe."

"And you as well." Silence embraced Colyne as he descended the steps to the cellar, the musty air thick and rich with the aromas of age and earth. He moved behind the stairs and opened the door.

"Who goes there?"

The rich softness of Alesia's voice ignited a need for her that far exceeded the physical. He frowned. Alesia had made it clear she didna want him to speak with her father. Should he respect her wishes and, when he left, never see her again?

Could he?

"'Tis Colyne." He entered. Need slammed him as he saw her sitting on the bed. Embraced in the glow of several candles, Alesia radiated beauty. Everything he wanted in a woman.

And more.

Colyne closed the door with a steadying breath. "A ship is in port and preparing to sail on the morrow. I must go."

Panic flashed in her eyes and then shifted to hope as she stood. Her shoulders relaxed. "We are leaving?"

His heart ached at their parting, at the possibility that he might never see her again.

Then he thought of her betrothed.

A man she'd vowed to wed but didna love.

When he spoke with her father, could he convince the powerful lord to release Alesia from an unhappy future? And if her father agreed, he would expect Colyne to offer for her hand.

He tensed. As daunting as the thought of again trusting his heart, he acknowledged that she had awakened sensations he'd never believed possible.

But did they equal love?

Before he met with her father he would be sure. "The vessel is nae designed for comfort but speed."

A relieved smile touched her mouth as she reached for her cloak. "Comfort matters not."

"I am going alone," he stated. "'Tis too risky to take you along."

She pulled on her cloak. "As if we have not already faced more than our share of dangers?"

A sword's wrath. "Before we did nae have a choice."

Her eyes widened in panic. "I must sail for France immediately."

The blend of fear and sadness in her voice had him moving closer. "The bishop will ensure you board a ship soon on which you will be safe."

"But—"

"I will nae argue." At her stricken expression, needing to offer her comfort, Colyne strode to her and claimed her mouth. His body trembled beneath the onslaught of emotions she inspired, needs that shook him to the core. Grief at having to leave her tearing through him, he pulled away. He stroked his thumb against her cheek. "I shall miss you greatly."

Marie drew in a shaky breath and fought back the tears. How could she convince him to take her with him to France? It would give them a few more days together. Not long, but when faced with being apart for a lifetime, she would claim each moment possible.

She cringed at the idea of becoming another man's wife, allowing intimacy with someone other than Colyne.

"I must leave."

The raw emotion in his words stopped her cold. As if in compliance, Marie removed her cloak, and then tossed it on the bed. She despised the secret of her heritage, of the threat it had brought to Colyne's life. Would there ever come a time when her royal blood wouldn't dictate her fate?

Neither could she forget her greatest need—to reach her father and explain her abduction. It outweighed everything else.

Even her love for Colyne.

His expression softened into regret. "I do nae want to leave with anger between us. Know that if I could take you with me, I would."

At the weariness on his face, she reached out. "I know. Kiss me," she whispered.

"I . . ." He muttered a curse. Then Colyne caught her mouth in a fierce kiss.

Marie gave in to her desire until her body ignited beneath his in a hunger only he could quench.

On a rough breath, he broke away. "'Tis time to go. I have already stayed overlong."

Sadness washed through her. He believed he was keeping her safe, but what he didn't understand was that her own mission outweighed the protection the bishop offered. Each passing day brought greater peril to Scotland's cause.

Aware of what she must do, Marie watched Colyne prepare to go. Once he left the cathedral, with the materials she'd found within a desk shielded by the cloth, she would ink an explanation of her actions to the bishop so he wouldn't worry about her disappearance. After, she would follow Colyne to the docks. Somehow, she would make her way aboard.

"My blessings for your journey." They wouldn't be parting, but he didn't know that.

A muscle worked in his jaw. "I wish it could be different."

"As do I."

"I care about you, Alesia. I am trying to keep you safe."

"I know, but you will not always be there for me."

As the door closed behind Colyne, Marie dipped the quill in the ink and wrote a missive to the bishop explaining her absence. Setting her note on the bed, Marie tugged on her cloak and slipped into the hallway.

Empty.

Anxiousness slid through her. Had he used the cellar door? The main cathedral exit above? Mayhap he'd left through the back of the building? She started forward.

"He is gone," the bishop stated, his steps a confident tap as he descended the stairs.

Marie halted, surprised by the cleric's appearance, further unnerved by the seriousness of his voice. He spoke to her as if he knew who she was. She frowned. Which was impossible. They'd never met.

"I was hoping to catch up with Colyne."

"You are safe here."

At the emphasis of his words, she swallowed hard. If he had recognized her when introduced, wouldn't he have used her proper address? Slowly, praying she was wrong and he hadn't identified her, she turned.

The bishop had halted several paces away, his face cast in shadows.

She wished she could see his expression. "I deeply appreciate your offer of protection," she said, grateful her voice revealed none of her distress. "Colyne has informed me of your making arrangements for my departure. I am thankful to you for those as well."

"'Tis my pleasure. I only wish that danger wasna about and I could offer you a room more deserving of your station."

Unease trickled through her. "The chamber you provided is adequate."

He stepped into the light, his gaze shrewd. "It would be if your father was nae King Philip."

Chapter 14

Marie's legs trembled, but pride held her still. "You know who I am?"

The bishop gave a slow nod. "I visited your father two years past. While there, I saw a painting of you in the solar." His mouth settled into a tempered frown. "Why have you nae told Colyne?"

As much as she wished to deny the truth, 'twould serve no purpose. "At first," she admitted, "because he was a stranger."

"After Elizabet, your deception will be a great blow to him." He quirked a brow. "I assume you know of her?"

Grief welled inside her. "I never meant to hurt him."

His mouth tightened. "But you will."

"I must. If my father learned of our . . ."

"Indiscretions?" the bishop supplied.

Heat warmed her face. "*Oui.* If my father knew, he might unleash his anger by demanding Colyne's life. A risk I cannot take."

"I have known Colyne since childhood. He is a good man and holds a formidable title. Mayhap if I speak with your father, 'tis possible—"

Marie shook her head, gathered every ounce of courage as she faced this man of God, needing to admit her sin. "I am betrothed to Gaston de Croix, Duke of Vocette." Her heart ached as she waited for the bishop to speak, to mete out the condemnation she'd earned.

His fingers rubbed the cross hanging from his neck as sad understanding shadowed his gaze. "Colyne cares for you more than he realizes." He watched her closely. "And what of you?"

A traitorous tear slid down her cheek. "I am in love with him, but it excuses me of naught."

"You have nae told Colyne of your feelings?"

"*Non.* It would only complicate an already dire situation."

Strain tightened the bishop's face. "After what has passed between the two of you, Colyne has the right to know your identity."

"Under normal circumstances, I would agree. But with my father being the king of France, nothing about this situation is normal. And telling Colyne will change naught. It is safest for him if I disappear."

"Is it? I am nae so sure." He motioned toward the hidden chamber. "Try to rest. I will ponder the situation. A night's sleep may offer a solution you have nae considered."

With her throat clogged with emotion, Marie nodded but found little enthusiasm at his words. Turning away, she reentered the chamber, frustrated by the delay. Regardless of the fact that the bishop had recognized her, naught had changed. As planned, she would wait a few moments and then slip out.

Colyne reached the docks as the first wisps of dawn cut through the layer of clouds. The scent of the sea hung in the air, thick with the promise of rain. He gave a rueful smile. He'd outmaneuvered the English duke's men again.

Beneath the wavering torchlight, Logan's sailors hustled to load crates aboard the Kincaid. Several paces away, another man staggered up the plank, as if having celebrated too much throughout the night.

From the shadows, Colyne studied the ongoing activity, taking in every nuance but hunting for . . . there. In the far corner, near a stack of crates, several English knights lurked, and three more stood guard near the ship.

He'd anticipated the English duke having instructed his men to keep watch over the port, but he'd hoped he was wrong. Their presence complicated everything.

A splotch of rain slapped his face. Thunder boomed and the rain pounded the docks. The knights' bolted for the overhangs of nearby buildings.

Taking advantage of their preoccupation, Colyne tugged his cloak tighter and stepped onto the wharf amongst the sailors, who, used to the adverse weather, continued to work.

As he neared several men carrying a container, he hefted an edge, kept his face toward the cargo, and fell in step. At the Kincaid, he hurried up the plank.

Near the top of the quarterdeck, a muscled sailor with a scraggly rain-sodden beard blocked his path. "State your business."

Though shielded by the rain, the coming dawn would aid in exposing him to the English. Colyne stepped forward. "I need to see Lord Logan immediately."

Cold warning flashed in the sailor's eyes a second before he unsheathed his dagger. "The captain is busy."

Before the sailor realized his intention, Colyne snared the man's wrist. "Tell your captain Lord Strathcliff requests his presence." The wind gusting through the wharf calmed, and the rain began to ease. To his right, English knights moved onto the docks. "Now!"

"Colyne?"

At Logan's voice, Colyne dropped his hold on the sailor's arm. "Aye."

"Let him pass," the captain ordered.

"A warm welcome," Colyne muttered as he strode on deck and clasped hands with his friend, whose long black hair and piercing ebony eyes reminded him of a brigand's. A title against the English his friend often fulfilled.

The captain's gaze narrowed on the English duke's knights, scouring the pier below. "They have been combing the wharf ever since I arrived in port. Whoever they search for, they are determined to find."

Colyne grimaced. "They want me."

Amusement trickled into his friend's eyes. "Come to my cabin where we can speak freely."

In his private quarters, Logan shoved back his hood. Water dripped onto a wooden deck stained by salty sea spray and the passage of time. "I am surprised you are in Glasgow. When I saw you a month past, you were headed to the Highlands."

Colyne shook the rain from his cloak. "Which is where I was until an issue forced my hand."

"An issue?" He lifted a brow. "Would it have anything to do with the abduction of King Philip's bastard daughter?"

"So you have heard?" Colyne asked, nae surprised. Like the bishop, his friend had many well-informed connections.

"Do nae worry. 'Tis nae common knowledge. The information came to me through . . . how shall I say it? Discreet but reliable channels."

Humor tugged at Colyne's mouth. "Robert Bruce needs to have your ear on more than random occasions."

Logan folded his arms across his chest. "My mistress is the sea."

"There is a comfort to be found on land as well," Colyne said, intrigued to find the proposition of spending time with Alesia brought him only happiness. "Do you think you will ever give up sailing?"

"Never. I have all I need beneath my feet."

Colyne understood his friend's reason for finding succor out to sea—the woman who'd broken his heart.

If asked a month before, Colyne would have agreed that his duties as earl and to his country's fight for freedom fulfilled his needs. Alesia had changed everything. "Mayhap you shall meet a woman who will convince you otherwise."

The captain uncrossed his arms. "Are those the words of experience, my friend?"

He nodded and gave a rueful grin. "Her name is Lady Alesia."

"Ah. Perhaps 'tis nae only the king's business that brings you to Glasgow, then?"

Colyne sobered at the reminder of his mission, along with Alesia, whom he'd left at the cathedral. "Nay. We met en route. She and other missionaries had delivered supplies to Beauly Priory. While traveling through the Highlands, their party was attacked."

"By the English?"

Colyne nodded, remembering Alesia's horror at the telling, and aching at her loss. "Aye."

"The bastards."

"I couldna leave her alone."

"The blasted cur. 'Tis nae a sight for anyone to witness, much less a lass." Logan paused. "Has she nay family nearby?"

"Her party sailed from France."

"France?" His friend scratched his chin. "'Twill put a burr beneath King Philip's arse when he learns of the attack."

"If only the attack on the missionaries was the French king's biggest problem."

"Has his daughter been found, then?"

"Not that I am aware."

He grimaced. "You are fortunate to have caught me in port. I would have departed yesterday, but I awaited several shipments of wool. They have arrived and my men are loading them now. I sail for Portugal with the morning tide." He studied Colyne with interest. "And how did you know where to find me?"

"The Bishop of Glasgow."

Logan gave a hearty chuckle. "I see I am nae the only one with his ear to the ground. So, what is it that I can do for you? That is why you are here, is it nae?"

"I need to sail to France."

"France?" He winced. "Bloody hell, why do you need to sail there?"

"On a matter of grave import."

"Ah . . . So you are delivering the writ to King Philip?"

Why had he believed his friend wouldna know? "So much for keeping my mission a secret."

A wicked grin curved his friend's mouth. "An educated guess." Deep lines furrowed his brow. "Though I had heard Robert Bruce sent Sir Douglas for the task."

Colyne swallowed hard. "The English duke's men caught him. He is dead."

"Christ's wounds. Douglas was a decent man."

"Aye, he was. Which is why I must depart for France immediately."

Logan swore as he walked to the table. He turned, his eyes blazing. "If anyone else had asked me to divert the Kincaid, he could go to the devil."

"I know."

"What of the woman you escorted from the Highlands? Will I have a lass in tow as well?"

As much as he wanted to bring Alesia with him, travel aboard the Kincaid was too dangerous. After he'd delivered the writ, Colyne would find her. "Nay. Robert will care for her."

"That is something, then," he muttered.

"How many hours before the morning tide?"

A hard rap sounded on the door.

Colyne slid a questioning glance toward Logan.

The captain shook his head in silent warning. "Enter."

A sailor they'd passed earlier hurried inside. "Captain, the knights who were here yesterday are demanding another search."

Logan cursed. "I will be along in a moment. Ensure they do nae come onboard until I arrive. As before, inform them I will escort them through the ship personally."

"Aye, Captain." The sailor hurried out.

"Another search?"

Logan quirked his brow. "Indeed."

Colyne's temper spiked. "How can you be calm when they are sure to find me? Or do you think they will nae want to be checking every inch of your ship?" With nae way to escape, within the next few minutes he could be imprisoned.

Or dead.

The captain walked to a chest in the corner of his cabin, shoved it aside. A trapdoor lay beneath. He opened the hatch. "I will have one of my men hide you in a crate on the docks until the knights have departed."

Relief swept through him. "My thanks."

"Go on with you now, while I deal with the Sassenach."

Colyne smiled at his friend's less than flattering term for the English. "Aye, I will." He slipped through the opening and landed in the cargo hold. He disliked that his presence aboard the Kincaid added to the dangers his friend faced by daring to sail into Glasgow harbor. But Logan entered port prepared for trouble. Unlike Alesia, a noblewoman stranded in a foreign country.

However much she believed otherwise, her strong will and determination wouldna defend her against those who, for whatever their reason, sought her.

Climbing out through a hatch, Colyne worked his way down a rope ladder to the dock. The English duke's men would have been informed of his past association with Logan, no doubt a fact that had led them to again search the Kincaid.

Logan came into view at the top of the gangway and started speaking with one of the knights as a sailor who'd helped him above quickly pulled up the woven rope

Noting his friend's easy stance, Colyne relaxed. They'd nae seen him leave. If they had, the English knights would have seized the ship. Thankful, he tugged up his hood and followed one of Logan's men toward a large stack of crates.

By the time one of Logan's men helped Colyne from the crate and told him it was safe to board, waves, spawned by a brisk wind, raked the bay. Above the water, the sun appeared as if a circle of fire. Blood-red rays seeped through the jagged clouds that dared slide across their path. The bastards had taken their time in their search of the Kincaid.

Nerves tingled up his neck and he searched the street behind him.

Naught. Unable to dispel the feelings of unease, he tugged his hood close against his face and followed the sailor through the bustling crowd.

Halfway down the pier, two of the English duke's men stepped into view.

Colyne tensed. As he moved past, he caught part of their conversation. From one of the men's description of a charming wench he'd bedded last eve, their interest at this moment far from involved searching for him.

On the Kincaid, he noted Logan giving orders to a sailor.

The captain spotted him, made a subtle gesture for him to hurry aboard, then resumed his task.

"Over here!" a knight shouted from behind him.

They'd seen him! Colyne reached for his sword, hidden beneath his cape. When the pounding of steps grew distant, he turned.

The knights ran toward the alley.

Relieved, he picked up his stride, heading for the plank. The diversion would allow him to board without event.

A woman's scream ripped through the shouts.

Alesia? His heart pounding, he whirled, stared past the sailors now halted in their tasks and straining to see who the knights had captured.

It couldna be her.

He'd left her safe in the cathedral hours before.

"Hurry up," Logan called to him.

"A blasted moment." Dread filled Colyne. Alesia was anxious to reach her homeland, but was she desperate enough to follow him and put her life at risk?

Worry had him striding down the dock. He forced his way through the sea of sailors toward where the English duke's knights congregated around a cloaked figure.

The ranks of the knights broke.

One of the men hauled their prisoner hard against his chest.

His captive flailed her arms in an attempt to break free. The hood fell back.

Alesia's pale, terrified face came into view.

Chapter 15

Terrified, Marie twisted in an attempt to escape her captor. She must reach the ship!

The knight tightened his grip. "Be still!"

She dug her nails into the man's face. Angry trails of blood streaked down his cheek.

"Curse you!" He wrenched her hand behind her back.

Pain shot up her arm. Marie sucked in air to scream and he clapped his hand over her mouth.

The duke's men moved closer, their bodies shielding her from the view of the men on the dock.

She strained to see past the knights to where she'd caught sight of Colyne moments before. Naught. Her heart sank. He'd boarded the ship.

"Take her down the alley," a burly knight ordered the man holding her.

She fought against her captor, but he hauled her into the narrow street. Mortared stone blocked her view of the pier. Non! *She must reach Colyne!* Marie bit her captor's hand.

He swore and released her.

"Help!"

The blustering workers, the screeching of seagulls, and the clatter of goods being hauled across wood drowned out her scream.

"No one is going to help you," the man snarled as he clamped his hand over her mouth once more.

Again, Marie tried to sink her teeth into his flesh.

With a snarl, he wrapped his fingers around her throat, squeezed. "You will be regretting that, King Philip's bastard daughter or not!"

She gasped. A veil of gray coated her vision. *Colyne, help me!*

Groggy from lack of air, she slumped against the man. He eased his grip and she began to cough.

"Try to escape again and next time I will not be so gentle." He tugged a piece of cloth from his garb, secured the gag over her mouth. Another knight stepped forward and wrapped a blanket around her, casting her into blackness.

The bitter cloth dug into her mouth, and Marie struggled to work the gag free. She couldn't untie it.

By the grace of Mary, what was she going to do? Colyne didn't know that she had followed him to the docks. Bishop Wishart believed her asleep and wouldn't notice her disappearance for hours. After reading her brief explanation as to why she'd left and believing her safe with Colyne, even if the bishop sent a runner to ensure she'd reached the ship, he'd not find her now.

"Go," a man's deep voice ordered. Leather boots slapped against the wet stone as the knight holding her walked.

"Colyne!" she called against the twisted cloth. Marie listened for any sign of possible rescue. Except for the sounds of men in the distance and the grumbles of the knights trudging by her side, work on the docks continued without interruption.

Refusing to give up, she wriggled her hands in the hope of loosening her bonds. After several fruitless attempts, the skin on her wrists burning, she stilled.

Why hadn't she remained hidden in the alley a few seconds longer? With the ship's departure imminent, Colyne would have been forced to take her with him.

She'd seen the English duke's men, but wearing the cloak of a commoner and having been ignored by the few people she'd seen en route to the docks, she hadn't anticipated trouble. If a sailor carrying a large sack hadn't stumbled into her and sent her sprawling, the knights never would have seen her.

What would the English duke's men do with her now? After her previous escape, they wouldn't relax their guard again.

Or would they remove any risk of her slipping free and kill her?

Marie tried to remain calm, but a sob built in her throat. She hadn't told Colyne that she loved him. Now, she would never have the chance.

And what of her father? Had the English duke reached him? Filled him with lies? Had he begun severing financial ties to the rebels? Without France's much-needed support, how much time would pass before Scotland fell to English hands? Months? A year? Unless a miracle occurred, without France's financial backing, it was only a matter of time before King Edward seized Scotland.

Angry shouts erupted in the distance

Had someone witnessed her abduction? No. By keeping a safe distance and following Colyne in the shadows, she'd ensured that.

"To arms!" a man called out, this time closer.

"Stop them!" a deeper voice called but yards away.

Hope ignited. Someone had noticed!

The knight holding her turned. Without warning, he shoved her away.

Blinded, Marie stumbled back. Steel hissed against leather at her side. A hand grabbed her. Before she could struggle, her blanket was torn away.

Colyne stood before her, his chest heaving, panic in his eyes. "Dinna move!"

The glint of his knife flashed past her face and the gag fell away. Blissful air raced into her lungs.

"Stay behind me!"

She obliged. Her hope of fleeing faded as she assessed the number of English knights around them. How could they escape?

Shouts filled the air as workers wielding daggers stormed the English duke's men.

The Kincaid's whistle pierced the din.

The ship couldn't leave without her and Colyne!

Three knights charged Colyne.

He sank his blade into the nearest aggressor, turned, and with several well-aimed thrusts, dispensed of the other two. "When I tell you to, run down the alley!"

The alley? Marie glanced toward the end of the pier where several sailors were untying the mooring lines in preparation to sail. They needed to head toward the ship. If they didn't board, they would be left behind.

From the corner of her eye, she caught Colyne wielding a defensive blow. Sweat streaked his face and his arms trembled with exhaustion. Angling his sword, he caught his next opponent's thrust. Colyne twisted his hilt, shoved the man back, and then glanced toward her. "Go!"

"Not without you!" She searched for something she could use as a weapon, grabbed a sword lying beside a fallen knight.

One of the English duke's knights spied her. Charged.

Her pulse racing, she raised the sword to block his blow, braced herself for the impact.

Before their blades met, her aggressor's fierce expression twisted to shock. His weapon clattered to the wet stone and he lay unmoving, a dagger buried in his back.

A stranger with long black hair stepped from the mayhem. Ebony eyes glittered with anticipation as he retrieved his dagger from the fallen man.

"Logan," Colyne called.

"Aye," the stranger replied as he sheathed his blade.

"'Tis safer if I take her through the alley to the ship. I will meet you at the other side of the pier."

The stranger nodded.

With a hard thrust, Colyne drove his sword into another attacker and then withdrew his blade. He grabbed Marie's hand. "Run!"

The slap of their steps echoed around them as they sprinted toward freedom.

"Why did you leave the cathedral?" Colyne demanded.

"I told you," she said between breaths, "I must return to France."

He shot her a hard look. "Once we reach the Kincaid, you will explain what was so bloody important that you would risk your life—all our lives—for it. Is that clear?"

Marie kept running, resigning herself to her fate. Once onboard, she would tell him the truth.

Embraced by the decaying streets, with the clang of swords their backdrop, the love they'd made seemed but a dream, his tenderness more so.

The ship's whistle pierced the air, announcing the vessel's imminent departure.

They weren't going to make it. Marie slowed, but he tugged her forward.

"We have to return to the docks. Otherwise we will be too late!" Colyne pointed toward a dilapidated building a short distance ahead. "We can cut through there. Then we will circle back."

They neared the hovel and found the door ajar.

He slipped inside, with her close behind, and then jerked the door shut. Darkness enveloped them, ripe with the scent of stale bread and ale. He navigated through the broken beams and rubble with sure steps, then led her into the next alley.

In the distance, the dark-haired stranger Colyne had called Logan stood at the edge of the dock. He waved them forward and then slipped over the edge.

The rub of wood groaned against the pier. Ropes splashed in the water.

Heart pounding, she shook her head. "The ship has left the pier!"

Colyne sheathed his sword. "Go!"

She pushed her tired body to keep pace. At the edge of the weathered dock, a small boat nudged the wooden post below. Relief swept her when she saw Colyne's friend sitting inside, hands ready at the oars.

The stranger glanced toward the other side of the pier, where a melee of men and swords continued. "Hurry!"

Colyne jumped into the craft, turned, and braced his feet against the hull. He reached for her. "Come."

She didn't hesitate, thankful when his powerful arms wrapped around her waist.

The small boat listed as Colyne shoved them from the pier. "Row!"

Water slid from the bow against the stranger's efficient strokes, each cutting deep into the sea to heave the sturdy craft forward.

Colyne helped Marie sit on the slatted wooden floor. With a relieved sigh, he dropped beside her.

She prepared for Colyne's wrath, evident by the deep lines on his brow. Instead, he embraced her, held her with such fierce compassion tears burned her eyes. Shaken at how close they'd come to dying, she sank against his chest, his strength a welcome balm against the day's uncertainties.

"When I saw the knights dragging you into the alley, I thought . . ." Colyne's lips trembled as he pressed a kiss against her brow. "You are safe now, 'tis all that matters."

"You were boarding the ship when the knights caught me," she said. "I did not think anyone saw me."

"I heard you scream." He cupped her face, his worried gaze adding another layer to her guilt. "Bishop Wishart would have made arrangements for your passage."

"I know, but I could not wait."

"A sword's wrath, you were almost killed!"

She nodded, still working to calm herself after her near capture.

"Oh, God." He pulled her to him and kissed her.

She tasted his fear, his vehemence to protect her. Marie returned his kiss and wished everything were different. That she could tell Colyne she loved him. That they could have forever.

The dark-haired stranger gave a victorious laugh. "I have nae tasted a brawl like that since Cádiz a year past."

Colyne broke the kiss and scowled at the man.

Undaunted, the stranger's smile widened. "You have hidden out in the Highlands too long." His brows rose with male appreciation as he studied Marie. "This is the fair Alesia, I take it?"

Colyne muttered a curse, which earned another laugh from the intimidating stranger.

"My lady," the black-haired man said with an easy calm, as if behind them the wharf wasn't tangled in a battle of flesh and steel.

Who was he? He'd helped them, so obviously a friend of Colyne's.

"Lady Alesia," Colyne offered, his expression far from amused, "may I present to you my friend, Thomas Kirketon, Earl of Logan, captain of the Kincaid."

"The captain?" Heat burned her cheeks.

The notorious-looking man winked at her. "Did you believe all of Colyne's friends to be as boring as he?"

Colyne grunted his dismissal.

Muscles bunched as the earl dragged the oars through the water. "The lad does nae understand the thrill found in battle. The satisfaction wrought from relieving English ships of their gold. Or arms."

She hesitated. "You are a brigand?"

Mirth twinkled in his eyes. "To some, perhaps."

Unsure what to make of this intimidating yet intriguing man, Marie slanted a look toward Colyne. Under his fierce stare, concerns about the captain and his disreputable endeavors faded.

As they neared the Kincaid, a sailor tossed down a rope.

"Stay here." With the grace of one long accustomed to moving in the confines of a boat, Colyne stepped to the bow. He picked up the floating line and pulled them closer as Logan stowed the oars inside the small craft.

With a muffled thud, they bumped against the ship's hull. Marie glanced back, relieved that the angle of the ship blocked them from the view of any onshore.

A sailor on deck dropped a rope ladder, which clattered against the side.

"Go on," Colyne urged Alesia. As she started up, he followed. A tremor rippled through him at the memory of how near she'd come to death. Thank God he'd heard her scream.

"That was blasted close," Logan said, his face flushed with excitement as he climbed on deck following Colyne. The captain studied Alesia with concern. "Are you well, my lady?"

"*Oui*. My thanks."

From her pallor, Colyne had his doubts. "I shall tend to her in your cabin."

"I will join you once we have safely cleared the harbor," Logan said.

Colyne nodded, then guided Alesia to the captain's cabin and closed the door. Alone, he hugged her, terrified at how close he'd come to losing her.

Alesia clasped her arms around him, her frantic pulse a testimony that she still relived her nightmare.

"I told you to stay with the bishop," he rasped. "I had made plans to ensure you sailed to France without danger."

A swath of pink stained her cheeks and she stepped back. "I appreciate all that you did for me."

"Do you?"

Hurt darkened her eyes, but she held his gaze. "I know you deserve answers. If you could accept without question my reasons for leaving the bishop's protection are sound, I would be indebted to you."

Colyne narrowed his eyes as he stared at her, the pain from her words immense. If she had tried, she couldna have hurt him more. "We made love, Alesia. I do nae want you indebted to me as if I were someone you could walk away from." He moved toward her, but to her credit, she held her ground. "On this I shall nae be swayed. Tell me why."

Her lower lip quivered, but she remained silent.

"Is it so hard to explain?" he asked, disheartened to find that after everything she would still hesitate.

"*Oui.*"

Her panicked expression had him damning himself over and again. "A sword's wrath. I am nae a merciless bastard set out to destroy your future." He gentled his voice. "If you did nae matter to me, the asking would be easy." He stroked his thumb across her cheek. "Do you think I do nae see the regret in your eyes?"

Her breath trembled out. "But if I tell you, you shall . . ."

"What?"

"Hate me."

Hate her? Merciful God. Never. He cared about her. More than was wise. And yet, by the self-condemnation in her eyes, she believed otherwise. In the silence, he watched her struggle for composure, noticing how she clung to her regal mien as a warrior would his blade.

" 'Tis a long story," she finally said.

The ship rocked comfortably beneath them as it cut across the windswept waters toward open water.

He dropped his hands to his sides, stepped back. "I have time."

Alesia stared out to where a stray beam of sunlight spilled over the swells to splinter into a million pieces. "I did not travel to Scotland to deliver assistance or much-needed goods to Beauly Priory," she said with solemn authority.

The hairs on the back of his neck tingled. He'd anticipated this possibility. "Continue."

"My name . . . is not Alesia." She skimmed her fingers over the aged wood of the opening, shot him a nervous glance. "Not the name I am known by, anyway."

His heart thudded against his chest. "What, then, would that name be?"

She lifted her head with a regal tilt. "First, you must swear an oath of secrecy that you shall not tell anyone what I am about to reveal to you."

"Demands?" His anger increased. The dictate sounded too easily given, as if she were used to her requests being granted.

"Please," Alesia said with solemn regard. "I must have your oath."

Colyne laid his hand over his heart. "I give you my oath that what you tell me stays between us."

Relief flashed on her face. Then she took a deep breath and exhaled. "My full name is Marie Alesia Serouge, and my father is—"

"King Philip," Colyne finished, as with heart-stopping clarity the fragments of clues she had revealed since she'd saved him tumbled into place.

Chapter 16

Colyne took a deep breath, overwhelmed by the full ramifications as each clue since they'd met became clear.

Finding her alone.

The men hunting a woman.

Her urgency to reach France.

Aye, he'd entertained the thought of her being the king's bastard daughter, and had dismissed the thought as quickly. A sword's wrath, why had he nae considered it further? He gave a frustrated sigh. As if it mattered now.

Her true identity explained her desperate act of following him to the docks, but it didna justify how she could have given him her innocence.

The writ he carried was but a document. Once delivered, it could be forgotten. "Why did you nae tell me who you were before?"

"When we first met, you were injured and a stranger and I dared not give you my trust. As we traveled and I found myself beginning to care for you . . ." She shook her head. "I was at a crossroads as to what I should do."

She reached for him, but he stepped back. He couldna let her touch him now and haze his logic with another surge of emotion. He needed time to think, to understand how Alesia could withhold from him something of such import.

Alesia?

Nae, Marie, King Philip's bastard daughter.

Colyne narrowed his gaze at the lass he'd never truly known, a woman who made him forget Elizabet, and a woman about whom he'd planned on speaking with her father to break her betrothal. Bedamned the entire situation! With a rough sigh, he nodded. "Continue."

Regret shadowed her eyes. "I was overwhelmed by everything you made me feel. Everything you made me want. I was unsure if my emotions were clouding my decisions. Neither could I do anything to jeopardize reaching my father."

As he remained silent, distress shadowed her face.

"Do you not think I wanted to tell you who I was? I hated my indecision. I despised holding back something so important to a man for whom I deeply cared. Every time I considered telling you the truth, I would think, what if I am wrong and he is loyal to England? With Scotland's freedom at stake, I could not take such a chance. Even," she said with a soul-searching look, "at the risk of losing you."

Colyne fisted his hands until his knuckles grew bloodless. "I took your innocence."

"*Non*," she countered softly. "That I offered you. You knew naught of my betrothed or my royal heritage. Had you known either, you would have left me untouched." She hesitated. "I wanted you, Colyne. More than anything. Caught up in my desires, too late I realized the consequences of our making love. At first I believed that my state of innocence mattered not in my marriage bed. Now I realize how foolish was that thought. It terrifies me to think of the reactions of my father and my betrothed if they learn the truth. Without intending to, I have endangered your life. You must understand, I was trying to protect you."

"By telling me lies?" he demanded, far from appeased.

"It was the only way I could think of to keep you safe. Once we parted, I would disappear. Even if you tried to find me, knowing the name Alesia, unaware of my royal tie and where I lived in France, you would never have found me."

A truth Colyne damned.

Tears glistened in her eyes and she wiped them away. "I expected you to become frustrated in your search for me and, in the end, grow to hate me. After the intimacy we shared, how could you not?" Her lower lip trembled. "But at least I would know you were safe."

Sincerity draped her words, a gut-wrenching honesty that had Colyne wanting to draw her into his arms. An action that would solve naught.

Moss-green eyes pleaded with his. "Though I do not expect you to forgive me, please try to understand why I did not tell you the truth."

Sadly, her reasons for withholding her royal tie made sense, which helped little.

"I am sorry."

As was he. "How did you escape from your abductors?" Colyne asked, as he struggled at how best to proceed.

Her brow wrinkled in surprise. "You heard about my abduction?"

"Aye. When the Duke of Renard's actions reached Robert Bruce, he called an emergency meeting in the Highlands, the area in which our spies believed you to be hidden."

"So you are aware of the reason as well?"

"Indeed." The twisted humor of the situation was nae lost on him. Here he'd traveled at a devil's pace to inform King Philip of the true culprit behind Marie's abduction when with his every step she'd traveled at his side. He shot her a wry smile. "You are the reason I am en route to France."

She frowned. "What?"

Colyne withdrew the leather-covered document he'd secreted from the Highlands. "'Tis an explanation from Robert Bruce, Earl of Carrick, Guardian of the Realm of Scotland to King Philip, explaining the Duke of Renard's abduction and his reason—to use you to enrage your father to the point of severing ties with Scotland."

"Back when we were almost caught by the stream," she said, her voice falling to a whisper, "you entrusted the writ to me when you . . ."

"Believed I was going to die."

She nodded, but Colyne didna miss the pain in her eyes that thoughts of his mortality brought her, and his anger melted further. "If naught else, from your selflessness during our first days together, I learned you were a woman whose word I could trust. As to your true identity, I should have believed my initial instincts."

"How so?"

"There were many clues," he said, "some subtle, others nae. To begin with, you are French."

"But I had given you a reason for my presence."

"Aye. Then there is your regal mien, which you wear like a cloak when you are upset."

Her lips narrowed at his comment.

"'Tis nae a trait you can change," Colyne said, "but something as essential to you as your next breath, as inherent as your strength and your caring for those in need." Her deepening frown assured him that she was debating whether his words were those to accept or discard.

"If you had suspicions, why did you never ask if I was King Philip's daughter?"

"Between your reason for being in Scotland and the likelihood of a king's daughter escaping the English duke's men, and the odds of my meeting you alone in the Highlands, I dismissed the possibility. Speaking of which, how is it that you escaped?"

"After we entered a castle in the Highlands that Renard had seized, his knights left me in a chamber with but one guard." Humor touched her face. "Like you, they believed me the spoiled and defenseless bastard daughter of a French king."

Colyne gave her an assenting nod. "True, I underestimated a king's bastard daughter, but nae Alesia."

At his confession, her eyes misted. "*Non,*" she agreed. "You never underestimated Alesia. And for that I thank you."

Another piece of the puzzle of this complex woman settled into place. Over the years, bearing the brand of the king's daughter, bastard or nae, how many had thought of her as a helpless lass who doted on her own selfishness?

Hadna he been as guilty?

Her words of the self-serving gentry were offered through firsthand knowledge. In her royal position, she would have witnessed and experienced a sickening dose of coddling. With her strong and independent nature, such treatment would have made her withdraw from that circle further.

That he finally knew the truth pleased him, but what reason would he give her father to allow Marie to end her loveless betrothal? It wasna as if he sought to offer for Marie's hand. Though thoughts of her as a part of his life brought a sense of peace, he didna love her.

Or did he?

Torn by the emotions storming through him, Colyne paced the deck, numb to the rush of waves breached by the honed wood of the bow. He cared for Marie deeply. She made him laugh, he enjoyed her quick wit, and with her in his arms he felt complete. But did that equal love?

Unsure, he stared at a fragmented strand of seaweed drifting on the water's surface. As it floated past, she moved to his side.

She lay her fingers on his arm. "However wrong, I shall cherish the memories of our making love."

Colyne stiffened, wanting her desperately. Yet he kept his gaze riveted on the sea. "Desire, however strong, is nae reason enough to give me the most precious gift a woman can offer."

"All my life men have sought my attention in hope of the royal connection marriage to me would bring. For once I wanted to experience the joys given by a man who sincerely cared for me, and one I cherished as well. That . . . you gave me."

He faced her, aching and wanting her with the same breath. "Now what? Or is there a choice?"

She dropped her hand. *"Non."*

A shout from outside the cabin reminded Colyne that they sailed to France. He needed distance. If he was wise, he'd go, consider all they'd discussed. Saddened at the thought of leaving her, he drew Marie into his embrace. After everything, how could she feel so right in his arms?

She rested her head against his shoulder, her breath warm against his neck.

Colyne pressed a kiss upon her brow.

"I wish it could have been different," she whispered.

As did he. Never in his life had he felt so helpless. A battle he could fight. Attackers he could fend off. With Marie pledged to another man and her vow sanctioned by a king, Colyne could do naught.

A thought slid through his mind and he stilled. "Marie, your father is in the position of making betrothals. By the same royal authority, he can break them."

Sadness shimmered in her eyes. "I have given my word to my father. I cannot break my vow."

A sword's wrath! "So you would marry a man you do nae love to please your father?"

Red crept up her cheeks. "You do not understand. Over the years my father was always supportive of me when, as a bastard daughter, he easily could have overlooked my existence. There is so much I am thankful to him for, and I will not shame him by requesting to break a vow after all he has done." She paused, her gaze searching his. "I have comfort in knowing he would never match me with a man who would be cruel."

"So you choose to live a life of servitude?"

Hurt darkened her eyes. "Regardless of how I might wish to be with you, my vow has been given. 'Tis too late."

"Nae!" He held up his hand when she made to speak. "You have a choice. You can settle and be unhappy or live the life you choose. Think about your choices. 'Tis all I ask. "

Marie remained silent.

However much he despised the thought of her marrying a man she didn't love, how could he intervene if he wasna ready to ask for her hand? Frustrated, Colyne paced the room. As he turned toward her, a new and troubling thought came to mind. "With the king's guard protecting you, how was anyone able to abduct you?"

Worried eyes met his. " 'Tis a question I have asked myself many times since I was taken. My conclusions were few and unsettling."

"What happened?"

"A young girl came to my home in the middle of the night. She begged for my aid, explaining that her mother was in pain and that her baby was coming. When I explained she needed to seek the healer, she said she had tried and was told she was away helping another." Marie shook her head, her eyes foggy with memories. "I accompanied the child to her home under the escort of my guards. When I entered, several men grabbed me."

"And your guards?"

Her gaze grew troubled. "I am unsure."

"What do you mean, you are unsure?"

"I heard no sounds of a struggle outside."

With a sickening twist he understood. "You believe the knights assigned to you were Renard's men and the girl's story was designed to lure you to where they waited?"

"*Oui*," she replied, anger sliding through her voice. "Which means someone within my father's trusted circle is a traitor."

Two days later, the ship groaned as storm-fed waves tossed the vessel higher before plunging it into the oncoming trough.

Water crashed over the bow with violent force. The solid mast severed the blackened sea rushing past. On the next swell, the craft was again hurled up.

Colyne braced his knees and clung to the line as another surge of seawater rushed past. "The rope is secure on this end," he shouted to a man tying a knot on the opposite side of a crate.

The man gave a final tug on the knot. "Secure here as well."

Another wave crashed over the bow. Water flooded the deck.

In an effort to keep from being swept overboard, sailors gripped the sides of the hull and braced their feet.

After the swell washed overboard, Colyne used the line and worked his way toward the stern.

"Is the cargo secured?" Logan braced himself as the ship angled downward and plunged.

Another huge wave swamped the deck and then poured over the side to join the churning water below. On a shudder, the ship again angled up.

"Aye," Colyne replied, but even preoccupied by ensuring everything was tied down, he couldna help worrying about Marie. Since the onset of the storm two days past, she'd become seasick. With each passing hour, she'd grown worse until now she couldna leave her bed.

He damned every second he spent away from her. The day before, she'd been unable to keep down what little she'd attempted to eat. With her body continuing to purge itself, she couldna tolerate much more.

Once the crates were anchored, Logan shouted for less essential men to get themselves out of harm's way, and then made his way to Colyne. "The sea is in a foul mood," he said with a nod at the towering swell rolling toward them.

"Aye," he agreed. "After two days I had expected we would have sailed out of the storm or at least left the worst of it behind."

Logan tightened his grip on the rope as the ship hurtled down the next trough. "There is nay telling with a spring storm. They can rush in all wind and fury and leave you within an hour. Or"—he scowled at the swirl of angry clouds—"it can stall and last for several days. We have wound up with a stubborn one."

Colyne scanned the turbulent sky. Until the storm broke, they couldna take their bearings and learn how far they'd been thrown off course.

The captain grimaced toward where several of his men worked to keep the rudder tight and the ship facing into the wind. "Hold her fast!"

"Aye, Captain," one of the sailors shouted back.

Colyne glanced toward Logan's cabin. "I need to check on Alesia." In deference to Marie, he'd kept her identity secret.

"I will go with you." Logan followed him. "I canna believe we saved those crates. When that last wave swept over the deck, I thought we had lost them."

"Or a piece of the ship if the cargo had ripped the rest of the way loose and slammed into the side."

The captain gave a grim nod. "Indeed." He opened the door to his cabin, keeping a tight hold. They entered, and he quickly shut it against the lash of rain outside.

As his vision slowly adjusted to the dim interior, Colyne crossed to Marie.

At their approach, she groaned.

Colyne met Logan's worried gaze.

"She is having a rough go of it," his friend whispered.

"Aye," he agreed, frustrated he'd exhausted nae only his knowledge on seasickness remedies but every other sailors' onboard. None of the herbs or potions had brought her more than a token of relief.

He'd witnessed untried sailors on their first cruise caught in the dregs of this malady. Each person's reaction was different. Some experienced a mild case of nausea while others grew so sick they couldna eat, drink, or stand. Any attempt to move agitated their already extreme condition. Upon the first port, the afflicted sailors disembarked, never to return to the sea.

"Colyne?" she murmured.

He knelt beside her and pressed a kiss on her brow. "I am here." A fine sheen of sweat coated her skin. She'd told him of her queasy stomach on her forced sail to Scotland. He surmised the storm raging outside had weakened her already fragile resistance.

Honey lashes flicked open. She stared at him with a groggy frown. "Y—you were gone."

"Aye, all hands were needed above." He would give anything to relieve her of this misery. He hated the helplessness, unsure whether the storm would end this day or thrive for several more.

Logan lifted her cup, frowned. "She is nae drinking enough water." Holding back a curse, Colyne stroked her hair. "She will try to drink more." They both were worried by her weakening condition. That his friend had come to check on her with the ship needing his guidance underscored the depth of his concern.

Marie's lids drooped, as if the act of keeping them open were a feat unto itself.

The brutal crash of another wave reverberated against the hull.

Logan grimaced as he glanced up. "I must return to the helm." Ebony eyes met Colyne's with intention. "Take care of the lass."

"I will."

After his friend left, Colyne helped her sit. The ship groaned against the battering swells as he held the cup of water to her lips. "Here."

She shook her head. "I cannot."

Her weak reply stoked his worry. "A sip. Please try."

Marie struggled to take a drink, but when she tried to swallow, she ended up coughing instead.

With a silent curse, he set the water aside. He drew her against his chest, feeling her every tremble, how fragile she felt in his arms. *Please, God, help her.*

As if mocking his helplessness, another wave buffeted the hull.

Colyne cradled her as the ship plunged into the next trough, and he prayed for the storm to pass. Hand trembling, he lifted the cup to her mouth. "A bit more."

With dull acceptance, she choked down a swallow. "Enough."

"For now." But he'd nae give up. He stroked her hair with slow, gentle sweeps, thankful when she succumbed to an exhausted sleep. But with each passing hour, as she grew more listless, fear clawed through him that even if the winds calmed, 'twould be too late.

Seized by her unending struggle against nausea, Marie lost track of time. Days hazed together, each laden with the stench of salt, the stale odor of wood, and the scream of the wind as the storm howled its outrage.

Bits and pieces of the past several days fragmented through her mind; the captain's concerned face, Colyne's urging her to drink and, at times, to eat. As she'd lain on the bed shaking and exhausted, she'd wanted to do neither, but for Colyne she'd tried. And through it all, as much as possible, he'd remained steadfast by her side.

"Are you awake?"

At Colyne's worried voice, she opened her eyes. A shaft of sunshine streaming through the window had her closing them. Then she realized the ship no longer was assaulted by the waves but rocked gently beneath her.

Slowly, this time prepared for the bright light, she gazed up at him. Though tired, the smile on his face warmed her soul.

He brushed his fingers across her cheek. "You have been asleep for a long time."

Marie frowned as she noted the sun's angle. 'Twas beginning to set. "How many days have passed since we left port?"

"Eight; we were thrown far off course."

Streaks of pink-orange rays cut through the blue sky, announcing the oncoming night. "They are all a blur."

"You have been very ill."

His fear for her roughened his voice, strains of exhaustion creased his face, and shadows haunted his eyes. A testimony to his own sacrifice. "You need sleep," she said, moved that he'd jeopardized his own health by remaining awake to tend to her.

"I needed you more."

Marie's hand trembled as she reached out for him.

Colyne entwined his fingers with hers and drew her to him, his kiss as soft as dew upon heather in the first morning light.

Overwhelmed by this amazing man, she poured out her love for him in their kiss. How would she ever be able to face life without him, to wake up each day and not find him at her side?

Colyne's words haunted her. *You can settle and be unhappy or live the life you choose.* Could she ask her father to end her betrothal?

As quick as the thought came the guilt. The daily demands of her father's kingdom kept him sequestered in meetings to ensure the stability of the crown, along with his many other concerns. And with England and Scotland caught in a desperate clash, and King Edward making threatening noises toward France, her father had enough on his mind without complications from her.

Colyne broke their kiss and traced the pad of his thumb across her lower lip. "Your health is much improved, but rest will make you even stronger."

She gave him a pleading smile at odds with her troubling thoughts about her future. "I want to feel the wind upon my face, and the cleansing warmth of the sun. And I need to get out of bed for a short while before I go mad. Please," she added as a frown began to work across his mouth. "Afterward, I promise I shall rest."

He hesitated. "If you eat first. And then only for a short while."

Before he changed his mind, she pushed herself up in the bed. With zeal, she ate the porridge, then a chunk of bread. With a satisfied sigh, Marie swiped the cloth napkin across her lips, dropped it into the empty bowl, and smiled at him. Her head spun and her legs threatened to give way as he helped her stand, but she didn't complain. Cloistered within the confines of this cabin, however temporary, she'd do anything to escape.

Colyne steadied her as she wove slightly as she started forward. When they reached the deck, sunshine exploded around her in a flood of golden light, the shimmering bands of light spreading upon the swells in a brilliant wash.

The unsettling thoughts of moments before fled. Marie basked in the warmth, inhaling the scent of sunshine and the sea, marveling at the aqua sky punctuated by streaks of the oncoming night. "It is as if Merlin has cast a spell," she whispered, moved by nature's masterpiece.

Colyne arched a curious brow. "Merlin?"

Warmth filled her as the memories rolled past. "When I was eight summers, after my father returned from one of his many travels, he gifted me with a book filled with stories about King Arthur and the Knights of the Round Table. From then on, whenever he visited, he would read me one of the tales before he departed."

As Colyne guided her across the deck, she reveled in the warm press of his hand against her lower back.

He halted, and she leaned against the rail and then smiled when he settled beside her, lacing his fingers with her own.

"Your father must love you very much."

Her heart swelled as she remembered the precious times they'd spent together during her youth. "*Oui.* A love that is returned, I assure you."

Colyne stroked his thumb across her palm. "King Philip is nae widely known for his gentle nature."

"*Non,*" she agreed, closing her hand over his. "My father's position demands a staunch ruler. Beneath his terse countenance, he is a kind and gentle man." She leaned against Colyne's chest, soothed by the steady pulse of his heart. She could stand here forever as the sea slid past with a magical whisper. "When did the storm end?"

"Late last night. With the gentle roll of waves, you would never believe that hours ago the water raged with a brownie's wrath."

"A brownie?" She arched her brow. "Another of your Scottish fairies?"

"Aye," he said, but Colyne's smile didn't erase the lines of fatigue on his face.

As much as she wanted to remain outside, he was all but asleep on his feet. She yawned to give credence to her words. "I am tired and ready to return to bed."

"Nae worrying about me, are you?" he said with uncanny insight.

"She is up, then?" The captain's deep voice boomed as he strode toward them, his long black hair secured in a leather strip, his swagger that of a man used to riding out rough weather, and his ebony eyes bright with devilment. As he neared, his sharp gaze settled on her, as if assessing her condition.

"For the moment," Colyne replied.

Logan halted before them. "I will have one of the men bring you some stew, my lady."

"Thank you." After the food she'd eaten, she was unsure whether she could swallow more, but she would try. Before they reached port, she needed to regain her full strength. "When will we arrive in France?"

"The stowaway wishes to debark in France?" He winked. "Colyne told me of your determination to return home."

She froze. What else had been shared?

"Alesia is a determined woman," Colyne said, his use of her second name calming her to a degree.

"*Oui*, I am anxious to return," she said with a forced calm. "My father will be worried about me."

Logan gave her a charming smile. "We should arrive in port with the morning tide. Once we have docked, I shall make any arrangements either of you need."

Colyne nodded and then gave Marie a pointed stare. "We will be traveling together."

"If I had such a beautiful woman at my side, I would nae let her stray far from me either," the captain teased. Logan studied her for another moment. "You look tired. Go below and rest, my lady. I will ensure your food arrives soon."

"My thanks."

"Never let it be said I have treated a lass with coarse manners." The captain gave a formal bow and then headed toward the aft of the ship, where one of the crew members labored around a pot hung on a tripod of steel. Below it, set upon a thick, smoothed patch of sand, a fire burned.

Marie turned to Colyne. "He is right. I am ready to lie down."

"Still worried about me?"

She scowled, frustrated he'd seen through her intention. "Over the past few days, you should have slept instead of remaining awake at my side. And do not deny it. Except when you helped secure the crates, every time I awoke, you were holding my hand."

He quirked an amused brow. "Was I?"

"Do not be so difficult."

With a chuckle, Colyne helped her return to the cabin. By the time he'd tucked her into bed, a crewman appeared in the entryway.

"I have brought food for you both," the sailor said.

Colyne walked over and accepted the bowls. "It smells like a fine stew."

"The cook added a bit of onions and sage, and the fish is fresh. I caught it me self." Beaming with pride, he left.

Colyne settled beside her, filled the spoon, and lifted it to her mouth. "Here."

She shook her head. "I am still full from the earlier meal. Go ahead."

"You need to eat more to regain your strength," he urged, worry weighing his words.

"I will eat once you are finished."

A muscle worked in his jaw. "I shall not eat unless you share this meal with me."

She gave a long sigh. "You are stubborn."

A smile touched his mouth. "Determined. After we are finished, if you are still hungry I will bring you more."

Marie took the offered bite, along with a wedge of bread. She chewed slowly and then swallowed as Colyne ate the next scoop before refilling the spoon.

He lifted the broth to her mouth and his hand stilled.

She met his gaze and her breath caught, the desire within making her aware her own pulse had begun to race. Marie accepted the food. "'Tis your turn," she breathed, her need for him almost stealing her breath.

"So it is." Colyne leaned forward and claimed her mouth, his warm taste nourishing. As quickly, he drew back. "I am sorry. You are too weak to—"

"I need you," she whispered as she learned toward him, but he caught her shoulders, his hold gentle but unyielding.

"There are other reasons why we should nae," he said.

"I know I am wrong to ask you, more so to never want what we have to end." She stroked the strong curve of his jaw. "Make love with me, Colyne. Let us have this one last time together."

"You are still weak."

"Please."

"I—" On a groan he claimed her mouth with a gentle kiss, and she surrendered completely. The light clatter of the bowl echoed from some faraway place, but she didn't care. As the Kincaid continued to sail over the pristine waters of the North Sea, he pulled her to him, his kisses becoming more desperate, and all she knew was that at this moment, she'd never felt more alive.

A sharp knock sounded on the door. "Colyne," Logan called from outside the cabin.

Marie's blush tempted Colyne to ignore his friend. Instead, he pulled on his garb as she hurried to dress. He'd nae meant to make love to her, especially with her just recovering from her bout of seasickness, but throughout the night when she'd turned to him with a tender touch and quiet whispers, he'd succumbed to what he doubted any man could deny.

If he was damned for taking her, so be it. But before he'd given in to his yearnings, he'd made a decision. Once he'd finished delivering the writ from Robert Bruce, he would beseech her father to release her from her betrothal. If he agreed, he would court Marie. He wasna sure, but at this moment, with her in his every thought, wanting her as he never had any other woman, he couldna let her go.

"Aye," Colyne called to his friend once they were both dressed.

Logan strode into the cabin, his face taut. "We have a problem."

The hull of the Kincaid rubbed against the wooden pier, announcing that they'd arrived in port. The shouts of the crew securing the ship echoed from outside.

Colyne tucked the writ to King Philip into the hidden fold of his undershirt. "What is wrong?" He leaned over and grabbed his cloak as Marie picked up hers.

"Renard's men are here."

Marie gasped.

With a curse, Colyne strode to a hidden vantage point and scanned the decks.

In the mix of sailors, cargo, and merchants bartering on the dock, moved the English duke's knights.

"A sword's wrath, I canna believe they are here!"

"Aye," Logan agreed. "My guess is that they were sent to each port in hopes of intercepting you."

Panic shimmered in Marie's eyes. "What are we going to do?"

"We shall find a way to slip past them," Colyne stated.

Her lower lip trembled. "Can we set sail and anchor farther down the shore?"

The captain shook his head. "We have already moored. To depart without unloading any cargo would raise suspicion."

"We will have to disembark here," Colyne said.

"How?" Marie asked.

"We shall hide you both inside our cargo," Logan explained. "When we unload the ship, I will have my men set the crate you're hidden in at the end of the wharf, behind several other supplies. Once the knights have departed, my men will take you to wherever you need to go."

"A fine plan," Colyne agreed. Danger would exist, but without the threat of the English duke's guard, 'twould be lessened substantially.

A sailor slid to a halt at the entry. "Captain."

Logan whirled toward his man. "Aye?"

"Several knights are on the gangway demanding to search the ship."

"They can kiss the devil," the captain growled.

"'Twas my exact thought as well," the sailor agreed with a dry look, "but they are sporting King Philip's seal."

"Which gives them explicit authority to make a thorough check of every vessel arriving," the captain spat, "including the right to break open and inspect any sealed cargo."

A sword's wrath! They couldna take the risk of hiding inside a crate and being discovered. "The duke must have spoken with King Philip." Underscoring the reason they needed to reach King Philip without delay. Colyne prayed time remained to undo whatever treachery the English noble might have spawned.

"Aye," the captain agreed. "You can be assured if Renard's men find you, they have orders nae to be handing you over to King Philip."

Or Marie, Colyne silently added. They would kill her as well, and then return her body to the Highlands to be found as proof of their foul accusations.

"I will have to allow them to board." Logan gestured to his man. "Go above and ensure our *guests*," he drawled, sarcasm lacing his words, "are nae allowed on the ship until I arrive."

"Aye, Captain." The sailor hurried out.

Worry clouded Marie's eyes as she glanced from one man to the other. "What are we going to do? We cannot stay here, but there is no way to escape."

Logan hesitated. "There is another way for you to reach shore."

"Nay." Colyne understood his friend's intention, but he refused to jeopardize her life. "She has barely recovered and is too weak to try."

"Too weak to try what?" she demanded.

Colyne scowled at Logan. "Naught."

"Unless you wish to be caught or we fight and try sailing from port, 'tis your only choice," his friend insisted. "I did nae say that you had to like it."

Marie straightened her shoulders and glared at the two men. "If there is another way off this ship, we shall take it." She shot Colyne a challenging look. "Whatever it involves, I will hold my own."

Chapter 17

By Colyne's dark scowl, he understood exactly what method of escape the captain was suggesting and didn't like it. But with English knights on deck demanding a search, it mattered little what he approved of. She narrowed her gaze. "Tell me."

At Colyne's stubborn silence, the captain cleared his throat, his face grim. "You must escape through a hatch on the side of the ship using a rope ladder. I will have one of my men secure a small boat at the bottom to—"

"Nay." Colyne glared at her with a look that clearly stated she was nae going anywhere. "She is too weak."

"How dare you dismiss my involvement in this?" Marie argued, furious he'd try.

Red slashed Colyne's face.

Raised voices echoing from the guards emphasized the fact that little time remained to escape, much less to argue. "I understand your worry," Marie said, gentling her voice. His stubbornness came from concern for her.

"Unless you want to chance hiding aboard ship," the captain said, his voice tight, "there is nay other choice."

Marie kept her eyes locked on Colyne's. "As they have authority to search any sealed containers, there is not." After the carnage they'd witnessed at the massacre of his friends, Marie held no illusions as to hers or Colyne's fate if caught. If climbing down the side of the ship would keep them safe, she'd do it.

She drew herself up to her full height, recognizing her gesture as regal, as Colyne had claimed. "Have the ladder lowered over the side," Marie said to the captain with quiet authority.

The captain arched an amused brow toward Colyne. "Aye, my lady."

Colyne's scowl deepened, but he nodded his assent.

His protectiveness warmed Marie, but Colyne must accept that he wouldn't always be there to defend her.

"I will delay the guards until I receive word from my crew that you are on your way," Logan said, "then I will allow them to search the ship."

Colyne exhaled a rough sigh. "I shall leave my mail within your chest."

"Should the guards ask," Logan said, "I will claim it as my own." He clasped Colyne's hand. "Godspeed."

"Godspeed to you, as well."

The captain pressed a chaste kiss upon Marie's knuckles. "Take care, my lady."

"Thank you. I will ensure my father learns of your bravery."

"Nay, lass, my aid is given freely." Devilment sparked in the captain's eyes. "Besides, I need nae for my name to be bantered about before your father or any other powerful lord." With a roguish smile, he left.

"Logan has had several encounters with outraged noble fathers," Colyne explained dryly as he removed his mail and stowed it within the hewn wooden chest.

That she could believe. "Where now?"

"A sword's wrath, you are nae fit to be climbing down a rope ladder."

"A fact you ignored last night," she charged, not that she wasn't as guilty for asking him to make love. With no secrets between them, a peace had enveloped her with his every touch. She only wished for more time with him.

And that he loved her.

Fragile hope swirled within her of the possibility of their sharing a life together. A life out of reach unless she spoke with her father and asked him to end her betrothal. Torn between duty and wanting Colyne, she was at an impasse. By the Grace of Mary, never would she upset her father, but loving Colyne, could she settle for a life without happiness?

Sadness weighed upon Marie as she followed Colyne through the storage hold. Within a day they would reach her father. Then Colyne would leave and she'd never see him again.

How could she live without him?

How could she break her vow?

Fighting back her emotions, she hurried to where a sailor waved them toward the hatch. At their fast pace, her breathing grew labored and her legs rebelled, but she pushed herself. A cramp in her side forced her to slow.

With a scowl, Colyne caught her shoulder. "You are nae well enough to do this!"

The footsteps of the armed men thudded on the wooden planks overhead.

"Bedamned." He swept her into his arms.

"I can walk."

He gave her a quelling stare. "You will be needing your strength soon enough."

As he carried her, she remained silent. Arguing would yield naught and possibly gain them notice from the knights searching the ship. And she was tired. Every muscle in her body ached. Once they'd reached the small boat, she would welcome the opportunity to rest.

"Take care as you climb down," the sailor cautioned as they reached his side.

Colyne set her on her feet.

"The boat is secured below," he continued. "Be careful as you board. If it breaks free, the strong current will pull it away." He pointed to a stand of trees crowding the shore where branches, thick with leaves, canopied to scrape the water's surface. "Row beneath them and secure the craft there. We will retrieve it after dark."

Relieved by the sailor's thoughtfulness, Marie's spirits rose. "My thanks."

Impatient footsteps clattered above, this time closer to the entry that would lead them to the storage hold.

"Hurry on with you now," the sailor urged. "From the sound of it, the captain is nae going to be able to keep them from coming below much longer."

Colyne moved to the exit. "I shall go first. Climb down after me, but stay close."

She nodded.

Once he'd disappeared over the side, the sailor helped Marie onto the rope ladder. Her arms trembled as she clung to the tightly bound hemp, the full extent of how weak she'd grown during her illness becoming unnervingly clear.

"Marie?"

The worry in Colyne's voice had her forcing herself to take a step down. "I am coming." Her arms trembled as she started her descent. After several steps, she made the mistake of looking down.

Far below, waves bumped against the side of the ship.

Nausea clenched in her gut. She closed her eyes and leaned her head against the rope, her brow slick with sweat. She could do this.

She had to.

"What is wrong?" Colyne called up.

"I am fine." She wasn't, but she wouldn't tell him that. She opened her eyes, focused on the hewn wood of the hull, then started down. Rope scraped her hands as she caught the lower rung. Waves continued to slap the scarred hull, and the cries of the seagulls overhead echoed as if to mock her.

As she started to lower her foot, her vision began to blur. She clenched the rough twine, held tight.

"Marie?"

"I . . ." Her stomach rolled. She was going to be sick.

"Hold on!" The ladder twisted as Colyne climbed to the rung below her. He wrapped his arm around the small of her waist. "We are going back."

She wanted to argue, but with nausea rising in her throat, all she could do was nod.

The hatch above slammed shut.

Colyne's muttered curse matched Marie's thoughts exactly. "Let me go," she said, frustrated when her voice wavered. "I can make it down."

"You are trembling," he countered, sounding far from convinced.

Her delay placed them in greater danger. "I needed a brief rest. I am fine now."

The ladder shifted as he moved.

A bead of sweat slid down her face as she struggled to follow. Her vision again blurred and her foot missed the lower rung. By sheer will, she focused long enough to snag the rope with her slipper.

"You are doing fine."

Colyne's voice reached her from somewhere in the distance. A gust of wind pummelled her body and merged with the storm building in her ears. *Focus,* she ordered herself. But her eyes refused, and then her body started to shake.

And the world began to fade.

"Colyne!"

At the panic in her voice, Colyne leaned to the side until he could see her face. Her skin had grown chalky white. "Marie? Marie, look at me!"

She didna respond.

"Hold on. I am coming up."

Above him, her body sagged.

Why had he listened to her? He never should have allowed her to attempt to climb down. As he started to cradle her body against his, her right hand lost its grip; she fell.

Colyne caught her hand.

Barely.

Now dead weight, she dangled at the end of his arm. The muscles in his injured shoulder screamed as he strained to keep hold. "Marie?"

"Colyne?"

At her weak whisper, his heart pounded. "Do nae move!" His grip on her was precarious at best.

A thump sounded near the hatch above. Another bump echoed inside the hull farther away.

The guards must be searching each crate. Thank God they'd nae made it back and tried to hide.

Marie moaned. Then, as if becoming aware of her precarious position, with her free hand she lunged for the rope.

The ladder lurched violently to the left.

"Colyne!" She clawed for a better grasp. "I cannot hold on!"

Her fingers within his slipped. "Stay still!"

Raw terror filled her eyes. "I am losing you!"

To brace himself, Colyne jammed his boot against the side of the rung. With the ladder swinging wildly, he missed. Off balance, he lunged to catch a rung as he fought to keep hold of Marie.

Her arm flailed. On a wild grab, her free hand caught his leg.

The ladder twisted violently.

Colyne lost his grip. Air, sharp with the tang of salt, rushed down his throat as he plunged straight down, Marie falling at his side.

"Help me!" she screamed.

"Keep hold of my hand when we—"

Cold water enveloped them with a roar, the force tearing her away. Bubbles streamed around him in a sheet of broken white and erased her from his view.

Colyne used his hands to slow his descent and then kicked to propel himself up. Water exploded around him as he surfaced. Gasping for breath, he scanned the blur of waves building beneath the wind's brisk flow.

Where was she?

A hint of white flashed through the inky depths.

God, nay!

Sucking in a huge gulp of air, he dove. Colyne reached out, his fingertips grazing hers. His lungs screamed for air, but he kicked deeper. This time, he snagged her cloak. He pulled her toward him.

Marie's form bumped against him like a limp doll.

Heart pounding, he kept his grip on her as he swam up. They broke the surface, and she started to cough.

She was alive! His throat tightened with emotion as he pulled her against him as he treaded water. "I have a hold of you. You are fine now." Safe was another matter.

At least with the steady wind, the waves would continue to build. If any of the English knights scanned the bay, the waves would provide a fairly effective shield.

"Where are we going?" she asked, her words sluggish.

"I am taking you to the boat." He fought for calm as he swam with her in his arms. He'd almost lost her. What if he hadna seen her below the waves? Nay, he wouldna think of that. "Hold on to me."

In reply, her hand tightened on his neck.

He didna care that she didna speak. She was alive, that was all that mattered. Using his free arm, he swam toward the boat.

Instead of closing on the craft, it drifted farther away.

To his right, floating on top of the water, he noticed the slack line. The sailor's warning came to mind. When they'd fallen into the bay, the impact of waves must have tugged the line free. "A sword's wrath!"

"What is wrong?"

At the exhaustion in her voice, he steadied himself. The last thing he wished was to alarm her further. "The boat is loose, 'twill take but a moment to catch it." Colyne swam after it, holding Marie afloat at his side.

The small craft bobbed in the water with cheerful abandon, the gap between them quickly expanding to several fathoms.

Refusing to give up, he swam harder, his fear growing with each stroke. The boat had become caught in the current.

Eyes raw with fear turned on Colyne. "We are not going to catch it, are we?"

"Aye." Colyne swam harder. His muscles screamed. Water swirled past.

The distance between them and the boat grew.

Breathing hard, he paused, began to tread water.

"What now?" she murmured, her pallor increasing his worry.

He scanned the docks, then the Kincaid. They couldna risk being caught. "We will swim with the current to shore."

With sure, steady strokes, he moved near the pier and kept them within the shadows of the moored ships. Thankfully, the crowd on the wooden dock above, along with the height of the growing waves, shielded them.

By the time they reached the shelter of the trees near shore, Marie's body was trembling uncontrollably.

As if she had the strength to try to swim in the first place.

His guilt grew. She hadna recovered from her bout of seasickness—nae that he had allowed her proper sleep last night. But when she'd returned his kiss, he'd become lost in the passions she aroused.

In his entire life, nay one had ever responded to him with such completeness. And with her every word, her every touch, she filled the emptiness that haunted him. Now, because of his selfishness, he'd put her life further at risk.

His boot grazed a rock and he stood. Water streamed from their bodies as he lifted Marie and carried her up the steep embankment.

Her teeth chattered and she groggily lifted her head. "Co—cold."

"I know. You shall be warm soon." And with her watching him with such belief, he'd do whatever it took to make his claim true.

Through the shield of leaves, standing on the pier, holding the rope to the small craft, Logan, accompanied by several English knights, came into view.

Colyne sighed with relief. Their mishap had been a blessing in disguise. At least his friend had recovered his boat, and 'twould end any suspicions the knights might have had of their presence aboard the Kincaid.

Now he must find Marie dry clothing and shelter. Turning, he ducked under a low limb. He kept beneath the overhanging branches as he made his way along the bank. After stealing a blanket and clothes for her from a line behind a battered hut, Colyne hid within an abandoned shelter and helped her change. "Marie?"

She frowned at him in confusion.

Panic welled in his gut. She scrutinized him as if a stranger. "Marie?"

Silence.

A sword's wrath, her exhaustion combined with the coldness of the water from their swim was making her lose consciousness.

He said a silent prayer as he wrapped her in the blanket and cradled her against his chest. He had to find shelter, a healer, and warm her fast. Colyne pressed a kiss to her brow. "I am going to take care of you. I promise."

Concern for her deteriorating condition pressed him to take risks; he entered the village he'd wanted to skirt around. He darted through alleys he would have otherwise avoided. At times he caught the interested stares of the people living in this dangerous part of town. Colyne shot them warning glares to keep their distance and moved on.

He wove through several streets, thankful he'd visited this area on a few occasions. At least he knew his way around, along with which parts of the village the duke's men would most likely ignore.

As he rounded a corner, a decrepit inn came into view. By its fallen state, he doubted they boarded many patrons. Exactly the type of place he was searching for. The fewer people who saw them the better.

Marie moaned.

"We are almost there." He hugged her to him and hurried inside. Wood creaked and then settled with a thunk as Colyne shoved the door shut. The scent of tallow candles stung the air as his vision adjusted to the dim, narrow chamber. A small hewn table sat to the right, the accompanying chairs designed for durability nae beauty, but overall, the inn was cleaner than he'd expected.

"What would you be wanting?" a woman's rough voice demanded.

He glanced toward the middle-aged woman whose black hair was twisted into a haphazard braid. "A room," he replied, nae making any gestures she would deem threatening.

"My husband has yet to remove the sign; we no longer accept guests."

Even better. Anyone searching for them would never look here. "My wife is ill and needs to rest. Please, any room will do. I have money to—"

"*Non.*"

Colyne retrieved two coins and held them up for her inspection.

She sniffed. "I have a small chamber, but it has naught but a bed and a hearth. You can stay there for the night."

Thankful, he retrieved five more coins, more than sufficient payment for a stay at the finest inn in Glasgow. "Three days?" Time, he prayed, that would allow Marie to recover.

A frown creased her brow as the woman studied him. After a moment, she nodded.

Thank God. Desperate at Marie's weakening condition, he'd already decided, willing or nae, the innkeeper would allow them to remain. Her cooperation made everything simpler. He laid the money in her palm.

Like a woman seasoned in dealing with less than savory characters, she quickly stowed the coins within the thick folds of her faded dress.

"Follow me." After a quick glance at Marie, she headed toward a back chamber. At the entry, she opened a door.

The musty scent of an unaired room assaulted Colyne as he carried Marie inside. What he'd give to take her to a chamber befitting her station; a bed with the finest linens, a hearth ablaze with a roaring fire, and a fresh pot of herbed tea. At least the bed appeared clean.

More important, they were safe.

Now to address his next problem. "My wife needs a healer. Someone discreet," he added with a knowing glance.

Worry flickered in her eyes as she studied Marie.

"I shall pay whatever fees are necessary."

"I will fetch her." Her dress rustled as she departed.

As the door closed, he dismissed the notion that woman might have recognized Marie. Her wariness came from dealing with unscrupulous patrons. On this side of town, nay doubt she dealt too often with a seedy lot. Colyne walked over to the bed and turned back the coverlet.

Marie moaned against his neck.

Worry rode him as he lay her upon the thinly covered straw mattress and pulled up the blanket. He pressed a kiss on her brow. "A healer is on the way." As much as he wished to strip her of her clothes and add his body heat to hers, he couldna until after the healer left.

Marie coughed.

At her continued trembling, Colyne built a fire and then lay by her side and drew her against him. "Easy now, lass." He combed away the wet hair clinging to her face. And with her every shiver, her every rough cough, his fear at her declining condition grew. Terrified, he closed his eyes.

And prayed.

The healer's brow sagged into a haggard frown as she examined Marie. "How long has she been this weak?"

Colyne ignored the sharpness of her tone, thankful for her competence and the fact that she genuinely seemed to care. "Since this morning."

He didna explain Marie's bout with seasickness. Though he doubted the information would interest the healer, he wasna taking any chances of word reaching Renard's knights of a man and a woman arriving by ship and staying at this inn.

As if able to read his mind, the healer's eyes narrowed on him. "Has she been sick?"

Her cool stare fueled his unease. They were too far from the royal palace where someone would recognize the king's bastard daughter. Their recent flight from the Kincaid prodded his suspicions.

"Her clothes are ill fitting," the woman pressed at his silence.

"Aye, a few days past, but she had begun to recover. Then, this morning, while delivering goods to the docks, a fight broke out. My wife accidentally fell into the water." A reasonable explanation for the smell of the sea on her garments, as well as their sodden state.

The healer grimaced. "See that she is kept warm and drinks plenty of water. I will leave herbs that should keep her from developing a fever and help her sleep."

Marie appeared so fragile. "Will she live?" Colyne asked, unable to keep worry from trickling into his voice.

The woman studied him a long moment. "I am not sure."

Fear balled in his chest, a keening so deep it tore through his heart. "I canna lose her. Please, if there is anything else you can do to help her . . ." He knew he sounded desperate, but he didna care.

"God and time will decide her fate."

"Stay," he all but demanded.

Tired lines marred the healer's weathered brow. "I have done all I can and have others who need my attention."

Colyne wanted to argue, order her to remain. In the end, he came to a compromise. "Can you return on the morrow?"

"I will. If a fever begins, I am to be sent for immediately. Ask the innkeeper; she will fetch me." She eyed him with a shrewd look. "You will be staying with her?"

"Aye."

"You are a Scot?" she asked with conversational ease as she reached over to the basket of herbs she'd brought and removed several pouches.

Wary, he hesitated. Within her gaze, he read bored interest. "We are here on business."

"Your reasons are your own," she said with a shrug. She measured a small amount of herbs and set them on a small platter. After loosening the pouch of another sack, she took a pinch of a white powder and sprinkled it atop the crushed leaves. With care, she mixed them. "Hold her head up while I give her these."

He complied as she fed her patient the concoction, and then encouraged her to drink some water.

In her groggy state, Marie struggled to swallow, but finally, she finished the last of the herbs.

The healer stepped back. "Now she needs to rest."

"She will." He started to reach inside his clothing for coin to pay the healer.

She shook her head. "We will settle anything owed on my return. For now, take care of her. 'Tis what is important." In silence she

160 • *Diana Cosby*

packed her supplies away with neat precision and then started out. At the door she turned, her wizened gaze leveled on him. "She is not to be moved."

At her emphasis on the last, another shard of unease trickled up his neck. "Aye."

After the healer departed, Colyne secured the door, his disquiet about the healer lingering. Why? Her aged eyes had scoured Marie with experience, she'd asked prudent questions, and she was knowledgeable in her craft, proven by how she had selected the necessary herbs without hesitation. In fact, during her brief visit the healer had acted more like a doting mother than a stranger.

He stilled.

Had she recognized Marie? Would she send word to King Philip? Shaken, he looked down.

Marie's chest rose and fell in a steady rhythm, her breaths even; she slept.

Colyne dismissed his worries. With fatigue weighing heavily on his mind, having eluded Renard's men for days on end in addition to his fear for her life, he searched for deception at every turn. Now, when he found a woman who cared about those she tended, he branded her a threat. The tension in his body eased and the room wavered before him.

More than ready to catch a bit of rest, Colyne stripped off his wet clothes and crossed to the bed. He climbed in beside Marie, removed her sodden garb as well, and then drew her against him.

Her every shiver speared him like a lance. "I am here," he whispered. The fire he'd started earlier heated the room with a meager efficiency, but it didna offer the warmth she needed.

He cursed the fact that circumstance had forced him to choose such a dismal hovel and he couldna trust anyone here to send word to King Philip of Marie's safety. She needed the best care possible. Instead, she lay freezing beside him.

Nestled against his chest, she murmured incoherently and continued to shiver.

The hours passed, each one stoking his fear. *Please, God, make her well.* She meant everything to him.

And more.

Shaken by the depth of his feelings for her, Colyne stared at Marie as if seeing her for the first time. His heart trembled.

He wanted her.

Needed her.

Forever.

On a hard swallow, he awaited the surge of fear, the rush of panic at thoughts of permanence.

Instead, he found renewed strength and a need so deep any thought of walking away from Marie left him devastated. . . . He loved her!

An anguished moan fell from her lips.

"There, lass." Colyne willed her to overcome the misery she suffered as he embraced his newfound feelings, overwhelmed, overjoyed, and anxious to share his realization. "I love you, Marie."

At his soul-drenched whisper, she frowned.

As if in her state he'd expected her to reply? But he'd told her, would continue to tell her how much he loved her until she could understand.

Memories rolled through him of when she'd admitted how she cared for him deeply. With the way she'd given of herself when they'd made love, how she'd touched him, caressed him with infinite care, he refused to believe she didna feel more.

She shivered in his arms.

"I love you, Marie." He stroked his fingers through her hair. From the flames in the hearth illuminating the chamber, he noted a light sheen of sweat had begun to cover her forehead. He pressed his fingers against her brow. A sword's wrath! She'd begun to run a fever.

He must send for the healer. And if she couldna be found, he'd find a horse and ride with Marie this night to her father. Bedamned the risk; he'd do whatever he must to ensure Marie lived.

Colyne gently slid a gown over her head and then tucked her beneath the covers. "I shall be but a trice." He kissed her cheek. As he pulled on the last of his garb, a soft knock sounded on the door.

With a grimace, he unsheathed his sword and crept to the door. "Who is there?"

"The healer. I have returned to see your wife."

Relief poured through him. Thank God. He secured his blade and started to open the door. "I was about to—"

The hewn wood was ripped from his grasp.

Swords raised, several armed guards bearing the king's colors stormed inside. The nearest knight seized his wrist. Another caught his wounded shoulder. They slammed him against the wall.

Stars erupted in Colyne's head.

"Lady Marie is over there," the healer spat. "This Scot claimed to be her husband, but he is lying. She has helped me treat the sick for many years."

The healer had worked with her? Colyne remembered Marie telling him that she lived near the coast and helped a healer who aided those who could nae afford proper care. With regret, he recalled how earlier he'd dismissed his unease at the woman's mothering presence.

The elder glared at Colyne as if he were the devil's spawn. "No doubt he is one of the rebels behind her abduction."

"Wait," Colyne gasped, "I can explain!"

"Explain what?" the man clenching his left shoulder growled. "How you kidnapped Lady Marie and are hiding her until your demands to King Philip are met, or how you have mistreated her until she is near death?"

A sword's wrath, they had it all wrong! "I am Colyne MacKerran, Earl of Strathcliff, a messenger sent by Robert Bruce, Earl of Carrick, Guardian of the Realm of Scotland to deliver a writ to King Philip," he explained, keeping his voice calm, refusing to give in to the fear clawing through him. "I found her in the Highlands and was escorting her home."

The healer scowled. "Another lie."

"Nay, I am telling the truth! She became seasick as we sailed to France. When we docked, she hadna fully recovered. By accident, she fell into the bay," he explained, damning the fact that his voice trembled. "Terrified for her life, I carried her here and called for the healer." Colyne scanned the guards' faces. Each one glared at him as if they wished to slice open his gullet and feed him to the dogs. "The last thing that I, or my country, would wish is harm to befall her."

With a curse, the guard he'd surmised as being in charge strode forward. "A well-crafted lie." Cold satisfaction curved his mouth as he grabbed Colyne's throat. "In the name of King Philip, you are under arrest for the abduction of Lady Marie."

"Wait," Colyne choked out as the room started to blur, "I have proof!"

The guard's nostrils flared in disbelief.

Colyne struggled for his next breath. "'Ti—'tis hidden in my tunic."

The guard's eyes narrowed. "Try to escape and I assure you 'twould give me the excuse to drive my blade into your heart." He nodded to the men holding him. "Release him."

The guards let go and stepped back.

Colyne gasped for air as he reached within the concealed pouch of his undershirt. He'd nae thought of the writ since they'd escaped from the ship. His fingers scraped across leather. Thank God 'twas still there!

His hand trembled as he removed the parchment from the sodden leather cover, displaying the unbroken seal. "As I have explained, I have nae abducted Lady Marie but am returning her to France. This document holds proof that the words I speak are true."

The knights eyed him with disbelief.

Their leader raised a skeptical brow. "Open it."

Colyne shook his head and lowered the rolled parchment. "'Tis for your king's eyes alone."

"Seize it," the lead knight boomed.

Before Colyne could prevent them, two guards pinned his hands against the wall. He struggled to break free, but the lead knight stepped forward and snatched the writ from his hands.

"Now," he drawled, his words like ice, "we shall see what truths you deliver." He grunted, as he studied Robert Bruce's seal. "'Tis fine craftsmanship"—his eyes flicked up—"whoever made it."

A muscle worked in Colyne's jaw. "I am telling the truth."

The knight gave an indignant snort.

A movement from the bed caught Colyne's attention. With soft words, the healer wiped Marie's brow.

A sword's wrath, she needed rest, nae to be subjected to angry words bantered about. "Open it," Colyne charged. "But King Philip will call for your head when he learns of your deed."

Without hesitation, the guard broke the seal. He unrolled the wet parchment and skimmed the writ. Face taut, the knight lifted his gaze, his eyes black as the gates of Hades. "Take him to the dungeon!"

"Wait!" Colyne struggled against the guards. "Did you nae read it?"

"Read what?" he hissed between clenched teeth, "smeared words as if written by a child?" Parchment crinkled as he shoved the writ before Colyne's face.

Colyne's knees almost gave way. The message penned by Robert

Bruce nay longer graced the page. Instead, ugly black stains streaked the parchment, the words illegible. During the crossing of the swollen river, or when he and Marie had fallen into the bay, the writ had become soaked, the ink smeared.

"You will regret you ever dared abduct Lady Marie," the lead knight growled.

Colyn's heart slammed against his chest. "You are wrong. I need to speak with King Philip!"

"The only person you will be visiting is the king's executioner." With contempt, the knight cast the writ into the hearth. The flames greedily licked the sodden paper, blackening and then destroying the fragile parchment until it crumbled into the embers beneath it, the chips of wax bubbling within the fire like molten blood. "Take him away!"

The guards hauled him toward the door.

"You are mistaken!" Colyne shouted as he fought them, but they tightened their grip and continued. Frantic, he glanced at Marie.

Caught in the throes of a fever, she twisted on the bed.

He couldna leave her!

"Move." One the guards behind him jammed his foot into Colyne's back, shoved.

Panic tearing through him, Colyne stumbled into the hall. Due to their false charges, he'd never see her again, hold her, or see her eyes light up when he told her that he loved her.

And without the writ as proof of his innocence, upon learning his daughter's abductor had been captured, King Philip would believe he was one of the Scottish rebels involved with her abduction and sever his support to Scotland.

Disgrace tainted his every breath, self-condemnation more so. He'd failed his country, failed Marie.

And with the damning facts in hand, the king would order what he believed a just sentence.

Colyne's death.

Chapter 18

Marie opened her eyes, wincing against the pain. Dismal gray light embraced her. The soft tap of raindrops striking a windowpane echoed through her misery. She pushed back another wave of discomfort, frowned as she realized she lay beneath a coverlet. Where was she? And why did her body ache?

Frowning when no answers came, she scanned the room. A silk tapestry woven in reds, blues, and greens, creating an image of a distant castle, adorned the far wall. Within a stone hearth, framed on each side by intricate marble carvings of lions standing guard, a fire roared, offering warmth. Angled on a ledge sat a volume of tales of King Arthur, the leather binding worn from use. To her left, atop an aged wooden chest, sat a doll given to her when she was a child.

A smile curved her mouth. *Her father's home.* This was the chamber she used whenever she visited him.

Marie inhaled the scent of fresh rushes entwined with the aroma of wood and rain cleansed air as peace wove through her. The feathered mattress against her skin cradled her as if in a dream.

"You are awake?" Relief filled a familiar deep voice.

Tenderness enveloped Marie as she faced the noble figure standing in the doorway of her room, his surcoat and vermeil mantle lined with ermine. "Father."

King Philip strode over and brushed a kiss upon her cheek. "I have been worried about you."

"Worried; why?" She fumbled for a reason. Vague images of a man with whisky-colored hair and deep blue eyes flickered to mind. Memories of being chased. Of hiding. As quickly, they faded.

Lines furrowed her father's brow. "You do not remember?"

"I . . ." More fragments slid into place. The howling of wind. Pounding seas.

Her father watched her, expectant.

"There was a storm."

"You were abducted by the Scots." Anger lingered within his words.

"Abducted by Scots?" She grimaced, somehow finding his statement incorrect.

"The incident is not a topic for you to dwell upon. You are safe; that is what matters.

Mayhap, but she saw the exhaustion hidden in his eyes caused by worry. Touched and needing to offer reassurance, she lay her hand on her father's arm. "I am well—"

"You are not. You have been ill since your arrival two days past. During the night your fever finally broke." He covered her hand with his own. "You must continue to rest. In time your memory will return."

The soft tap of approaching steps drew her gaze to the doorway.

A tall, dignified man entered. He walked toward her, his heraldic surcoat spun of royal blue silk and embroidered with gold fleur-de-lis. His straight brown hair scraped the edge of his shoulders, hard angles outlining his square jaw. Hazel eyes met hers, softening in relief.

Did she know this man? From the confidence in which he entered her chamber, 'twould appear so. But she had no memory of him.

"Sire," he said as he bowed to her father. He faced Marie, a tender smile touching his lips. "It is good to see you awake." Disquiet shadowed his gaze as he glanced toward the king, then back to her. "And we are thankful for your safe return."

"Marie, may I introduce to you Gaston de Croix, Duke of Vocette, your betrothed."

Betrothed! Marie clutched the bed linen, unable to shake her disquiet at this meeting. "We have met before?" Her heart pounded as she awaited his confirmation.

"*Non*," Gaston replied as he lifted her hand. He pressed a kiss on her knuckles. "'Tis my pleasure, my lady."

Heat stroked her face because she wasn't sure what to say, and was even more confused by how her pulse raced. Why would meeting her betrothed cause her such distress? She must have been aware of her upcoming marriage.

"I am sorry," Marie said, fighting for calm, "I am having difficulty remembering."

"Understandable after your ordeal," the duke said.

Ordeal. He meant her kidnapping, an event of which she had no memory. "As we are affianced, please, use my given name, Marie."

He nodded. "Please do me the honor of calling me Gaston."

"Of course." Why did thinking of him in a familiar light leave her on edge?

Her father's gaze shifted to the duke. "You have taken care of the task we discussed?"

"*Oui*, Sire." His jaw tightened with anger. "He will be dealt with this day."

A chill swept through Marie at the coldness of her betrothed's words. She glanced at her father. "Who will be dealt with?"

The king's mouth thinned into a hard line. "We have caught one of the Scots involved in your abduction. Before I am through, he will name all who are involved."

"An action they shall regret," Gaston stated.

A shiver slid through Marie. Though she'd never witnessed the methods her father's guards used to extract confessions, she'd heard of the rack, flogging, and other techniques employed to loosen an unwilling tongue.

A sense of urgency filled her, but the grogginess coating her mind smothered her ability to find the reason. "Father, I . . ." Why couldn't she recall the past weeks? And when she did, would she wish otherwise?

The king leaned closer. "What is it?"

A low pounding built in her head as she struggled to remember. "It has something to do with the Scot."

"I should not have spoken of your capture," her father said. "I have upset you when you need to keep calm and rest."

"*Non*, I . . ." She pushed herself into a sitting position. "There is something important that I must tell you, it is only that . . ." Her mind blurred.

"Marie, I must add my agreement to your father's," the duke added. "You are still weak."

King Philip waved his hand in a subtle gesture, and a thin, somber man stepped into view. "See that she is given herbs to help her sleep."

The man bowed. "*Oui*, Your Majesty."

She recognized her father's personal physician. "I would rather not—"

"You are to rest," her father stated. "We shall discuss this later."

Her betrothed again raised her hand to his mouth and pressed a kiss on her knuckles. "I shall return to visit after we sup." With a formal bow, he departed, his stride sure, that of a man confident in his abilities. A man who took care of what was his.

Coldness crept through her at the thought of the latter. Why? She should be pleased at his protectiveness, a trait so like her father's.

"My lady." Her father's physician held out a cup of water warmed over the fire and sprinkled with herbs; steam drifted upward in wispy tendrils.

Exhausted, she accepted the healing brew. After a sip to ensure it was not too hot, she gulped the liquid in three swallows and then returned the cup to the side table.

Her father nodded his satisfaction and dismissed the physician.

Alone, the king knelt beside her bed, his brow wrinkled with worry. "I will return once I am informed you have awakened." He pressed a kiss on her cheek and then exited the chamber.

A lethargic warmth slid through her. Marie embraced the numbness, sinking into the luxurious comfort of her bed. As she gave in to blissful sleep, a nagging that she'd forgotten something of great importance persisted.

Beyond Colyne's dank cell, the distant calls of prisoners echoed with macabre finality. Outside, rain continued to batter the castle.

Sprawled on the floor, he struggled against the blackened void of pain that threatened to suck him back under. How long had he lost consciousness this time? Somewhere between when they'd dragged him back to his cell and now, the red-orange rays of sunrise had become smothered by the angry churn of gray.

A chill cut through his body, then another. He scanned his surroundings, the stench almost making him sick. Except, after the last several hours of being tortured to gain a confession, he couldna scrape up the energy to move, much less retch.

He awaited the echo of steps announcing the guards' arrival. They would return again and again, until he admitted his part in Marie's abduction.

Even if 'twas a lie.

Colyne gritted his teeth as another spasm of pain tore through his body. His vision hazed, but he forced himself to remain awake.

A sword's wrath; why was he even bothering? He should let go, succumb to the dark void. At least then he wouldna feel. Or remember these last few days of misery.

Since the king believed him one of the Scottish rebels who had taken part in his daughter's abduction, he would never be able to see Marie again or tell her that he loved her.

Regret dragged his grief deeper as he thought of her battling a fever as the guards had hauled him from the inn. He stared at the gray walls marred by aged blood and the rust of forgotten chains.

Steps thudded past his cell. A short distance away, they paused.

Muted voices.

The creak of a door opening.

A curt order.

A man's plea to spare his life reverberated through the dungeon.

Colyne fought to quell his fear, the feeling of inevitability. How many times since his incarceration had he heard the same, or the din of the crowd outside as they cheered for the executioner to swing his ax? He swallowed hard. 'Twas a fate he could envision all too well.

Footsteps again sounded. This time they halted outside his cell. Keys grated in the lock, a heavy, loud clank.

He braced himself.

The door opened with a shuddered groan. The thud of boots against the stone floor announced he had a visitor. Several, in fact.

"Look at me," a guard ordered as he shoved his boot into Colyne's side.

Gritting his teeth against the pain, he complied. Instead of the grizzled face of a dungeon guard, a well-dressed man stared down at him. Framed by golden hair the color of sunlight were eyes so filled with hatred, if he'd claimed to be the devil, Colyne would have believed him. Stunned, he recognized the man dressed in a surcoat and a mantle of vermeil—*King Philip.*

As the monarch studied Colyne, his expression grew more ominous. "Lift him to his feet." Venom raked his words.

The guards hauled Colyne up.

At the agony raging through his body, he smothered a scream.

Another man with straight, shoulder-length brown hair strode to the king's side. Caustic hazel eyes bored through him.

Colyne didna recognize the man, but the gold fleurs-de-lis sewed on his surcoat, along with his arrogant stance, ended any doubt. *Marie's betrothed.* His heart slammed in his chest. The man she would wed.

Colyne wanted to scream that Marie belonged to him. That he loved her. "Sire," he forced out, trying to make his tongue create the words, aware this was his only chance to explain the misunderstanding.

The king nodded to his guard.

The man's fist lashed out; Colyne's head snapped back.

"How dare you abduct my daughter?" King Philip boomed.

The coppery taste of blood filled Colyne's mouth. By the grace of God! King Philip didna know the truth; Marie must still have a fever, as he'd suspected. Or . . .

God, nay!

His knees buckled and blackness threatened. Colyne struggled for consciousness. She couldna be dead. "I—"

The king again nodded to the guard.

The man's fist rammed into Colyne's gut.

On a groan, he doubled over. Before he could catch his breath, Marie's betrothed grabbed Colyne's hair and jerked his head up.

"But that was not enough for you, was it?" The duke nodded to a guard.

The man drove his fist into Colyne's jaw.

Bones crunched. A ringing reverberated in Colyne's ears and the room began to spin. Needing to explain, he pulled himself back to consciousness.

Barely.

"My physician has informed me that my daughter has lost her innocence," King Philip charged with lethal menace. He shoved Colyne's jaw against the stone wall. "She had bruises around her neck, her wrists, and others on her body. You will regret having tied her up and raped her!"

Visions of making love with Marie slid through Colyne's mind, of her beauty, of her sensual awakening. Nae the brutality her father painted or her betrothed believed. "Nay, we . . ." Colyne fought to explain that she'd acquired the bruises when the Englishmen had seized her on the dock in Glasgow as well as their escape from the ship, but pain crushed his words. *We made love*, he silently finished.

"Admit the truth," Marie's betrothed demanded.

Colyne stared at King Philip, forced his mouth to form words he wished to tell Marie instead. "I love her."

"You love her?" The king's indignation boomed through the cell. His nostrils flared. "How dare you twist your depraved actions into self-serving righteousness."

"Nay." Colyne's mind blurred. Somehow, he had to make her father understand. "Marie—"

"Silence! How dare you speak my daughter's name? You are unworthy to breathe. Now," he said with deadly authority, "you shall pay for your transgressions!"

Colyne tried to speak, but his tongue, swollen and parched, hindered his labored attempts. "I did nae abduct her," he managed to force out. "The Duke of . . ." His throat worked as he fought to speak. "The Duke of Renard—"

"Enough of your lies!" the king's roared.

"Aye," her betrothed agreed with disgust. "The Duke of Renard warned us the Scot would try to accuse him of such treachery."

"Ask your daughter," Colyne rasped as he frantically looked from one man to the other, his fears of the English duke having reached the king's ear before he'd arrived tragically true.

An ominous smile slanted across King Philip's face. "I have. Thank God she remembers naught. But you—" His glare pierced Colyne like a dagger rammed into his chest. "You will regret the day you dared touch her." The king stalked to the open door. At the entry, he glared at Colyne. "At dawn, behead him."

Like enraged hornets swarming around their hive, the drone of the crowd cut through Marie's slumber. Groggy, she glanced around.

Her blanket lay rumpled, as if she'd tossed and turned while she'd slept. Nearby, a jug of water sat half full, and her cup lay overturned, further evidence of her disturbed sleep.

A sound blared from the courtyard.

The crowd cheered.

"Papa?"

She remained alone.

With a frown, she rubbed sleep from her eyes, frustrated that she couldn't rid herself of the sensation that something was wrong.

Another cheer from outside piled onto her disquiet.

Marie turned to the open window, the shutters pulled wide, exposing a pale, cloudless, blue morning sky.

As she'd slept through the night, on one of his visits after the storm had passed, her father must have opened the window.

Cheers rose again.

She shoved her remaining covers aside. Her head swam as she stood.

"Marie, what are you doing out of your bed?"

At her maid's worried voice, she started. "Felyse." She fought to conceal her weakened state as her maid entered her chamber, not wishing to worry her further. Over the years they'd become friends. And whenever she'd taken sick, Felyse fussed over her as if she were her own child.

"You should not be out of bed, my lady," she gently chided. At another distant cheer, the slender woman with her graying hair neatly secured in a braid scowled at the window. Fury blazed in her eyes as she walked over and closed the shutters with a quick snap.

Somber light smothered the room.

"Is it the Scot being executed?" Marie asked.

Her maid stiffened. *"Oui."*

Disturbed by the thought, Marie rubbed her arms against the sudden chill. Even with the window closed, she could hear that the increasing shouts had taken on a fevered pitch, the jeers and calls for death seeping into the protected silence. "How many men have they caught?"

"Only the one."

Somehow, she had known. "I would like to see him when he walks through the crowd." Mayhap his face would prod her memories.

The maid pursed her lips in displeasure. "It is unwise for you to be up and about, nor would I wish you to endure further distress."

"For a moment. Please."

"I should insist you return to bed." The maid hesitated, as if mulling the wisdom of conceding, and then nodded. "For a short time." She opened the window and grudgingly stepped aside.

Prickles of tension wove through Marie as she crossed the chamber, her feet sinking into the burgundy woolen rug spread on the cold floor. At the window, she clenched the stone, still cool from the rain.

Below, the crowd spread out before her like a macabre sea to witness a man's execution.

Sickened by their grotesque fervor, she looked past the throng filling the bailey to where an elevated wooden platform stood. A large hooded man with an axe waited near the center. She searched the crowd for a man being led through by her father's guards.

Why did thoughts of her abductor cause her such concern?

Her maid touched her forearm. "You are trembling. You must return to your bed."

"A moment more."

"Not a whisper longer, my lady."

Marie's pulse raced as she scanned the path to the dungeon.

The throng jostled and then shifted back.

Her father's guards moved forward, others in their wake. Between them, a man stumbled into view.

The prisoner.

Jeers rose from the crowd as he was led past.

At the high-pitched scream for the Scot's death, Marie leaned out the window in hopes of seeing him better. She still couldn't make out his face.

Frustrated, she withdrew, halted. Angled on a ledge near the hearth sat the volume of tales of King Arthur her father had gifted her with on her eighth birthday. A book rich with tales of Arthur and the Knights of the Round Table.

Like floodwaters as they rushed to engulf all within its path, memories flooded her mind. Her journey across Scotland with Colyne. Their ensuing voyage to France. How they'd made love. And how much she loved him. Tears blurred her eyes.

Mon Dieu, how could she have forgotten him?

She started to shake.

Felyse caught her by the shoulders. "I should not have condoned your getting up. You need to rest, not worry about a man who is better off dead."

The writ! She was mistaken. The man below couldn't be Colyne. Once he'd shown the guards the document from Robert Bruce, they would have immediately escorted him to her father, who would have read the Guardian of Scotland's warning of the English Duke of Renard's treachery.

Except her father had not mentioned the writ. And his references to the Scot had been filled with disgust. "On with you now. 'Tis rest you need, not staying up and tiring yourself further."

Foreboding filled Marie. "Tell me the man's name!"

The older woman scowled. " 'Tis the Earl of Strathcliff."

It couldn't be! "What about the writ?" At her maid's blank stare, she understood. Her father hadn't seen it. Had Colyne lost it when he'd swum with her to shore? "There has been a mistake. The Earl of Strathcliff did not abduct me; he saved my life."

Her maid cast a frantic glance toward the window.

Mon Dieu! On shaky limbs, Marie pulled free and ran to the door. At the entry, she caught a guard's shoulder. "Find the king. He must stop the execution."

"*Oui,* my lady." Steps echoed as the guard rushed to do her bidding.

A cheer echoed from below. Then a chant for death rose from the crowd.

Panic swept her. Colyne must be nearing the platform. If she waited for her father's intervention, it might be too late!

Ignoring her body's protests, Marie bolted down the corridor. And prayed she wouldn't be too late.

Chapter 19

The guard shoved Colyne. "Move along."

Weakened from days of torture, Colyne stumbled. He righted himself. Barely.

"Kill him! Kill him! Kill him!" the onlookers chanted as they parted before him like an angry sea.

An overripe apple slammed the side of his face, the foul juice smearing his cheek. A clump of mud splattered against his chest.

On trembling legs, Colyne wove forward.

"Move back," a king's man bellowed.

Instead, spewing curses and threats, the crowd surged forward. Hands tore at Colyne's clothes, his hair, stripping him of whatever they could yank loose. Beneath the assault, he collapsed to his knees.

Fists beat him.

A boot slammed into his ribs with a crack.

Pain exploding inside, he started to collapse. On a curse, he jammed his hands into the muck and fought to remain conscious.

"Get back!" the guards ordered, shoving between Colyne and the attackers, slowly forcing the crowd back.

His blood pounding, Colyne regained his focus. A fresh gash lay across his chest, his ribs ached, and blood from several cuts seeped into a puddle of water below him, framed in the muck.

He clenched his jaw against the pain and struggled to his feet. With the crowd around him fading in and out, he forced his legs to move.

As he trudged forward, he scanned the tower windows. He willed Marie to be there.

To see him.

To remember.

The windows remained empty. A painful ache built in his chest, as he fought the grief consuming him. He'd never see her again, ever. When her memory returned, 'twould be too late. Numb, he stumbled forward.

As if in answer to his wish, a woman's figure appeared in one of the central tower windows. Honey-colored hair fluttered in the light breeze.

Marie! Hope exploded inside.

The woman moved from view.

His heart slammed against his chest. Had she nae seen him?

"On with ye." The guard shoved.

Muck spattered his face as Colyne slammed to his knees. He wiped away the grime and refused to give up hope. By God, she'd seen him!

On a shaky breath, he locked his elbows and looked up. Instead of Marie's window, the executioner's platform blocked his view.

Dread crawled through him as he scanned the scarred steps, the planks worn down by his predecessors, the hewn wood tainted by their blood.

At the cheers of the crowd, he looked over.

A hooded man, his arms thick as oxen, stood on the center of the platform. As their eyes met, his fingers on the axe tightened.

Colyne sucked in a raw breath, fought the churn of panic. A guard caught his arm, hauled him up. "Move."

His boot clunked on the bottom step with morbid finality. He swallowed hard as he forced his foot up the next rung and faced the truth.

He'd been wrong.

The woman in the window had been another lass.

Any hope of telling Marie that he loved her vanished.

Panic wrenching through her, Marie elbowed her way through the crowd. "Colyne!"

The rumble of excited voices smothered her shout.

Mon Dieu! Water and mud streaked the hem of her gown and slapped against her legs as she pushed another person aside. As she rounded the well, through the sea of people, she caught a glimpse of the man she loved. "Colyne!"

He collapsed atop the platform steps.

Non!

The crowd cheered.

Fury swept her. *He would not die!*

"Marie!"

At her father's shout, she turned.

With his long robes surrounding him, he stood on the distant steps of the castle, her betrothed at his side. His face red, her father motioned her toward him.

Panicking, she turned toward the platform.

Colyne swayed as a guard hauled him to his feet.

She fisted her hands. Why hadn't her father halted the execution? As the crowd jeered, dread filled her and she understood. With the size of the gathering, the guard had been unable to deliver her message. "Father, halt the execution!"

Her father frowned and then motioned his guards toward her.

Tears burned her eyes. There wasn't time to make her way to him and explain. She shoved her way forward.

A woman stepped back.

Marie slid past. A gap opened ahead and she rushed through.

A man and a woman shifted in front of her, craning their necks in an effort to see the macabre spectacle unfolding on the platform.

"Move aside!" Marie shoved between them.

The man whirled, recognition flared, and his outrage transformed into rapid apologies as he backed away.

She hurried ahead.

A cheer filled the bailey.

Panic whipped through her as she glanced forward.

In the distance, Colyne stumbled toward the center of the platform.

Mon Dieu! "Stop the execution!" Shouts from the crowd drowned out her command.

The guard seized Colyne's wrists, wrenching them behind his back.

Another man secured his hands.

Tears blurred Marie's vision as she pushed forward.

With his wrists bound, a guard pushed his head against the block. Cold, rough wood dug into Colyne's cheek. He leveled his gaze on his executioner. If he were to die, 'twould be looking his executioner in the eye with the courage of a Scot.

On a hard swallow, he clung to the fact that once Marie regained her memory, she would tell her father the truth. Then the bastard Renard's attempt to dissolve Scotland's ties with France would fail.

With a grunt, the shrouded man swung his axe.

Steel dug into the block with a deep thud a hand's width from Colyne's face.

A roar erupted from the crowd.

His heart pounding, he thanked God for having blessed him with Marie.

Rumbles of excitement swept the throng as the headsman raised his axe.

The blade's shadow fell over Colyne.

An expectant hush fell upon the crowd as all awaited the final swing, the slice of steel against flesh.

On a prayer, Colyne inhaled one last time.

"Non!" Marie's scream pierced the silence.

Blood pounding hot, Colyne jerked his head free and scanned the crowd.

With a curse, the executioner lowered his blade. "Hold him down!"

"Wait!" Colyne shouted as two men caught his head, slamming him against the wood. "Did you nae recognize the king's daughter's call?"

The executioner grunted with disgust. "Quiet! The woman's screams were nae for you. No one will save your worthless arse!" With a scowl, he raised his blade. "This Scottish rebel who would dare threaten our king," he bellowed, "will now feel the bite of justice!" With a grunt, he began his downward swing.

"Halt, in the name of King Philip!" Marie commanded.

Jarred by the woman's furious demand, the executioner lost the smooth rhythm of his swing. The axe sank a finger's width away from Colyne's neck.

Surprised murmurs rippled through the crowd as Marie, dressed in a gown of white and splattered by mud, broke free of the angry throng before the platform.

Relief swept him, along with a burst of love. "Marie!"

"Colyne!" Tears rolled down her face as she struggled up a step and then began to weave.

Bedamned! Colyne lunged against the guard's hold to reach her.

Strong hands held tight. "Be still!"

Colyne twisted against the hold, cursed as another man helped to restrain him.

Gasping for breath, Marie clasped the rail and pulled herself up step by step.

"Marie, stop!" Her father's indignant roar echoed through the bailey. Horses whinnied.

People scattered as King Philip rode toward the platform.

Her betrothed cantered in his wake, his face red with fury, his cape waving with uneven slaps.

Gasping for breath, Marie reached the top, her eyes dark with terror. She glared at the guards holding Colyne. "Release him!"

Mouths opening in shock, the men scrambled back.

"Look at you!" she gasped as she crouched beside him as he shoved to his knees.

Joy, relief, and love stormed him. "Marie, I—"

"Look at the cuts, the bruises," she sobbed as she tore the bonds from his wrists.

Trembling, Colyne wrapped her in his arms. "'Tis fine, you are here now."

"*Non!* Look at what you have been forced to endure, because," she said on a sob, "I temporarily lost my memory. Forgive me."

"Marie," he rasped, her scent filling his every breath, her bravery his soul. "'Tis nae your fault." Oh, God, there was so much he needed to tell her, so much they needed to discuss.

"Marie!"

At King Philip's furious call, she pulled back, concern darkening her eyes. "We shall explain together."

Colyne had seen that stubborn expression before. 'Twas the same throughout their journey when she'd made a decision and would nae back down.

Few women would have dared to escape after being abducted, or journeyed across Scotland to preserve a country nae her own. He swallowed hard. How could he ever have contemplated living his life without her? Or have hesitated in giving her his love?

She caught his arm, her fingers digging into his muscles. Together they stood and faced her father.

King Philip dismounted. His face red, he strode toward them, the duke in his wake.

A thousand eyes focused on them, the expectancy thick enough to carve with a sword.

As he reached the top of the platform, the king's gaze was riveted to Marie's hand clasped on Colyne. Outrage mottled his face.

Gaston's eyes narrowed as he took in Marie's protective stance.

Colyne braced himself. Though he'd journeyed to France in service to his king, he'd nae only compromised King Philip's bastard daughter but another man's betrothed. "Sire." He struggled to bow at King Philip's approach, almost losing his balance. He straightened and then nodded at the duke. "Your Grace."

"Silence," King Philip commanded. Concern and love waged their own war in his expression as he scowled at his daughter. "Marie, I demand an explanation."

Pride shone in her eyes. "Colyne MacKerran, Earl of Strathcliff, has been wrongly accused," she said, her voice strong. "He did not abduct me, but risked his life to return me to France."

Stunned murmurs rippled through the crowd.

Her father's skeptical gaze shifted to Colyne.

Hope ignited that with Marie at his side, the king would listen. "The Duke of Renard was behind her abduction," Colyne rasped, his voice unsteady. "I carried a writ explaining the English noble's ploy."

"I have seen no writ," King Philip stated.

"After an accident," Colyne continued, "the writ became soaked and the ink smeared. The arresting guards believed I lied because the document was unreadable and tossed the missive from Robert Bruce, Earl of Carrick, Guardian of the Realm of Scotland into the flames."

Shrewd eyes turned to his daughter. "Explain how you came to meet and trust this Scot."

"I escaped the Duke of Renard's knights," Marie replied, pride in her voice. "En route to a port in Scotland, I found Lord Strathcliff wounded and tended him."

"She saved my life," Colyne said, his words somber. "Once I had healed, I escorted her to France."

Tears in her eyes, Marie nodded. "If not for the earl, I would never have safely returned. I owe him my life."

The king studied her for a long moment and then whispered to Marie's betrothed.

Irritation flashed on the duke's face.

King Philip strode to Colyne. "I owe you my deepest appreciation for saving Marie's life." He held out his hand. "And an apology."

Emotion filling him, Colyne clasped the king's hand. "Had I stood in your stead, Sire, I would have had doubts as well." With the threat of his imminent death over, Colyne wondered what her father's reaction would be when, later this day, he offered compensation to end Marie's betrothal and then sought her hand?

King Philip raised his hand before his subjects.

The crowd grew silent.

"'Tis come to my attention that the Earl of Strathcliff has been wrongly accused," the king announced. "The Scot did not abduct Lady Marie but saved her life." He nodded toward Colyne with gratitude. "For his bravery, he will be honored."

Surprise, then nods of understanding, rippled through the crowd.

King Philip faced Colyne. "After you have rested and have been cared for by my physician, we will discuss Renard's treachery in detail." He gestured to a nearby guard. "Ensure that the earl is placed in one of our finest chambers and brought food and a hot bath. Notify my physician to tend to him immediately."

"*Oui*, Your Majesty." The guard bowed and hurried away.

"I add my humble gratitude as well for saving Marie's life," her betrothed offered.

Colyne nodded, but he didna miss the frigidness of the duke's tone, nor did he doubt that the man's fury, if pressed, could turn lethal.

Chapter 20

Marie nodded to the physician as he left Colyne's chamber and then walked to the guard outside his door. "We are not to be disturbed."

He gave a curt bow. "*Oui*, my lady."

Still overwhelmed with the relief of Colyne's life having been spared, she stepped inside and closed the door.

Near a small table, the man who had rewritten her purpose in life stood with his back to her, pulling on a clean tunic.

Heat pooled inside her as she watched the ripple of muscles, the graceful power that was an integral part of him, a strength he wielded with fierce precision as quick as tenderness.

He shifted, and ugly bruises of yellow and black came into view, a potent reminder of how close he'd come to death. Of how even after all the challenges they'd faced, a future between them had not been ensured.

Coldness swept her as she remembered her betrothed's request for a private audience with her once they'd left the bailey.

Her father's concern that she needed to rest had delayed the inevitable confrontation. If Gaston learned of this visit with Colyne, given his upset at the favor she had shown Colyne, he would be furious. With an unsteady breath, she stepped deeper into the room.

At the soft scrape of her slipper, Colyne turned. Surprise crossed his handsome face, then desire. "Marie?"

Tears filled her eyes as she stepped into his warm embrace, the need to be with him as elemental as breathing.

"Oh, God." He wrapped his arms around her and brushed his mouth on hers, soft, slow, as if savoring her taste, as he shook with desperation.

She melted into his demands, giving everything and needing more. Mayhap she could hope for a miracle, that her father would release her from her betrothal. Most of all, she wished Colyne would want her forever.

His eyes dark with passion, he broke the kiss and stared at her, as if absorbing her every nuance. "I—I never thought I would see you again," he rasped, the toll of the past days shadowing his face. "There is so much I want to tell you." He swallowed hard. "I did nae think . . ."

"You are safe." Marie brushed her finger across a purple bruise on his jaw, and her guilt grew. "Look at your face, your body. I am so sorry. I—"

He caught her fingers and pressed them to his lips. "It does nae matter."

Shaken, Marie withdrew her hand. "It does. How could I ever forget you, even for a moment?"

"You were ill."

Mayhap, but to her it excused nothing. "Once my memory returned, I sent a guard to inform my father to halt the execution. Unsure if word would reach him in time," she said, needing to share her greatest fear, "I had to try to reach you."

"And you did."

He stared at her, his expression so intense she found herself believing he could forgive her when she struggled to forgive herself. How could he when she'd deceived him throughout most of their journey, and had made love with him without disclosing she was promised to another?

"Marie."

At the somberness of his tone, her breath caught. She was wrong, he'd forgiven her of nothing. He was going to tell her that once he'd spoken with her father, he was sailing back to Scotland. "What?" She held her breath.

"I love you."

At the same moment he spoke, torn by grief at his leaving, she blurted out, "I know you must return to Scotland. And I understand your not forgiving me, but . . ." His declaration echoed in her mind and she paused, stared at him in disbelief. "Y—you love me?"

Tenderness creased his face as his eyes darkened with need. "Aye, very much." Then his mouth captured hers in a long, hot kiss. As he drew back, he watched her, his eyes solemn.

Joy burst through her; she wanted him, needed him forever. "I love you so much. I was afraid that—"

"I need to explain. I knew I cared for you, deeply. As you lay ill and in a delirium at the inn, the thought of never seeing you again or making love with you 'twas unthinkable." Colyne brushed a kiss tenderly across her mouth. "The guards arrived and arrested me before you became lucid enough for me to tell you. Know this," he rasped. "I canna imagine my life without you, of nae sharing the smallest joy with you, or a day passing without seeing your smile." He swallowed hard. "As they led me to the executioner, my greatest fear was that I would never again see you, that you would never know how I feel."

At his heartfelt admission, tears blurred her eyes. When he started to speak, she shook her head. "I want to explain why I kept so much from you."

"Marie, I understand—"

"Please listen."

He nodded.

She released a long, unsteady breath. "Over the years I have learned that men wanted not me but a tie to my father. Throughout our journey, I hesitated to expose my true feelings because I was afraid to be hurt. After we made love I wanted to tell you, but you did not know who I was. Then I realized the gravity of my selfish actions. I was afraid for your life if my father or my betrothed learned of our intimacy." Her lower lip quivered. "I will never regret our intimacy. But with you unaware of the possible repercussions, I was wrong to continue to allow your ignorance. For that I am sorry. At least neither my father nor my betrothed are aware of my indiscretions."

"They know," Colyne said quietly.

Guilt swept her, and she despised her actions even more. "*Mon Dieu*, how can you ever forgive me?"

"How can I nae? I love you," he whispered. "Neither am I without guilt. We had nae said our vows before God within the sanctity of the church, yet I came to your bed."

Warmth swept her cheeks. "I gave you little choice."

His brow quirked with amusement. "I agree that your being an amazing and beautiful woman made my decision difficult. But," he said, his voice growing somber, "aware you were an innocent, I knew as well the responsibilities of my decision."

Mayhap, but considering all the facts, her actions far from absolved her of sin. "Now what?"

"Now," Colyne said, taking her hand, "I will be asking the woman I love for her hand in marriage."

Tightness squeezed her chest as she stepped back. Numb, aching, hating what she must say, she walked to the window, stared out. "As much as I wish it," she whispered, "as much as thoughts of a life with you fulfill my every dream, regrettably, it is not possible."

Colyne's quiet steps paused behind her.

A sob built in her throat.

He caught her shoulder and gently turned her. Eyes raw with torment scanned hers. "Why nae?"

A tear slid down her cheek in a cool path. With a sniff, she wiped it away. "You may be able to believe my father could be made to accept our indiscretion, but from Gaston's manner, I assure you that it is not possible."

His blue eyes narrowed. "Do you love the duke?"

She stared at him in disbelief. "How can you ask that after everything I just said? You have met Gaston, have seen firsthand his fierce intention to keep what is his."

A muscle worked in his jaw. "Is that what you are, a possession to be won?"

Marie bristled. "I am my own woman. But I also made a vow to my father, a man who raised me with love when many would never have recognized a bastard daughter. Never would I wish to hurt him."

"Would you nae hurt him more by marrying a man you do nae love?"

Marie stilled. Throughout her life, grateful for her father's love, she'd always complied with his wishes. When she reached marriageable age, without feelings for anyone and with his expectation of her to wed, she'd entered into an arranged betrothal without hesitation. With Colyne's question, she wondered what her father's reaction would be if she asked to be released from her agreement to marry the duke.

Her stomach twisted. Never before had she defied her father's bidding, but she was no longer a child. She took his hand, lay it over her heart. "I love you and I want a life with you. I will speak with my father and request he break the betrothal."

Eyes fierce, Colyne's gaze held hers. "I have nae found you only to let you go."

He crushed his mouth over hers, but however much she loved him, doubts haunted her that her father would deny her request.

Clouds shrouded the moon, casting the bailey in a feeble light. With a heart heavy, Colyne continued toward the stables.

Bedamned this night.

Bedamned the king's decision.

Bedamned that he didna have another choice.

Soft steps fell behind him and he turned.

Caught in a flicker of torchlight, Marie's slender frame approached.

He stiffened. "Return to the keep."

She halted, her stance fierce but her eyes glittering with unshed tears. "I needed to see you."

"After your father's decision this night to deny my request for your hand, 'tis unwise for any to find us alone. Go."

At his brisk order, that determined look he so loved hardened her face.

"Marie," he pleaded as inside a part of him died, "you must leave. Please."

In a flicker of moonlight, her eyes reflected her turmoil, anger, and grief.

A sword's wrath! He wanted to kiss her, make love with her, and keep her forever. With the king's refusal to break the betrothal, such a chance had ceased to exist.

To stand here with her a hand's width away did naught but add to the enormity of their heartache. With ground-eating strides, Colyne entered the stables where he could be alone, to think, to somehow find a way to deal with the pain of losing Marie.

And wondered if he ever could.

How did one move past losing the woman who was the other half of his soul? A woman who made his life complete?

Wisps of distant torchlight fractured the dark confines as he moved deeper. The familiar smell of horses and hay offered a soothing balm, the blackness an escape.

The soft scuff of slippers fractured the silence in his wake.

Colyne braced himself against the emotions the sight of her would always evoke. He turned. "Marie, I—"

She ran to him. Before he could warn her away, her mouth pressed over his with passion.

He fought the urge to return the kiss. But at the raw desperation in her touch, he succumbed.

At her soft moans, Colyne skimmed his fingers down to pull her flush against him. His body burning, he backed her against the stall, took the kiss deeper. She shuddered beneath him.

A horse to their right snorted. Another toward the back of the stable shifted restlessly.

Shaken at how she could strip his control, Colyne pulled free, his breath unsteady, his body hard with unspent desire. What was he thinking? Anyone could come upon them. He shook his head. "Nay, 'tis wrong."

"My father is mistaken not to end the betrothal," she rushed out, passion clinging to her words.

"He is a king who loves his daughter but has his country's interests to consider as well. Your betrothed is a powerful man."

"And a man I do not want," she said. "After you left, I begged, pleaded with him, but he refused to change his mind." She sniffed. "It is you I love, you I need."

As if he didna feel the same. The warmth of her tears stained his neck and melded with his own. For long moments he held her, savoring the feel of her body against his, the way her breath caressed his skin, how she brought peace to his heart.

After a long while, her sobs quieted.

On a rough sigh, he kissed her brow, damning his decision. "On the morrow I shall go."

She gasped. "Why? For your bravery, my father has invited you to remain a fortnight."

"And if I stayed, what? Can you guarantee we would nae meet again where none can see us? That we would nae make love?" He released her, paced to a nearby stall then returned. "I swore to myself nae to touch you. Yet, here, where any could come upon us, we risk the greatest sin. For if I believed 'twas safe, I would make love with you. You are a temptation I canna resist."

A gust of wind spiraled wisps of hay across the courtyard as the

188 • *Diana Cosby*

cry of a baby echoed somewhere in the night, mingling with the distant laughter of guards on the wall walk. Marie remained silent, but the flicker of torchlights in the bailey exposed the tears rolling down her cheeks.

"I have confidence your father will find those responsible for your abduction," Colyne said, needing to change the subject.

"I cannot lose you," she whispered.

A muscle worked in his jaw. "'Tis nae a choice."

Silence fell between them, cold, hard with the pain of truth.

She sniffed. "I hate this."

"As do I."

"If Renard is still in France," she said with vengeance, "he will regret that he did not flee to England when he had the opportunity."

"Aye," Colyne replied, through sheer will bringing his emotions under control. "But his involvement far from explains how he was able to bypass your guards and abduct you."

"A puzzle my father said he and Gaston have discussed at length."

At her familiar use of her betrothed's name, Colyne flinched, again damned that he could nae sway the king to end the betrothal.

"'Twas daring of the English duke to request an audience with my father to plant false accusations against the Scottish rebels."

"Aye, a brazen act that convinced King Philip of a lie."

"And one that persuaded Gaston as well." She paused. "Neither can I forget how Gaston reminded my father of the Duke of Renard's warning."

His jaw tightened as he recalled her betrothed's caution to the king. "I find it interesting that your betrothed was so adamant in giving an Englishman's word credence, more so with King Philip's support of Scotland."

"Mayhap," Marie said, "his claim was more out of his dislike for you than his belief in your reasons for coming to France."

Colyne grimaced, far from appeased. "Mayhap."

Her eyes widened. *"Mon Dieu!"*

He stilled. "What is it?"

What if," she whispered, "Gaston helped in planning my abduction?"

Tension thrummed through him. "Why would he, with your hand already promised to him? There was naught for him to gain by becoming involved."

She nodded. "My ramblings were those of a dreamer. If he had indeed conspired with Renard, my father would not hesitate to sever the betrothal."

As absurd as the idea of her betrothed involved in a treasonous plot against his sovereign seemed, Colyne couldna dismiss the thought. "His involvement would explain how your abduction transpired without event."

She grimaced. "It would, but it does not answer why Gaston would take such a risk. Even if he was involved, how could we find proof?"

"We?" Anger slammed him hard and quick. "I will nae allow you to endanger your life. If he conspired with Renard, I will find out."

"How?" she demanded. "You have no reason to be near my betrothed. As his intended, my presence beside him is expected."

"A sword's wrath! You will do naught to bring suspicion upon yourself." The stubbornness in her eyes assured Colyne that she'd nae heed his warning. He shot her a cool look. "I have decided to accept your father's offer to remain here for a fortnight. If your betrothed was involved, I will find proof."

A smile touched her mouth. "I can help—"

"You will do naught. I will have your promise!"

"Promise?" her betrothed demanded with a dangerous edge as he stepped into the stable.

Colyne whirled to face the duke, pushing Marie behind him as he grasped the hilt of his sword.

"'Twould be unwise to draw your weapon," the duke drawled. "If I were to kill you, 'twould be in self-defense."

At least he'd nae come upon them earlier when he'd kissed Marie. "'Tis unwise to eavesdrop."

"More so for a man to engage in a clandestine meeting with my intended," Gaston said with brittle coldness. "As you saved Marie's life, I shall grant you leave of this illicit assignation. But should I find you alone again with my betrothed, I will kill you."

Colyne grunted. If he were challenged, the bastard would die.

The duke extended his hand. "Marie, come here."

She stiffened behind Colyne.

Hating what he must do, he drew her forward. "We will speak later."

"You will not!" The duke's nostrils flared. "Except for public meetings, she is not to meet with you. I forbid it."

Marie's body shook with fury. "You will not dictate who I see."

"This is not a topic I shall discuss in public," Gaston stated with cold warning.

"Go," Colyne said.

"For you," she said under her breath as she passed him. With her head high, she walked to her betrothed.

Colyne damned the moment she placed her hand in the duke's, damned that decorum forced him to watch the woman he loved walk away with a man she despised. Neither could he risk losing his freedom. He had a fortnight to discover the truth. If Gaston had been involved in the plot to abduct Marie, he'd find out.

Chapter 21

The fading aromas of roasted boar, peacocks, and swans sifted through the air as the servants removed the remainders of the celebratory dinner. Laughter rippled through the great hall from the throng of well-wishers gathered within as Marie sipped the last of her spiced wine and returned the goblet to the table, dreading the festivities leading up to her wedding.

Beneath half-lowered lashes, she glanced to where Colyne sat finishing his meal.

Deep blue eyes locked on hers. Desire blazed from their mesmerizing depths as his fingers tightened around his cup.

Shaken, she looked down and found her own hand had curled into a fist. How could she go through with this mockery of a marriage? But what other choice remained? Two days past, in private, she'd again sought out her father and demanded that he break the betrothal.

Once again, he'd denied her. Panicking at the thought of losing Colyne, she'd threatened to flee to Scotland. And with his eyes leveled on hers with cold intent, he'd made it clear that if she foolishly tried, not only would she be caught and returned but Lord Strathcliff would be hanged. His face dark with fury, he explained that after learning the Scot had taken her innocence, regardless of her going to him willingly, only the noble's having saved her life had swayed him to allow him to live. Then he'd stormed out.

"You are finished, my dear?" Gaston asked from her side.

Marie started and met his gaze, unsettled by his nearness and wanting to be alone. "I am tired." The truth. The last few days, she'd felt lethargic, and at times her stomach had been a bit upset, no doubt due to her recent illness. Anxious to be away from his company, she nodded. "I shall be retiring now."

This night, once everyone was abed, she would sneak to Colyne's chamber. For three days, with fear of her father's promised repercussions, she'd not spoken to him beyond a brief and distant daily greeting. Since Gaston had interrupted their meeting in the stable, the duke had escorted her from dawn 'til dusk.

If only she'd waited to choose a suitor. To be fair, had she not met Colyne, with Gaston's striking looks and polite manner, theirs would most likely have been a peaceful relationship.

The discord between her and Gaston arose from her show of favor to Colyne when she'd halted his execution. She'd embarrassed the duke. His coming upon her and Colyne in the stable had served to increase her betrothed's ire. To further complicate matters, her suspicions of his involvement with her kidnapping added to her angst.

With the passing days, Colyne had not learned anything that would tie Gaston to her abduction. Not that her covertly spying on the duke had delivered anything of consequence either.

Marie stood.

Immediately, her betrothed rose at her side. "Sire, if you will allow me, I shall escort Lady Marie to her chamber."

With a frown, her father studied her. "Marie, you have been quiet throughout the meal and eaten little. Are you ill?"

She forced a smile to her lips. "*Non*, Father. Merely tired, and I have little appetite."

"'Twill take time to fully recover from your ordeal. Although," the king said, his eyes dark with meaning, "I wonder if your sleeplessness may have more to do with your upcoming vows."

Unsettled, she remained quiet.

Gaston gently took her arm. "Come."

She cast a yearning look at Colyne and, with regret, allowed the duke to lead her from the great hall.

A series of torches secured in ornate sconces illuminated their path as they climbed the worn steps. "I, too, am concerned at your silence this eve," he said as they reached the top and began to walk down the corridor toward her chamber.

Ahead of the duke, Marie spoke over her shoulder. "As I informed my father, I am tired."

"I see."

Mayhap, but she heard his doubts. Marie stopped at her door.

He took her hand, skimmed his thumb across her skin. "You are a beautiful woman."

Uneasy, she withdrew her hand. "I bid thee good night," she said, fighting to keep the panic from her voice.

Gaston leaned forward.

He was going to kiss her. A finger's width apart, she turned away, and his mouth skimmed across her cheek.

On a heavy sigh, he caught her chin. "I know you believe you care for the Scot, but 'tis because he saved your life. With time, your feelings for the earl will fade."

Marie didn't reply, aching at the thought of living without Colyne, the cold emptiness of her life ahead. She would never stop loving him.

At her continued silence, Gaston's gaze narrowed to dangerous slits, a crack in his well-polished veneer.

For the first time since they'd met, fear scraped through her that, if pushed, the duke would do her harm. "'Tis late and—"

"Listen well and heed my words," he hissed. "'Tis me you shall wed. I will not tolerate any appearance of impropriety. Until he leaves, never again will you speak with the Scot."

The pompous ass. She broke free. "How dare you talk to me with such disrespect? The king is my father and I shall—"

"Do naught." He caught her jaw, his fingers digging into her soft flesh as he jerked her toward him. "Do you believe I am ignorant of the child you carry?" he scoffed. "You should be thankful that I care little about your unfaithfulness. Marriage to you will gain me access to the throne."

Stunned, she stared at him, his words melding into one thought. The child she carried? She wasn't . . . The lingering tiredness, her inability to eat much as of late, and her aversion to the smell of many foods, all of which she had attributed to her recent illness. With his accusation, the signs of her pregnancy were clear.

Her heart stumbled.

A child.

A life she and Colyne had created.

Emotion swept her at the thought of his babe in her arms, of blue eyes watching her with wonder as tiny fingers wrapped around her thumb with a smile. Colyne would be so excited to learn . . .

Colyne.

Regardless of the duke's warning, he must be told they were going to have a child. And what of her father? Once he learned the news, mayhap he would end the betrothal?

Joy swept her at thought of a life with Colyne, the start of their family, of the years ahead and sharing their love.

"Did you think I would not find out that the rebel's seed grows within you?"

Gaston's harsh words dragged her to the fore.

He stilled, realization dawning on his face. He released her with a cold laugh. "Strathcliff does not know, does he?"

"*Non*," she whispered, her pulse racing as she rubbed her wrist where he'd held her. "My father—"

"Knows naught of the Scot's spawn. As your betrothed, and with the king unavailable due to pressing matters, the physician informed me."

She swallowed hard. This explained how the duke had learned of her condition.

"I assured him that I would pass the news to your father. But I chose to spare King Philip further shame."

Hurt tore through her. "He would love my child!"

"Another bastard?" Eyes narrowed, he leaned closer. "Do you not understand the disgrace your father has endured since your birth? Have you never asked yourself why he has kept you sequestered on the coast with but minimal protection? Or why you are rarely invited to visit?"

"You lie! His home is always open to me. He loves me!"

He drew himself to his full height with a cold laugh. "Does he? Is that what your desperate heart wishes to believe? Or your begging him to release you from our betrothal didn't reveal the obvious?"

Stunned, she stilled, the hurt immense. "He—he told you I pressed him to end our betrothal?"

"Indeed. He is anxious to have you out of his life." Pity shadowed Gaston's face. "He doesn't want you and never did."

Sickened, a sense of betrayal washed over her as her childhood memories collapsed in her mind. As a young girl when she'd shown an interest in herbs and healing, her father had arranged for her to live in the seaside village. In addition to allowing her to follow her passion for healing, it had given her freedom from suitors who'd sought her hand to gain a royal tie.

Marie understood her father's explanation that the responsibilities of the crown allowed her infrequent visits. When the opportunity arose for her to stay at one of his castles, hadn't he always visited with her at the start of each day, reading stories of magic and faraway lands?

A chill swept through her. What of her father's recent threat toward Colyne? Was Gaston right? "My father loves me," she said, but doubts filled her words.

He closed his eyes, shoved out a harsh breath. When he opened them, his gaze softened. "I am sorry I was overly harsh. 'Twas wrong of me to have shared some of your father's admissions to me with such candor. Forgive me."

Some of her father's admissions? *Mon Dieu!* What else had he told the duke? Her heart aching, she stepped back; all she wanted was to be alone.

A weary smile touched his mouth, fell away. "I have allowed jealousy to guide my tongue. But I see by the hurt in your eyes that you know my words are true." With a grimace, he gestured toward the turret. "Go, then. Speak with the king. Ask him if my claim is a lie."

No, it couldn't be true. Shaking, Marie knew she should move, should seek out her father and learn the truth. And yet her feet refused to move.

"Though you do not love me," Gaston said with unexpected tenderness, "I believe ours can be a comfortable marriage. I expect naught but your duties as my wife. Once an heir is born, if you choose, you will have your privacy. But I shall expect you at my side when an occasion requires such."

An heir, his child, when Colyne's grew inside her. A babe she wanted desperately.

"My only stipulation is that the Scot remain ignorant of the child," the duke said. "'Twould bode ill for his life if he dared again confront the king or me."

Fear rippled through her, and Marie lay a protective hand over her stomach where her babe rested. If Colyne learned of her pregnancy, he would do whatever it took to claim her as his wife.

"Think of what I told you," the duke said quietly. "On the morrow I will have your word that you will comply." He walked away.

Overwhelmed, she watched him go with a confident stride. Once he disappeared into the turret, she wrenched open her door and stumbled inside.

Her maid rushed toward her. "You are ill?"

"Non." She held up her hand to forestall the woman's approach. "Please, I need to be alone."

Felyse scowled. "I told your father it was too soon for you to be about, but he insisted it was your duty to spend time with your betrothed." She made a tsking sound. "If you ask me, the king is anxious for you to wed."

The woman's words chilled Marie further.

"Do not listen to me; worry is making me ramble." She gave her a comforting smile. "Let me help you to bed and then I will be on my way."

She remained silent. After her maid left, Marie curled into a tight ball but couldn't sleep. Gaston's harsh words repeated in her mind. Did her father love her, or had all he'd claimed been a lie? She hated the doubts, the misgivings that undermined her father's support, which she'd never questioned before.

And Colyne—he would be thrilled at the news. She easily envisioned him holding their son or daughter, the pride, the love in his eyes as he told their babe stories of the fey. But he would never know they'd created a child.

With a frustrated sigh, she shoved her bed covering aside and rose. There was no way she was going to sleep this night. Unsure of anything, she moved to the window and stared into the night.

A thin film of clouds shielded the stars overhead.

As she started to turn, a movement on the wall drew her attention. Narrowing her gaze, she tried to make out the murky figure. Failed. Someone was hiding in the shadows near an arrow loop.

Why?

An assassination attempt against her father?

Her pulse raced as she studied the covert stranger. Whatever his intention, she must inform the guards of his presence.

As she started to move back, she caught sight of another man hurrying down the wall walk.

Moonlight spilled from a break in the clouds, illuminating the lone figure.

Gaston.

She frowned, surprised by his presence, believing he'd returned to his chamber. Or, as troubled as she by the news he'd imparted, mayhap he couldn't sleep as well?

Marie steadied her emotions and glanced toward the man hidden in the shadows. As her betrothed approached, the stranger stepped from his hiding place.

He was going to attack Gaston. She started to call out a warning, but as the duke spotted the man, he waved him back into the shadows.

Both men slipped into the shield of darkness.

Unease rippled through her. A planned meeting. Why? Was Gaston's rendezvous somehow connected with her abduction? Shame filled her at the thought, one driven by fear. If indeed her betrothed was right, she'd lived a lie, her father's words of love naught but sympathetic offerings from a man who'd tried to appease an unwanted child. Tears welled in her eyes. Her foundation of love was but a story, conjured up like one of the tales of King Arthur.

King Arthur!

So caught up in her doubts, stunned by the realization of her pregnancy and devastated at losing Colyne, rational thought had fled.

Her heart pounding, Marie bolted to the hearth. Angled on a ledge sat the volume of King Arthur tales, its edges worn from use. She picked up the leather-bound volume.

With unsteady fingers, she flipped through the hand-penned parchment. Through the blur of her tears, she read the inscription.

My dearest, Marie. Your birth is a blessing. You are a daughter who fills me with joy and one whom I welcome into my life, home, and heart. One day, when you are grown, my greatest wish is that you too may be blessed with a child created by love.

Your father, Philip IV

The fragile parchment shook in her fingers. Marie closed the volume and slid it on the ledge, then clenched her fists.

Gaston had lied.

Anger knotted into a hard ball in her chest. The bastard thought he could convince her that she was unwanted, sway her to believe she could ever stop loving Colyne or the child she carried.

Her anger shoved up another notch. The bastard had played on her fears of love, her doubts that any man would want her if not for her royal tie. Before she'd met Colyne, she might have believed his words.

No longer.

Through Colyne's trust, friendship, and patience, he'd taught her that she was a woman a man could love, not because of the royal link but because she had a good and honest heart. With Colyne, she felt complete.

Marie glanced to where Gaston remained cloistered in the shadows with the stranger. What other devious decisions had he made? Did they extend to her abduction? Grabbing her cloak, she ran out the door.

Mon Dieu, she would find out!

Crouched in the shadows along the wall, Colyne listened to the hushed conversation between Marie's betrothed and a stranger who'd stood in the back of the great hall during the evening meal.

From the coat of dust clinging to the man's garb, he'd ridden hard to reach this assignation.

With quiet steps, Colyne edged closer.

He could now move without pain or dizziness, but his recovery did little to ease his troubled mind. Marie's celebratory dinner this eve had been a potent reminder of her impending marriage, a union that would transpire unless he found evidence linking the duke to her kidnapping.

An owl hooted in the distance. A gust of wind swept past, thick with the scent of rain.

He took in the clouds churning overhead, slowly robbing him of the guiding moonlight. Silver rays faded. Except for a wavering glow of light cast by the torches, blackness shrouded the castle.

The scrape of leather sounded nearby.

Bedamned! He flattened himself against the stone.

Caught within the wind, the soft murmurs of the distant guards and the chirp of crickets filled the night.

Colyne made another slow sweep. Satisfied the sound had come from a distance, he crept closer.

The rustle of clothing sounded from the entrance to the wall walk.

He stilled, his eyes narrowing.

With stealth, a cloaked figure moved from the stairs.

Another gust of wind whipped past. Fragments of moonlight cut through the break in the churning sky. The silver rays exposed several strands of honey-colored hair whipping about the secured hood. The clouds roiling overhead closed, smothering the person in blackness.

Marie!

With care, Marie edged closer to where the duke whispered in the shadows with the stranger, her anger at being made a fool still running hot. She strained to hear their conversation.

"I told you never to come here," Gaston snapped.

The man shuffled his feet. "Your Grace, I—"

"Silence! If anyone should hear, 'twould cost us both our lives."

Their lives? Anger melded with apprehension. She pressed closer.

"I am sorry," the stranger replied.

Her betrothed glanced around. As if satisfied no one was about, he faced the man. "Why are you here?"

"With our abduction attempt exposed, the Duke of Renard fears for his life. He beseeches you to arrange his passage back to England immediately."

"I told him I would take care of matters as soon as it was safe," Gaston hissed. "Inform him that he is to remain hidden, and I will send word when all the arrangements have been made. You will never visit me here again. Is that clear?"

"*Oui*, Your Grace."

Sickened, Marie closed her eyes. Her betrothed had participated in her kidnapping. Damn him, he would pay for his treachery.

Gaston shook his head and lowered his voice.

Marie leaned forward, but their words were too soft for her to understand. Keeping low, she crept closer.

"The Duke of Renard also states the remainder of the payment will be sent once he is safe."

Her betrothed cursed. " 'Twas not the agreement we made."

"I am but a messenger," the man rushed out, his voice trembling with fear.

"Be gone," Gaston snarled.

"Aye, Your Grace."

Mary's will! If they looked in this direction, they'd see her! Marie turned toward the tower, but her slipper caught against the stone. Her pulse racing, she steadied herself.

"Did you hear something?" the stranger asked.

Moonlight flickered to expose the harsh lines of Gaston's face. Fury, then macabre satisfaction settled in his eyes, leaving her chilled to the bone. "Marie. 'Tis a pity you have followed me."

Chapter 22

Shaking with a mixture of rage and fear, Marie stepped back from her betrothed, keeping his accomplice in sight. "You helped plan this," she said with contempt. "And what else are you involved in?"

The duke lunged.

Marie tried to run, but he caught her.

With a jerk, he hauled her against his body. "You should have gone to sleep as I insisted," he hissed. "Now, when they find you sprawled on the ground below, 'twill be with regret that I inform your father that your delirium returned." His expression mocked sadness.

She shook with fury. "When my father learns of your deceit, 'tis your life that will be—"

Gaston clamped his hand over her mouth, muffling her scream. "You worthless bitch! No one will be able to hear you until it is too late." He gave an indignant grunt. "Now you know too much. Had you listened to me, you, along with the Scottish bastard's child, would have lived."

Colyne halted as he inched forward, the duke's news slamming through his mind.

She was carrying his child?

At Marie's gasp, Colyne tamped down the elation and edged forward. He had to save her!

In the slashes of errant moonlight, terror widened Marie's eyes as her betrothed wrestled her toward the edge.

The bastard! Colyne charged Gaston.

"Your Grace," the stranger shouted, "behind you!"

The duke turned, giving Colyne much-needed time. Teeth clenched, he caught Gaston's neck, wrenching him backward.

Marie broke free.

"Run!" Colyne shouted as he plowed his fist into the duke's jaw.

Instead, Marie gasped. "Behind you!"

Colyne whirled.

Dagger in hand, the stranger charged.

With a quick twist, he evaded the man's attack. Before the assailant could slow, Colyne caught his forearm, jerked him forward. The stranger dropped to his knees, his hands scraping at the stone. Momentum slid him forward, and a cry ripped from his lungs as he tumbled off the wall walk. Seconds later, his body thudded against the earth.

Gasping for breath, Colyne rounded on the duke.

Deep lines savaged his face as the noble, his sword raised, charged.

Fury toward this man who had dared to threaten Marie's life backed Colyne's swing. Metal scraped metal as he deflected the aggressor's blade.

At the duke's next attack, Colyne ducked. Forged steel hissed over him by mere inches. Taking advantage of Gaston's lowered weapon, he charged.

Blades screamed.

Locked.

Colyne shoved. The duke stumbled back.

Sweat poured down Colyne's face as drove forward with a series of brutal swings. He would nae lose her. She was his life. "Cede!"

"To a Scot?" With a curse, Gaston bore down on Colyne, narrowed the gap, swung.

Colyne repulsed the blow, drove his blade forward. The slide of the duke's flesh against the honed steel offered its own reward.

In shock, Gaston gaped at the wound across his left arm, a clean line severing skin from bone. Brows slammed together in outrage. "For that you will die!"

The thud of steps echoed as the guards rushed toward them. "Halt!" one of the king's knights ordered.

Eyes blazing, the duke attacked.

Colyne repelled the blow. "This," he said between clenched teeth, "is for Marie!" He sidestepped and thrust, sank the tip of his sword deep into the noble's gut.

The duke's weapon clattered to the ground, slid across the stone, wobbled at the edge, and then tumbled over. Eyes wide with shock, the duke stared at the blood staining his tunic in a slow, sluggish trail and collapsed to his knees.

Colyne glared at the noble. He'd almost cost Scotland their much-needed aid, had played a part in both Stephano and his family's as well as Douglas's murder, had hurt Marie and had endangered their child's life. The bastard would never harm anyone again. Colyne lifted his sword to deliver the fatal blow.

Marie stepped forward. *"Non!"*

Colyne's fingers trembled on the hilt. "He deserves to die."

"He does," Marie agreed, her voice unsteady, "but his shame will be greater if his sentence is delivered by my father and witnessed by his own serfs."

As much as Colyne yearned to end the bastard's life, he lowered his weapon. He would allow the king to mete out the deserved punishment. "Why did you help to abduct Marie?"

Defiant eyes lifted to Colyne. Silence

"For the coin my abduction would bring," Marie said.

The duke glared at her.

"I overheard him and the man with whom he met."

Colyne motioned the guards as they halted around them. "Arrest the Duke of Vocette for conspiring against King Philip."

The knights seized him.

"When you are interrogated," Colyne stated, his words like ice, "'twill be intriguing to see what devices they choose to acquire your confession. Methods I have nay doubt will have you praying for death long before 'tis served."

Fear curdled in the man's eyes, and he tried to shove to his feet. His legs gave, and he landed hard. Wide eyes, panic swept his gaze. "*Non*," he begged, "if you have any mercy, kill me now."

"Mercy?" Marie said with disgust, "you have earned none." She nodded to the guards. "Take him to the dungeon."

"I will help you," Gaston pleaded, as the guards hauled him away. "Give you whatever amount of coin or lands you request."

The knights shoved the duke into the turret, his pleas for death echoing in his wake.

His heart pounding, Colyne drew Marie into his arms.

Her body trembled against his. "I was so afraid!"

"You are alive." Colyne swallowed hard, brushed the pad of his thumb against her cheek. "You are with child? I am—"

"Marie?" the king's voice boomed with fear.

With her in his arms, Colyne faced the powerful ruler.

Her father, followed by several of his knights holding torches, closed in. A pace away, they halted. King Philip's fierce gaze narrowed on Colyne. "I demand to know what is going on!"

"Colyne saved my life," Marie stated with pride.

The sovereign arched a doubtful brow.

"Sire," Colyne said, "there is a man lying in the bailey below. Moments ago, he met with the Duke of Vocette in secret, a rendezvous both Lady Marie and I overheard."

The king's eyes shifted to Marie. "Is this true?"

"*Oui*. They discussed my abduction. It seems Gaston was involved in the entire scheme, and it was he who led them to me."

A muscle worked in her father's jaw. "This explains why you were so easily taken."

"Aye," Colyne agreed. "His accomplice also revealed that the Duke of Renard is still in France. He is hiding until arrangements are made for him to sail back to England."

A humorless smile touched the king's lips. "Arrangements will be made, but far from those he expects. Renard will regret that he dared to try to sway my support from Scotland by abducting my daughter." Beneath the torchlight, the king's gaze grew somber as he assessed Colyne. "Twice now you have aided me. I offer you my greatest appreciation."

Colyne bowed.

His face taunt with worry, King Philip gazed upon his daughter. "I feared for your life. Had anything happened to you . . . I love you, Marie."

"I love you too, Father." Tears rolled down her face as Marie ran to him and gave him a big hug, her doubts and fears falling away. The bond between them was solid. Never again would she doubt that he wanted her in his life.

A sincere smile touched her father's mouth. "But I shall never become used to your independent ways."

Colyne stepped forward. "A fact I am more than willing to take charge of, Sire."

Brow arched, the king studied the Scot.

Pride filled Marie as Colyne held her father's gaze with fierce resolve.

"I am aware the situation is far from proper," Colyne stated, "but I am requesting permission for your daughter's hand in marriage."

"And your reason?" the king demanded.

Tenderness creased Colyne's face as he turned toward her with a look so filled with love that her heart ached. "Because, Sire, I am in love with Marie. I want to care for her, to help raise our child, and to cherish her for the rest of her life."

In the torchlight, wonder shone in her father's eyes as he glanced from Colyne to Marie. "Child? Is this true?"

Tears streamed down her cheeks as she nodded. "*Oui.*"

A happy smile curved her father's face. "In light of recent events, I hereby end your betrothal. You are free to marry the man you choose."

She gave him another hug. "You have made me so happy."

He nodded to Colyne. "You have my blessing." The king pressed a kiss on her brow, and then stepped back as Colyne moved to her side.

Happiness pouring through her, Marie turned.

On an unsteady breath, Colyne cupped her face. "I love you, Marie. I want to grow old with you, to share the happiness of our every day, and to hold you as we watch our children grow. Marry me; you are all I need to make my life complete."

Emotion tightened in her throat as she stared at the man who was her life, her love, and who she wanted to be with forever. She threw herself into his arms. "*Oui!*"

In the candlelit chamber, Marie stared at Colyne, their bodies still joined from making love. "When I think of you almost dying—"

Colyne silenced her with a gentle kiss, his taste stealing over her, tempting her to make love with him yet again. "'Tis over now. A fortnight has passed since Renard was captured."

Memories lingered of how, when her father had learned the location of the English noble's hiding place, he'd stormed off to personally make the arrest. "He will regret his part in the deceitful plot."

"Aye, with his life. But"—Colyne kissed her until her thoughts hazed—"I can think of many things to do this night besides talking of your father's anger, or of those who would try to usurp Scotland's freedom."

She shuddered against him, this moment fulfilling her every hope and dream.

"I love you, Marie. Never will I tire of telling you so."

"Nor I you. You are my heart, my life. Never did I believe I would find a man who would want me for myself." She smiled. "Then I was blessed with you."

Tenderness mingled with the passion in his eyes. "'Tis I who am blessed." He claimed her mouth in a tender kiss, and with excruciating slowness, he tasted her, unhurried, savoring. When he nipped at the skin along the curve of her throat, she could only groan as she basked in his every touch.

Hours later, Marie lay beside Colyne, her pulse still racing from making love. A smile touched her lips as she caught sight of her worn copy of the tales of King Arthur, which she'd received in her eighth summer.

Throughout her life she'd believed the brave knights who graced the pages were naught but characters crafted to entertain children and make grown women sigh. But it'd turned out they were true. Like Sir Lancelot, Colyne had ridden into her life, swept her away, and won her heart.

Be sure to read the first two books

In the Oath Trilogy

AN OATH TAKEN

And

AN OATH BROKEN

Available now

From

Lyrical Press

THE
OATH
TRILOGY

*In deception
lies desire...*

An
OATH TAKEN
DIANA COSBY

"Diana Cosby is superbly talented."
—Cathy Maxwell, *New York Times* bestselling author

AN OATH TAKEN

As the new castellan, Sir Nicholas Beringar has the daunting task of rebuilding Ravenmoor Castle on the Scottish border and gaining the trust of the locals—one of whom wastes no time in trying to rob him. Instead of punishing the boy, Nicholas decides to make him his squire. Little does he know the thieving young lad is really . . . a lady.

Lady Elizabet Armstrong had donned a disguise in an attempt to free her brother from Ravenmoor's dungeons. Although intimidated by the confident Englishman with his well-honed muscles and beguiling eyes, she cannot refuse his offer.

Nicholas senses that his new squire is not what he seems. His gentle attempts to break through the boy's defenses leave Elizabet powerless to stem the desire that engulfs her. And when the truth is exposed, she'll have to trust in Nicholas's honor to help her people—and to surrender to his touch . . .

An

OATH BROKEN

THE
⟫⟫OATH⟪⟪
TRILOGY

DIANA COSBY

"Diana Cosby is superbly talented."
— Cathy Maxwell, *New York Times* bestselling author

AN OATH BROKEN

Lady Sarra Bellacote would sooner marry a boar than a countryman of the bloodthirsty brutes who killed her parents. And yet, despite— or perhaps because of—her valuable holdings, she is being dragged to Scotland to be wed against her will. To complicate the desperate situation, the knight hired to do the dragging is dark, wild, irresistible. And he, too, is intolerably *Scottish.*

Giric Armstrong, Earl of Terrick, takes no pleasure in escorting a feisty English lass to her betrothed. But he needs the coin to rebuild his castle, and his tenants need to eat. Yet the trip will not be the simple matter he imagined. For Lady Sarra isn't the only one determined to see her engagement fail. Men with darker motives want to stop the wedding—even if they must kill the bride in the process.

Now, in close quarters with this beautiful English heiress, Terrick must fight his mounting desire, and somehow keep Sarra alive long enough to lose her forever to another man . . .

"Diana Cosby is superbly talented."
—Cathy Maxwell,
New York Times Bestselling Author

HIS CAPTIVE

*Divided by loyalty,
drawn together
by desire...*

DIANA COSBY

HIS CAPTIVE

With a wastrel brother and a treacherous former fiancé, Lady Nichola Westcott hardly expects the dangerously seductive Scot who kidnaps her to be a man of his word. Though Sir Alexander MacGruder promises not to hurt her, Nichola's only value is as a pawn to be ransomed.

Alexander's goal is to avenge his father's murder, not to become entangled with the enemy. But his desire to keep Nichola with him, in his home—in his bed—unwittingly makes her a target for those who have no qualms about shedding English blood.

Now Nichola is trapped—by her powerful attraction to a man whose touch shakes her to the core. Unwilling and unable to resist each other, can Nichola and Alexander save a love that has enslaved them both?

"Diana Cosby
is superbly talented."
—Cathy Maxwell,
New York Times
Bestselling Author

His
Woman

Some passions are too powerful to forget...

DIANA COSBY

HIS WOMAN

Lady Isabel Adair is the last woman Sir Duncan MacGruder wants to see again, much less be obliged to save. Three years ago, Isabel broke their engagement to become the Earl of Frasyer's mistress, shattering Duncan's heart and hopes in one painful blow. But Duncan's promise to Isabel's dying brother compels him to rescue her from those determined to bring down Scottish rebel Sir William Wallace.

Betraying the man she loved was the only way for Isabel to save her father, but every moment she spends with Duncan reminds her just how much she sacrificed. No one could blame him for despising her, yet Duncan's misgivings cannot withstand a desire that has grown wilder with time. Now, on a perilous journey through Scotland, two wary lovers must confront both the enemies who will stop at nothing to hunt them down, and the secret legacy that threatens their passion and their lives . . .

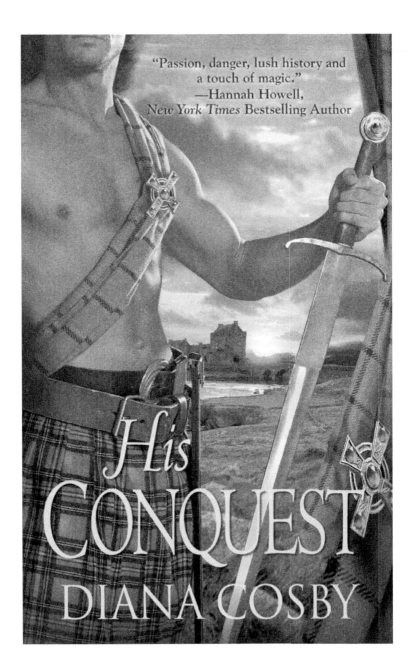

His
CONQUEST
DIANA COSBY

HIS CONQUEST

Linet Dancort will not be sold. But that's essentially what her brother intends to do—to trade her like so much chattel to widen his already vast scope of influence. Linet will seize any opportunity to escape her fate—and opportunity comes in the form of a rebel prisoner locked in her brother's dungeon, predatory and fearsome, and sentenced to hang in the morning.

Seathan MacGruder, Earl of Grey, is not unused to cheating death. But even this legendary Scottish warrior is surprised when a beautiful Englishwoman creeps to his cell and offers him his freedom. What Linet wants in exchange, though—safe passage to the Highlands—is a steep price to pay. For the only thing more dangerous than the journey through embattled Scotland is the desire that smolders between these two fugitives the first time they touch . . .

DIANA
COSBY

His
DESTINY

HIS DESTINY

As one of England's most capable mercenaries, Emma Astyn can charm an enemy and brandish a knife with unmatched finesse. Assigned to befriend Dubh Duer, an infamous Scottish rebel, she assumes the guise of innocent damsel Christina Moffat to intercept the writ he's carrying to a traitorous bishop. But as she gains the dark hero's confidence and realizes they share a tattered past, compassion—and passion—distract her from the task at hand . . .

His legendary slaying of English knights has won him the name Dubh Duer, but Sir Patrik Cleary MacGruder is driven by duty and honor, not heroics. Rescuing Christina from the clutches of four such knights is a matter of obligation for the Scot. But there's something alluring about her fiery spirit, even if he has misgivings about her tragic history. Together, they'll endure a perilous journey of love and betrayal, and a harrowing fight for their lives . . .

DIANA
COSBY

His
SEDUCTION

"Medieval Scotland roars to life in this fabulous series."
—Pamela Palmer, *New York Times* bestselling author

HIS SEDUCTION

Lady Rois Drummond is fiercely devoted to her widowed father, the respected Scottish Earl of Brom. So when she believes he is about to be exposed as a traitor to England, she must think quickly. Desperate, Rois makes a shocking claim against the suspected accuser, Sir Griffin Westcott. But her impetuous lie leaves her in an outrageous circumstance: hastily married to the enemy. Yet Griffin is far from the man Rois thinks he is—and much closer to the man of her dreams . . .

Griffin may be an Englishman, but in truth he leads a clandestine life as a spy for Scotland. Refusing to endanger any woman, he has endured the loneliness of his mission. But Rois's absurd charge has suddenly changed all that. Now, with his cover in jeopardy, Griffin must find a way to keep his secret while keeping his distance from his spirited and tempting new wife—a task that proves more difficult than he ever imagined . . .

DIANA COSBY

His
ENCHANTMENT

The MacGruder Brothers

HIS ENCHANTMENT

Lady Catarine MacLaren is a fairy princess, duty-bound to eschew the human world. But the line between the two realms is beginning to blur. English knights have launched an assault on the MacLarens, just as the families of Comyn have captured the Scottish king and queen. Now, Catarine is torn between loyalty to her people and helping the handsome, rust-haired Lord Trálin rescue the Scottish king . . .

As guard to King Alexander, Lord Trálin MacGruder will stop at nothing to defend the Scottish crown against the Comyns. And he finds a sympathetic, and gorgeous, ally in the enigmatic Princess Catarine. As they plot to rescue the kidnapped king and queen, Trálin and Catarine will discover a love made all but impossible by her obligations to the Otherworld. But a passion this extraordinary may be worth the irreversible sacrifices it demands . . .

About the Author

A retired Navy Chief, AGC (AW), Diana Cosby is an international bestselling author of Scottish medieval romantic suspense. Diana has spoken at the Library of Congress, appeared at Lady Jane's Salon NYC, in *Woman's Day,* on *Texoma Living! Magazine, USA Today's* romance blog, "Happily Ever After," and MSN.com.

After retiring from the navy, Diana dove into her passion—writing romance novels. With thirty-four moves behind her, she was anxious to create characters who reflected the amazing cultures and people she's met throughout the world. In August 2012, she released her story in the anthology, *Born to Bite*, with Hannah Howell and Erica Ridley. Diana looks forward to the years ahead of writing and meeting the amazing people who will share this journey.

Diana Cosby, International Bestselling Author
www.dianacosby.com

Printed in Great Britain
by Amazon

25890226R00131